A Time for Murder

A *Murder, She Wrote* Mystery

OTHER BOOKS IN THE *Murder, She Wrote* SERIES

Manhattans & Murder
Rum & Razors
Brandy & Bullets
Martinis & Mayhem
A Deadly Judgment
A Palette for Murder
The Highland Fling Murders
Murder on the QE2
Murder in Moscow
A Little Yuletide Murder
Murder at the Powderhorn Ranch
Knock 'Em Dead
Gin & Daggers
Trick or Treachery
Blood on the Vine
Murder in a Minor Key
Provence—To Die For
You Bet Your Life
Majoring in Murder
Destination Murder
Dying to Retire
A Vote for Murder
The Maine Mutiny
Margaritas & Murder
A Question of Murder
Coffee, Tea, or Murder?
Three Strikes and You're Dead
Panning for Murder
Murder on Parade
A Slaying in Savannah
Madison Avenue Shoot
A Fatal Feast
Nashville Noir
The Queen's Jewels
Skating on Thin Ice
The Fine Art of Murder
Trouble at High Tide
Domestic Malice
Prescription for Murder
Close-up on Murder
Aloha Betrayed
Death of a Blue Blood
Killer in the Kitchen
The Ghost and Mrs. Fletcher
Design for Murder
Hook, Line, and Murder
A Date with Murder
Manuscript for Murder
Murder in Red

A Time for Murder

A *Murder, She Wrote* Mystery

A NOVEL BY JESSICA FLETCHER & JON LAND

Based on the Universal television series created by
Peter S. Fischer, Richard Levinson & William Link

BERKLEY PRIME CRIME
New York

BERKLEY PRIME CRIME
Published by Berkley
An imprint of Penguin Random House LLC
penguinrandomhouse.com

Library of Congress Cataloging-in-Publication Data

Names: Fletcher, Jessica, author. | Land, Jon, author.
Title: A time for murder / Jessica Fletcher, Jon Land.
Description: New York : Berkley Prime Crime, 2019. | Series: Murder she wrote; 50 | "A novel by Jessica Fletcher & Jon Land; Based on the Universal television series created by Peter S. Fischer, Richard Levinson & William Link."
Identifiers: LCCN 2019011805| ISBN 9781984804303 (hardback) | ISBN 9781984804327 (ebook)
Subjects: LCSH: Fletcher, Jessica--Fiction. | Women detectives--Fiction. | Women novelists--Fiction. | Murder--Investigation--Fiction. | BISAC: FICTION / Mystery & Detective / Women Sleuths. | FICTION / Media Tie-In. | GSAFD: Mystery fiction.
Classification: LCC PS3552.A376 T56 2019 | DDC 813/.54--dc23
LC record available at https://lccn.loc.gov/2019011805

First Edition: November 2019

Printed in the United States of America
1 3 5 7 9 10 8 6 4 2

Jacket photograph of school corridor © vipman/Shutterstock
Jacket design by Ally Andryshak

For the fans of the *Murder, She Wrote* television and book series.
Thanks for coming along for the ride.

What the detective story is about is not murder
but the restoration of order.

—P. D. JAMES

A Time for Murder

A *Murder, She Wrote* Mystery

Chapter One

"When did you solve your first murder?" the reporter for the Cabot Cove High School newspaper asked me from across the table at Mara's Luncheonette just before the noon lunch rush began.

"Well," I said to wide-eyed senior Kristi Powell, who was doing a series on former teachers at the school, "that would go back to the first mystery I actually published, called—"

"Mrs. Fletcher," Kristi interrupted, taking off her horn-rimmed glasses and tightening her gaze on me, "I mean in real life, not in your books. Was it here in Cabot Cove?"

It's funny, but I'm not at all reluctant to talk about the murder cases I invent. On the other hand, I'm very reluctant to discuss the actual ones, which I'd much prefer to forget the moment they end. Call it the most common proclivity among fiction writers—a preference for the worlds we create over the one in which we're just as powerless as everyone else. Usually, I would have deflected or avoided the question altogether. But I hated to dodge an impressionable high school student, especially one who was already dreaming of a career in print. I figured it best to set a good example for her and be the best role model I could be by remaining as honest and forthright as I could without divulging more than I was comfortable with.

"No, it wasn't in Cabot Cove."

Kristi put her glasses back on and twirled a finger through some stray hair that had escaped the bun wrapped tightly atop her head—an odd way, I thought, for a high school senior to wear her hair. "Was your husband, Frank, still alive at the time?"

I nodded, impressed. "You've done your homework, Kristi."

She didn't look to be of a mind to accept my praise. "It's one of the first things that shows up in a Google search," she said.

Having never googled myself, I wasn't aware of how the Internet prioritized the various elements of my biography. If I were writing that, instead of one of mystery novels, it would be painfully short, perhaps no more than a page. My actual achievements in life make for a pretty thin list, since I've long preferred to live vicariously through my alter ego, who's far better at solving fictional crimes than the real me is at the occasional real-life one.

"What about that first actual murder you solved, Mrs. Fletcher?" Kristi said, prodding me.

Yes, she would make a very good journalist, indeed. I wondered if Kristi really needed those horn-rimmed glasses. She had the look of a young woman bursting with enthusiasm and excitement over chasing her dream through college and beyond—the kind of student who was an absolute pleasure to teach, as I recalled from my days in the classroom. She had dressed fashionably in a skirt and blouse, donning a restrained, professional appearance perhaps to make me more forthcoming with my answers. I've probably done a thousand interviews over the years without such a thing ever occurring to me, perhaps because this was the first time one of those interviews had been conducted by a high school student.

In any event, the ploy very nearly worked, because I almost, *almost*, told Kristi the truth I'd shared with extraordinarily few people over the years.

"Would you believe the first real murderer I caught was my own publisher?"

She looked up from her notepad. "Really?"

I nodded. "And the murder happened at a party in my honor—well, in honor of the publication of my first book."

"That would be *The Corpse Danced at Midnight*?"

"It would indeed. It was a costume party with everyone coming dressed as famous characters, the brainchild of my publisher Preston Giles."

"Then, he was the murderer?"

"Sadly, yes," I told Kristi, elaborating no further. "I'll spare you the details. I just happened to be in the right place at the right time. Or the wrong place at the wrong time, depending on your perspective."

"That seems to happen to you a lot, Mrs. Fletcher, especially right here in Cabot Cove."

"I don't keep a running tally."

"But your publisher, Preston Giles, he was the first?"

I sensed something in Kristi's tone, an edge that hadn't been there a moment ago. It reminded me of my own voice when I was about to spring a trap on a man or woman I was convinced had committed murder. So I pulled back a bit, the physical space between us at a corner table in the back of Mara's Luncheonette remaining the same, but the distance widening.

"For all intents and purposes, yes," I told her, splitting hairs.

"It's all right, Mrs. Fletcher. The *Eagle* is only a high school newspaper, after all." Kristi seemed hesitant, then pushed herself to continue. "It's just that the research I did turned up a death where you used to live, where you were an English teacher."

"*Substitute* English teacher," I corrected her, for the record. "And the town was Appleton, Maine, maybe a half-hour drive from Cabot Cove. That's where I met my husband, Frank."

"And the murder that took place there?"

"You called it a death before."

"But it was a murder. I mean, someone was arrested. That's right, isn't it?"

"There was a murder, and someone was arrested, yes, Kristi."

"Were you the one who caught him, Mrs. Fletcher?"

I reached across the table and patted her arm. "Who said it was a *him*?" I asked, smiling.

"Touché," she said, smiling back.

"Beyond that, I'm going to need to plead the Fifth."

"For legal reasons?"

"Personal ones. If you've researched me, you're aware that you're asking me about something I've never discussed publicly or in the media. With that in mind, I'd ask that we proceed to something else out of respect for those who don't need all this dragged back into their lives. People moved on, a town moved on, and having the story dredged back up by even the *Cabot Cove High School Eagle* could do harm to those who, if they haven't forgotten, have at least stopped remembering."

Kristi started to make a note, then stopped. "This would have been twenty-five years ago?"

I shrugged. "That sounds about right."

"And you were teaching high school at the time."

"*Substitute* teaching," I corrected her again, "yes."

She broke off a fresh corner of her blueberry muffin and chased it down with the iced tea she'd ordered with it. "This is a great muffin."

"Mara, the owner this place is named for, bakes them herself using wild Maine blueberries. I've teased her about expanding the business to produce her baked goods on a bigger scale."

Kristi took another bite. "That's actually not a bad idea. Do you have any food-based mysteries, Mrs. Fletcher?"

I laughed. "I leave the kitchen to other mystery writers, but I've done a few books where cooking plays a prominent role."

"Do you enjoy cooking yourself?"

"Less so as I've gotten older. When you live alone, it just doesn't seem to be worth the effort as much. And I've been living at Hill House for the past few months while my house is being repaired. I fear room service is going to be a tough habit to break."

"Well, there's always Grubhub," Kristi said, flashing a fresh smile. "That didn't exist when you started your career . . . or when you were living in Appleton."

"Clever," I complimented her, nodding.

"What?"

"The way you worked back to the original question, trying another way to get me to answer it."

She didn't bother denying that, but laid down her pen as if to concede my point. "Do you blame me?"

"Not at all. You're just doing your job."

"It's only a high school paper, like I said before."

"Maybe so," I told Kristi. "But you came here this afternoon better prepared, and with more challenging questions, than anyone who's interviewed me in quite a while."

"I'm sorry if I'm pushing too hard."

That sudden doubt—second thoughts, so to speak—exposed Kristi's vulnerability, reminding me that she was just a high school student. I wished I could tell her what she wanted to know, give her the scoop she was hoping for. I couldn't, though. Too many years had passed. Appleton might have been only twenty miles or so away as the crow flies, but for me it was another lifetime, another *life*. I think it was as much a matter of all that transpiring before I'd become a writer, while Frank was still alive, while we were raising our nephew Grady after his father, Frank's brother, had been killed in an accident and his mother needed some help.

Grady . . .

He'd been a little boy when I encountered my first murderer, and I guess he was one of the people I was trying to protect by refusing to discuss that time, with Kristi Powell or any of the reporters who'd poked me about the case over the years. There were some places in my past I didn't want to go, and this was one of them.

In the silence that had settled between us, I wondered whether the real reason for my reluctance to speak about the first murder I ever solved lay in the two separate lives I'd built for myself: my life with Frank and my life after him. His death had provided the impetus for my becoming a writer, and my writing was what had too often embroiled me in very real-life mysteries. It was as if I didn't want my life with Frank to be at all tarnished by that mess, which meant I needed it to remain wholly separate from my life afterward to keep the memories pure. All we had shared and done together needed to be left apart and not demeaned by such a difficult experience, which haunted me to this day. I'd stored those memories at the periphery of my consciousness, like a dream I couldn't quite remember, until they were occasionally dug up again by reporters with cigarette-stained fingernails and coffee on their breath.

Which, of course, didn't describe Kristi Powell even one little bit.

"Tell you what, Kristi," I said, starting in again without being prompted. "If I ever decide to share the details of the first murder case I was involved in, you'll be the first person I call."

She smiled. "Then I'd better make sure I give you my phone number, Mrs. Fletcher. I think you only have my e-mail address."

I hadn't thought in quite some time of Appleton or that town's high school or even the murder that was a prime inspiration for what would ultimately become my future career. Back then, I dabbled in writing as a beloved hobby without ever imagining I'd someday be the author of fifty mystery novels.

After giving up on my original dream of becoming a so-called "serious" writer, I submitted stories one after another to *Ellery Queen's Mystery Magazine* and *Alfred Hitchcock's Mystery Magazine* among others. While it's a testament to the enduring qualities of the genre that those magazines are still in existence today, I never received anything from them but rejection letters and renewal notices. A few articles on me have advanced the theory that it was coming face-to-face with murder in real life that allowed me to write not just a story but an entire book that I ended up selling to Coventry House. Little did I know at that point that my publisher, Preston Giles, would end up murdering one of the guests at a party in honor of my debut novel's publication, and that I'd be the one to ultimately catch him. Most mark that case as the first time I ever solved a murder, when in fact it was the second. But I don't think that experience made me a better writer, at least not directly; after all, I didn't plunge into the book-length work that became *The Corpse Danced at Midnight* until Frank's death, when I turned to the keyboard as a respite for my grief and loneliness.

Who knows, though? The subconscious is a strange and unexplored place where I guess it's more than possible that my experience with murder up close and personal in Appleton left an indelible impression that continues to influence me to this day. I like to believe all my stories spring entirely from the imagination, but my proclivity for finding real-life crimes to investigate inspires me to do justice to the process and always pay proper respect to the victims. When you've seen so many up close, often with people with whom you're personally acquainted, murders are bound to leave their marks on you.

I picked up my mail at the front desk of Hill House upon my return from Mara's. I'd enjoyed my months living there, but looked forward to the day when I'd be able to return to my beloved Victorian home on Candlewood Lane. The reconstruction in the wake of the fire that had almost claimed my life was coming along nicely, after the contractors had encountered some initial setbacks, and they'd assured me that in a few short weeks I'd get a fresh look at all the progress they'd made. While Hill House had proved to be such a blessing during those months, there was no way to surround myself with books the way I could at home. And the first thing I intended to do upon my return to 698 Candlewood Lane was restock my refurbished bookshelves.

The stack of mail, containing the usual circulars and junk, also included an oversized stiff envelope that appeared to contain an invitation of some kind. I opened that envelope first and slid out its contents, a single card with big black text in fancy script.

You are cordially invited to

a retirement party in honor of . . .

I scanned the rest of the invitation without absorbing all of its content.

A name I recalled well followed, but the words my eyes fixed on next stoked memories long dormant, until earlier that day, thanks to my interview with Kristi Powell of the *Cabot Cove High School Eagle*:

. . . Appleton High School.

I'd been a substitute English teacher there for more than five years, up until a quarter century ago. It was where I looked murder in the face for the first time and tried to stare it down.

Tell you what, Kristi. If I ever decide to share the details of the first murder case I was involved in, you'll be the first person I call.

Right now, though, those details came roaring back front and center in my mind, starting at the very beginning.

Chapter Two

Twenty-five years ago . . .

"You'll catch your death, Grady," I warned my young nephew, who'd refused to put on a sweater or even one of those hooded sweatshirts he had become increasingly partial to.

"It's my life, isn't it?" he challenged me, looking up from cornflakes drizzled with powdered sugar and with bananas floating in the milk, just as he liked.

"Well, yes."

"Then it should be my death, too," he pronounced in a fitting example of logic, courtesy of an eight-year-old.

"He's got a point, Jess," my husband, Frank, noted, lowering the morning paper to reveal his grin.

It didn't take much for Grady to get Frank to grin, and that was more than enough for me to be grateful for the boy's presence in our lives. Our marriage was complete in all ways, save for one glaring exception: the fact that we'd never had a child. It wasn't that we hadn't tried, but we'd never bothered to seek professional expertise on why we'd continually been unsuccessful. Neither of us wanted to blame the other, and both of us believed such things were a matter of fate more than of science. If it was meant to be, it would happen. And the fact that it hadn't after so many years meant it never would. But raising Grady in the wake of his father's death and his mother's belief that the boy would be better served living with Frank and me for a time had wondrously filled that void, even as it filled our lives with fresh responsibility neither of us had ever imagined.

As Frank was fond of pointing out, though, we'd "acquired" Grady absent the three worst words in the English language: "some assembly required." He'd been part of our Appleton, Maine, household for two years now and, after an initial rough patch, he'd adjusted marvelously to his new environment, including Appleton Elementary, where I was acquainted with any number of the teachers. I'd substituted there occasionally in the days before Appleton High principal Walter Reavis brought me on as a full-time sub to step in for teachers who were gone for extended absences. I much preferred this to the daily grind, since it gave me an opportunity to get to know the kids and actually teach them something on my own, once their initial resistance to a substitute wore off.

Teaching gave me time to continue pursuing my passion for writing—a torch that had been lit during my days freelancing for whatever newspaper or magazine I could convince to consider my work. I actually fancied myself a real journalist, even though my portfolio was painfully thin on bylines in journals more prestigious than the *Appleton Daily Sun* or *Maine Monthly*. I'd like to say at least it paid the bills, but the meager sums I made freelancing didn't even come close to that.

The move from journalism into short stories came at the same time Walter Reavis hired me as a full-time sub at the local high school. I was still making only about half what the real teachers made, without any benefits to boot. Coupled with Frank's income from giving flying lessons at a local airport and his Air Force pension, it was more than enough for us to get by. The costs of raising Grady, meanwhile, were covered by his late father's insurance policy, giving us no worries there either.

And it was a good thing we weren't relying on my fiction writing to bring in any income, since it hadn't so far. I'd gotten one story published in a local literary magazine that was typed, instead of typeset, my one true career highlight having been making a sale to *Yankee* magazine.

It had been Walter Reavis who'd gotten that story to a friend who worked at *Yankee*. I'm not sure I've ever been more grateful to anyone in all my life. I hadn't asked Walter to do it, hadn't even known he had a friend there. He'd done it on his own after reading that particular story and liking it enough to go out on a limb for me. If you want to be a writer, you need a little help along the way. Nobody makes it entirely on their own, particularly not a substitute English teacher with no more than a dream and a Royal typewriter. I resolved to use the first income I made off my short stories to purchase a computer. So, needless to say, I was still using the Royal.

"Why do they have school when the weather's sucky if everybody gets sick?" Grady asked, spooning up the last of his cornflakes.

"'Sucky' is not a word, Grady," I said.

"How do you know?"

"Well, I am an English teacher."

"But you're not *my* English teacher, Aunt Jess," he said, at which point Frank raised the newspaper in front of his face again.

"Thanks for the support," I said to him, and I could see the paper rustling as he stifled a laugh behind it.

Grady pushed his chair out from under the table. "I'll go get a hoodie, Aunt Jess," he said, giving me a hug that I took as an apology for his smart remark.

That's the way it was with Grady. He had too kind a nature to let even the most casually flippant or derogatory remark stand for very long. I believe it must've had something to do with a fear of losing the people he had left in his life. The death of his father had left him with a keen, even obsessive inclination to avoid any behavior that might create distance between him and anyone else vital to his life. He was that way with his teachers and friends, too, never the one to start trouble or finish it. Afraid even at times to stand up for himself or respond in kind out of fear of losing a single friend or acquaintance. I learned pretty fast that you can't reason out such things with a six-year-old, much less an eight-year-old even more set in his ways two years later. There were times when I thought Grady was surviving more than living, but other times when he seemed like the happiest little boy in the world. Occasionally I thought he might be faking it to reward Frank and me for our love.

"Peanut butter and jelly," Frank pronounced, setting Grady's brown paper lunch bag before him. "And a surprise!"

"What? What?" Grady asked eagerly, practically bouncing up and down.

"If I told you, it wouldn't be a surprise. And you know the rules."

The boy frowned and blew the wavy hair from his face.

"Don't look until lunchtime," Frank reminded Grady. "No cheating?"

"No cheating, Uncle Frank," the boy agreed.

Frank then placed my bag in front of me, and I asked, "I don't get a preview? I don't get a surprise?"

"Chicken salad on whole wheat. Hold the celery."

"What about the surprise?"

"That will have to wait until later," Frank said, stopping just short of a wink, which left me wondering what he was hinting at.

I slung the strap of my shoulder bag, which doubled as a briefcase for books and papers, over my shoulder and picked up my lunch bag, minus the surprise, just as Grady reappeared with his sweatshirt on backward so the hood was pulled over his face.

"What do you think, Aunt Jess?" he asked before banging his leg against a chair. "Ouch!" the boy rasped, pulling the hood down.

"Enough said."

Frank wasn't holding the newspaper anymore, so he just turned away this time before fetching his keys and leading us outside to his car.

"Looks like I'm going to need you to fill in for Bill Gower awhile longer, Jessica," Walter Reavis greeted me when I arrived that morning with the buses. "You're earning rave reviews teaching remedial English, by the way."

"Don't call it that."

"What?"

"Remedial."

"But that's what it is."

"It makes the students feel inferior."

He scolded me playfully with his eyes. "They know they're inferior. That's why they're taking *remedial* English."

"You make it sound like a badge of shame, Walter."

"Well, Mrs. Fletcher, you're looking at a proud graduate of remedial English. You see me wearing a badge of shame anywhere?"

"You must have left it at home."

"I'll make sure to check the drawers tonight."

The bell rang, signaling the beginning of homeroom, which meant I had to get a move on.

"Thank you," I said to him.

He was good-looking, with strong, rugged features that made him attractive to women and an easy smile that made him approachable to men. "For promising to check my drawers for that badge?"

Now it was my eyes doing the scolding. "For this opportunity."

He nodded, clearly not used to that kind of compliment. "I'd like to speak to you about another one. You're free sixth period, right?"

"Why, yes," I managed.

"Perfect. Come by the office then."

I was filling in for a longtime teacher named Bill Gower who taught three remedial English classes and one advanced honors class to sophomores. The previous week I had distributed to that sophomore class a short story I'd recently written, photocopied at my own expense at Staples. Normally, I would have used one of the high school's twin copying machines, of which one was almost always down on a rotating basis. Since this particular short story wasn't on the lesson plan left by Mr. Gower, however, I couldn't justify spending taxpayer dollars and forked over the twenty dollars for the copies plus stapling.

Today was the day I'd put aside to discuss the story with a sophomore class that had most recently wrapped up "Rappaccini's Daughter" by Nathaniel Hawthorne and "The Masque of the Red Death" by Edgar Allan Poe.

"I don't think the story knows what it wants to be," a straight-A student named Missy noted.

"Could you expand on that a bit?" I asked her, hoping to see more hands shoot up into the air.

"Well, it's trying to say something important."

"You agree, Ben?" I asked a boy who was one of my go-tos in the class, but seldom raised his hand.

"Maybe. It may be trying to say a whole lot of things," he responded, "but it ends up saying nothing at all."

Ouch, I thought.

"And I didn't like the characters," Ben continued.

Double ouch.

"Maybe you're not supposed to like them," I pointed out.

"I didn't say it right," Ben said, trying again. "I don't know how I'm supposed to feel about them, so I never really cared."

"It's like, well, they're boring," suggested a Goth girl named Becky. "They never do anything. Nothing ever happens."

"Except that one part with the car accident," noted Will from inside his ever-present football letterman's jacket. "That was cool, 'cause there was nobody behind the wheel, so what happened to the driver?"

"Why'd he run away?" Missy asked.

"Maybe he was never there," suggested a boy named Trevor who delighted in carving his name wherever he went, like a dog marking its territory.

Will again: "Maybe he was running from something. The accident happens, and he has to run before he gets caught."

"What do you think he did?" Missy wondered.

"Killed someone!" a voice rang out.

"Dealt drugs!"

"Stole money from his boss!"

Right before my eyes, the discussion had veered hopelessly off track, fixating on a small, relatively insignificant part of the story. And, try as I might, I couldn't get the class's focus back on the subject at hand, which was the story as a whole.

"Is this a mystery?" Missy asked finally, restoring a semblance of order to things.

"What makes you ask?" I said.

"Everything comes back to that car accident, the missing driver. It has to be one of the other characters, right? That's what the story, the mystery, is about. Figuring out who the driver is. But it ends with us never finding out."

"Ugggghhhhhhhh," Becky added to the pronouncement Missy had just made. "I hate when writers do that."

"Too bad we can't ask the writer who the driver was," Ben lamented.

"Mrs. Fletcher," Missy said, holding up the photocopied set of pages, "who is the writer? There's no name on this."

"You know," I said, "I forgot the author's name. Nobody well-known—that's for sure."

* * *

I lived with my students' comments for the rest of the day, playing them over and over in my head after making the bold move of teaching one of the unpublished stories I had lying around. Craving some kind, however limited it might be, of feedback.

Is this a mystery? Missy had asked.

Maybe it was. Maybe that was the problem. Maybe I wasn't the writer I thought I was or wanted to be.

Except that one part with the car accident. That was cool, 'cause there was nobody behind the wheel, so what happened to the driver?

I didn't know and had never really thought about it until now. But I spent much of the rest of the day thinking about nothing else, concocting an entire scenario that swept the story away in an entirely different direction, if not on paper, at least in my imagination.

Until sixth period, that is, because sixth period was when Principal Walter Reavis had asked to see me in his office.

I rushed down to the main office, located at the back end of the building, as soon as fifth period ended, just before one o'clock. Walter's secretary, Alma Potts, was out sick that day, and her harried replacement was juggling phone calls, so I headed down the short corridor to his private office and knocked on his open door.

"How's your first day as a full-time teacher going, Jessica?" he asked, grinning broadly after I'd sat down before his desk.

I was so excited, my knees wobbled and I literally felt faint. The sun streaming through the open blinds forced me to squint and then shield my eyes to regard him. Alma Potts made it a habit tc close those blinds every single day, but since she was out today, there was no one to save visitors to Walter's office from the bright rays of the sun.

"If Bill Gower stays out, I'm going to make you a permanent part of the faculty," he continued.

"Wow," I managed.

"He and I are speaking in the next hour. I should have news for you by the end of the day," said Walter, framed by the sun's bright glow. "Stop by before you leave the building."

I raised a hand to shield my eyes. "I . . . I don't know what to say, Walter."

He rose behind his desk, a clear signal it was time to take my leave. "End of the day, Jessica?"

I stood up, too. "End of the day, yes."

After school ended, I sat at my desk—well, Bill Gower's desk—on the pretext of correcting papers. But I ended up continuing to think about what had happened to the driver in the story my sophomore English class had skewered and why he, or she, had fled the scene of an accident. How would the story read if it opened with that scene and went from there? Maybe that was why this story, and many of the others I'd penned, had proved so hard to write. Maybe I was fighting my instincts, trying to be a different writer from the writer I really was.

But *mysteries*? Really?

I kept fixating on that to the point where I forgot all about Principal Walter Reavis having asked to see me at the end of the school day.

The light was starting to bleed from the late-afternoon Maine sky when I stuffed my belongings into my shoulder bag and raced to the main office, my shoes clacking against the tile floor, drawing a tinny echo in the now-empty building. The main office was still open and lit, even though Alma Potts's replacement had left for the day. I moved to Walter's office and found the door closed. I was about to knock when I heard his voice boom from inside.

"Stop!"

Followed by a pause.

"Absolutely not! I'll have no part in this—you hear me?"

Another pause came, the absence of a second voice telling me this must be a phone conversation, a particularly heated one.

"Was that a threat? Because if it was . . ."

I felt like I was snooping, prying, like some local gossip hound or something. I knew I should go take a seat in the front section of the office, but his voice trailed me when I started backing away from his door. Slowly, as if to draw out the last of his heated remarks.

"Maybe you didn't hear me clearly," Walter's voice continued to rage. "And don't threaten me! I'm not going to warn you again."

I thought that was it, the call done. But then Walter's voice returned, softer but just as intense.

"Over my dead body."

Chapter Three

The present

The ringing of a phone broke my trance, and I groped absently for my cell phone before realizing it was my landline that was chiming away.

"Where are you?" Seth Hazlitt asked by way of greeting as soon as I answered. "We were supposed to meet at Mara's."

"I was just there."

"Well, come back. Afternoon pie and coffee are nothing without my afternoon-pie-and-coffee partner."

I checked my watch. Where had all the time gone? Could I have lost this much in my reminiscing about my days back in Appleton? I guessed so.

Cabot Cove's resident family doctor had a simple prescription for living a long and happy life: a piece of pie and a cup of coffee every day at three o'clock. Call it the luxury of a small-town physician able to make his own hours in the company of a writer able to do the same.

I pulled my new bicycle out of the Hill House shed, where I'd placed it after returning from Mara's. I'd purchased something called a Crosstown bike, from a company called Pashley, after my older Schwinn was destroyed in a riding accident. A front slot fitted for a wicker basket was what had first attracted me to it in the store, my interest also stoked by some of the very qualities that turned others way. First of all, it was heavy and came standard with an abuse-proof frame that promised to last a long time and even withstand any further encounters I might have with nefarious pickup trucks. I took the Pashley out for a spin and fell in love with it instantly. Its heft had an old-fashioned feel to it. Not the choice to make if you intended to be racing around, and since I didn't, I'd purchased it on the spot.

Deep fall was already in the air, and before I knew it, my Pashley would be tucked away in the shed for the entire winter. I resolved to get out riding as much as I could before the conditions deteriorated further and the temperature started regularly drifting below freezing, as was typical for mid- to late fall in Maine. One day you're out in your shirtsleeves, and the next there's snow in the forecast. I looked forward to that first scent and feel of winter in the air with both wonder and dread: wonder for the beauty and quiet, dread for the isolation and being stuck inside without my daily bike rides or walks to invigorate me.

The summer season had long since passed, yielding the roads of Cabot Cove back to its residents, with the summer people having departed at long last. I didn't miss them, but I did miss the weather that brought them in droves to our once-quaint seaside village, which was now a haven for the privileged masses. I often wondered how such a thing came to pass: how a town could go from well-kept secret to traffic snarls seemingly overnight.

It's not like there was an article in some fancy magazine or Cabot Cove was featured on some popular TV network. Word had gotten out because, well, word had gotten out, almost like we'd paid for the privacy we'd been fortunate enough to enjoy for so long by losing it in a proverbial heartbeat. Went to bed one night with the town our own and woke up the next morning to find we had been inundated.

When I chained my bike up outside Mara's in the same spot where I'd left it that morning, I could see Seth seated at a table through the window. Not surprisingly, an empty plate sat before him, Mara's daily special long gone.

"Well, Jessica," he said, flapping the cardboard invitation before him, "you're always complaining you never get invited to anything."

"I am?"

"Maybe not," Seth noted, frowning. "Maybe it's me." He regarded the invitation again. "A retirement party, eh? Not yours, of course."

"Writers never retire, Seth."

"Neither do doctors, at least not the small-town variety. Then again, Cabot Cove isn't as small as it used to be." He handed me back the invitation. "So, are you going?"

"Well, it is being held right here, at the Cabot Cove Country Club."

"No such venue in your former hometown, as I recall."

"Appleton does have the theater, though," I reminded him, referring to the place where I'd first met Frank while we'd been working as volunteers on the same production.

"Not the greatest place to host a retirement party. So, how well do you know this"—Seth stopped to review the invitation anew—"Wilma Tisdale?"

"Not very. We taught at the high school around the same time, and she came to a book signing a few years back. Beyond that, if she walked into Mara's right now, I'm not sure that I'd know her."

"And yet she invited you to her retirement party. Hmmmm," Seth added, touching his chin.

"You sound like you're trying to solve a mystery."

"What, you think you're the only sleuth in town?"

His question brought me back to the interview Kristi Powell had done with me in this very restaurant just a few hours earlier.

When did you solve your first murder?

Even Seth didn't know the answer to that question. Neither did Mort Metzger or Harry McGraw. They were almost surely the three people with whom I was closest in the world, and I'd never shared the answer with any of them. So why did I suddenly feel guilty about not sharing more of the story with a high school student?

"Seth," I started, pushing my chair back out, "there's something I need to do."

"You haven't gotten your pie yet."

I started to reach for my cup of tea for one last sip, but decided against it. "You finished yours before I even got here," I said, standing up.

"I was going to order another."

"Have mine."

Seth's nose wrinkled at the prospect. "You know I hate lemon meringue, Jess."

"Oh, yes. How could I have forgotten? Next time I'll be sure to order one of your favorites."

I had no intention of sharing the truth of my first murder investigation with Kristi Powell, but I felt I owed her more of an explanation than the one I'd given. I made it a habit never to dodge questions during an interview, believing strongly in the old adage that if you always tell the truth, you never have to remember what you said. While I hadn't lied to Kristi, I hadn't been totally upfront either. Had she been an adult eking out a living on her byline, I wouldn't have given my sin of omission a second thought. But she was a high school student, impressionable and idealistic. And as a former high school teacher, I felt I owed her more than I'd initially provided.

I recalled Kristi saying something about being on deadline, which meant the chance existed that she was still at the high school even several hours after dismissal. So I rode my bike over there from Mara's and waited to be buzzed into the building, smiling toward the camera mounted over the main entrance. I heard the buzzer, followed by the click of the door opening.

Back when I was teaching in this building, I'm not even sure they locked the door at night, and now this was what we'd come to? I was glad Cabot Cove had at least been spared the metal detectors common now even in similar suburban high schools, but bemoaned the fact that any security precautions were deemed necessary. Was there no place we could consider safe anymore?

Cabot Cove High principal Jen Sweeney emerged from the school office, lugging an armful of books, just as I entered the building.

"Mrs. Fletcher, what a nice surprise!" She caught me spying the books she was toting. "Oh, this . . . I make the rounds every day, picking up left-behind library books before they accidentally get tossed away. Budget cuts being what they are, we can't afford to lose a single book from our shelves."

"As president of the local Friends of the Library group, Ms. Sweeney, I can't think of a more noble pursuit, and I applaud your efforts."

"So, what brings you down to our humble school? Are you mentoring anyone in the senior project this year?"

I shook my head. "Guess this year's class lacks the token scribe to take under my wing."

"A pity no student thought to take advantage of one of this town's true treasures."

"That would be the coastline," I said.

"I hope you don't mind that I gave our new advanced-placement and creative writing teacher your e-mail address."

"Not at all. I'd be happy to speak to the kids anytime."

"Wonderful, Mrs. Fletcher!" I watched Jen Sweeney switch the books from her right arm to her left. "Now, what can we do for you here at Cabot Cove High today?"

"One of your students interviewed me earlier today for an article in the school paper."

"The *Eagle*'s won awards, you know."

"Actually, I didn't."

Ms. Sweeney nodded, smiling. "New England High School Newspaper of the Year three times running and Maine's six times running. Talk about a dog catching a ball every time you toss it to him. Who interviewed you for the *Eagle*?"

"Kristi Powell."

"She's won several awards herself, including Feature Story of the Year."

"I didn't know that either."

"I'm surprised she didn't mention that or the paper's success, Mrs. Fletcher. Seems a bit strange."

"She was probably just being humble."

Jen Sweeney didn't look convinced of that at all. "'Humility' and 'high school' are seldom used in the same sentence."

"I suppose. Anyway, she mentioned she might be working on deadline. I thought I'd see if I could catch her. You see, Ms. Sweeney, I'm afraid I may have been a bit short with her on one of the lines of questioning she was pursuing, and I've been feeling guilty about it ever since."

"I'm sure it was nothing."

"Maybe. But if I want to sleep tonight, I need to make this right, maybe make it up to her in some way."

"I'm sure taking the time to come down here will be more than enough to accomplish that," Ms. Sweeney said, laying the books she'd been toting down on a wooden bench set in front of the office. "I can get these back to the library later. Why don't I show you to the newspaper office?"

Have you ever noticed that all high schools smell the same? The hallways are inevitably filled with a mix of stale cleaning solvent, linoleum, paper, age, and sun-scorched tile. During the school day, those odors might be blocked by perfume, cologne, body sprays, and the like, but after hours, when the building empties, the original scents return to take hold.

"Here we are," Principal Sweeney said, reaching an open door near the far end of the first-floor corridor.

Inside, I could hear the steady, rhythmic clack of fingers flying across computer keyboards—on deadline, as Kristi Powell had put it. Young, creative minds still believing anything was possible. I might have spoken to English and writing classes here occasionally, but hearing that sound made me fondly recall that stretch when I'd moved to New York to teach writing and criminology at Manhattan University, the first time I'd been back in a classroom since leaving Cabot Cove High. I don't think I've ever had a more rewarding or enlightening experience, and I gave it up only because I missed Cabot Cove too much. Since I'd kept my Manhattan apartment, I did get back occasionally to the school for a week here and there, though it wasn't the same. What I had enjoyed more than anything else was getting to know my students and watching them grow as they learned; popping in occasionally didn't permit that luxury.

"Mind if I come in?" Jen Sweeney asked those students gathered before her in the newspaper office. "I have a surprise for you all. I'm sure you've all heard of Cabot Cove's own resident bestselling author, Jessica Fletcher."

I missed my cue and was late making my entrance through the door. I'd been distracted, wondering if it was time to finally answer, once and for all, the question I'd been dodging for twenty-five years, most recently earlier that day during my interview with the award-winning Kristi Powell.

When did you solve your first murder?

If it was time to come clean, what better way to do that than by letting a high school student be the first to tell the whole story of my final days at Appleton High? There was a curious, fitting symmetry to that, and I came to believe, as I stepped into the office of the *Cabot Cove High School Eagle*, that Kristi's interview with me might come to serve a greater purpose. Maybe she'd even win another award. That thought brought a smile to my lips—making some good come from an experience I'd long banished from my memory.

I didn't spot Kristi initially among the room's eager young faces.

"Kristi, Mrs. Fletcher would like to have a word with you," Principal Sweeney said to a girl seated in the corner before me.

My breath seemed to freeze.

I'd never seen that girl before in my life.

Chapter Four

"Now, that's a strange one, even for you, Mrs. Fletcher," Sheriff Mort Metzger said, sitting across from me behind his desk at the Cabot Cove sheriff's department.

"Why *Mrs. Fletcher* today, Mort?"

"Because we're in the office. That makes this an official visit, and I like to impersonate a professional police officer from time to time."

"You spent twenty-five years with the NYPD," I reminded him.

"And I can't help but remember my predecessor, Amos Tupper, didn't provide any notion of what I was in for when I accepted this job."

I settled back in my chair. "So, what do you think?"

"That I should drive you back to Hill House, so you don't have to bike there in the dark."

"I was talking about the young woman who impersonated a high school newspaper reporter."

"Is that even a crime?"

"You tell me, Mort. You're the sheriff."

He laid his ever-present magical memo pad, which never seemed to be out of paper, down on the worn desk blotter before him. The blotter had so many coffee cup ring stains that some of the stains had stains. "Why exactly would someone impersonate a high school kid?"

"To get me to talk," I told him.

"And did you, Jessica?"

"This isn't business anymore?"

Mort rose from his chair and sat down closer to me on the front of the desk. "Did you speak with the real Kristi Powell at the school?"

"Yes."

"And?"

"Truth be told, I don't think she'd ever even heard of me."

"But she really has won awards for her work?"

I nodded. "Is that important?"

"I have no idea what's important here, Jessica, because none of this makes any sense." He looked down at me from his new perch, pondering the situation further. "You didn't ask to see any ID?"

"No."

"And how did this young woman claiming to be Kristi Powell contact you?"

"By phone."

"Your room at Hill House or cell?"

"Hill House. If she'd called my cell, I would've been suspicious, wondering how she'd gotten the number."

"An intrepid high school journalist? She probably has all kinds of contacts on speed dial. You know, lunch ladies, the custodial staff, building security guard—the kinds of folks who know where the bodies are buried."

"This isn't funny, Mort."

"I know, but I'm not sure what it is. And you let a perfect stranger into your home without doing any due diligence whatsoever."

"We met at Mara's, Mort."

"I was speaking figuratively. Maybe you should come to my public safety coffee klatches once in a while. And I'm going to need to talk to Kristi Powell."

"I told you—I have no idea who she really is."

"I'm talking about the real one."

"Is that really necessary?"

"What do you think? Maybe the impostor contacted her, dug some background info out of her to better seal the deal."

"I don't think so. Like you said, the real Kristi has won awards, something the fake one never mentioned, something she surely would have done if she'd done her homework."

"No pun intended, given this case centers around high school."

"The impostor was no high school student, Mort. She was only made up to look like one."

"So how old might she have been?"

"How can you tell these days? I have no idea."

"And you call yourself an investigator."

"I call myself a writer."

"Hmmm, you sound testy."

"It's been a long day, that's all," I said, thinking of that invitation to the retirement party for a colleague from my days at Appleton, on top of all those questions about my involvement in my first murder investigation. "I have a feeling the past is catching up with me."

"What's that mean?"

"I'll let you know when I figure it out myself. But there was this murder. . . ."

"Now there's something I've never heard before."

"It happened twenty-five years ago when I was a substitute teacher in Appleton."

"Never heard of it."

"It's not even a half hour from here, Mort."

"Oh, that Appleton. You're saying there was a murder *at the school*?"

I nodded. And then, in that moment, I figured something else out—an anomaly I should have noted before but had somehow missed.

"You've got that look, Mrs. Fletcher."

"What look is that, Sheriff Metzger?"

"The one that says there's something you're not ready to tell me yet."

"It's probably nothing."

"With you, it's *never* nothing."

"We'll figure all that out . . . when I'm ready to tell you, Mort."

I met Seth for dinner back at Mara's.

"I think I'll have the meat loaf," I said, closing the menu.

"You always get the meat loaf."

"No, I always get the special, which just so happens most of the time to be meat loaf."

He closed his menu, too. "Club sandwich for me."

"Turkey, of course."

"You really are a sleuth, aren't you?"

"You always order the same thing, too."

"We're nothing if not predictable, Jess." Seth set his menu down before him and regarded me with a serious stare. "Could you tell me about Wilma Tisdale?" he asked, referring to the woman who'd invited me to her retirement party, scheduled for the coming Saturday.

"Not much to tell"—I shrugged—"or at least not much that I remember. She taught math, and we ate lunch together a lot because she started out as a substitute, too."

"You weren't close?"

"Not particularly. I left all my friends behind when Frank and I moved from Appleton to Cabot Cove."

"With good reason, I suppose," Seth said, sipping his water.

"Well, there was a death involved."

"A murder, more specifically, right?"

I nodded, sipping the tea the server had already set down before me.

"There's always a murder with you, Jessica, but this is one I don't recall you ever going into much detail about."

"There's a reason for that, Seth."

"Which is . . . ?"

"There's not a lot to say."

"There's *always* a lot to say when it comes to murder."

"Not this time. I've never thought about this before, but it's almost like talking about my experiences with real-life murders became a lot easier once I started writing about fictional ones."

Seth nodded. "The experience in Appleton is unique because it happened before you were published."

"Mysteries, anyway."

"You'd published something else?"

"I was a journalism major at Harrison College, you know."

"That doesn't answer my question."

"Yes, I've published things other than mysteries. Not much, but some."

We ordered our meals, Seth looking primed to change the subject once our server, Clara, left the table. "I've never heard of anyone impersonating a high school student before."

I sipped some more of my tea. "Nothing aroused my suspicions during the interview, nothing at all. She must've been very comfortable in the guise."

"If you were writing about this in one of your books, what would you say she wanted?"

"Well," I said, thinking with my words, "I'd home in on what her primary focus was, based on her line of questioning."

"Okay . . ."

"And in this case, that would be Appleton."

"The murder?"

I nodded. "When I think back to our conversation, it seems she must've already known the answer to her own question and was after details."

"For a murder that happened before she was born, in all probability. Why, pray tell?"

I shrugged again. "If I had to guess, I'd say that something new has been added to the equation, something I'm not aware of yet."

"I can drive you to Appleton tomorrow afternoon, *ayuh*, if you want."

"Let me think about it."

"Is that a no?"

I shook my head. "It's a 'let me think about it.' I'm not so sure there'd be anything to gain from that after so many years. There'd be only a handful of teachers left at most who were there back then, and I'll probably see all of them on Saturday night at the retirement party."

"You're going, then."

"I haven't RSVP'd yet."

"But you're going for sure now. Because it's business."

"You mean murder, Seth."

"Same thing in your case."

Mort had dropped me and my Pashley bike at Mara's, but I insisted on riding it home, against Seth's protestations.

"Don't blame me if the next time you look at me is from a hospital bed in the ER."

"I promise."

"Because I can't treat bad judgment. They don't make a pill for that, and I don't want to see anyone scraped off the sidewalk."

"Your bedside manner could use some work, Seth."

"Really?" he said, his gaze turning playful. "Because I don't care one bit about anything you say."

I biked to the Cabot Cove library, instead of straight back to Hill House. Doris Ann, our wonderful librarian, greeted me with her customary enthusiasm and pointed me in the right direction for the old Cabot Cove High School yearbooks.

My thinking was that, given her knowledge of our town, the young woman who had impersonated Kristi Powell might be a former resident who had attended the high school. Even though

I'd be looking at pictures that had been taken anywhere between five and ten years, if not more, since the impostor graduated, I recalled enough of the young woman's features to be confident I'd be able to spot her amid posed headshots of the members of several senior classes. I started four years back, figuring she'd likely at least have finished college, and stacked ten yearbooks before me, since I didn't think she was older than twenty-eight or so.

Two hours later, blurry-eyed and with my fingers lined with paper cuts, I finally abandoned the effort. The general resemblance among people that age, at least in their yearbook photos, had never struck me before to this degree. By the time I finished, the faces were running into one another, and I feared I'd see rows and rows of them all night in my sleep. There were as few as five and as many as twenty female faces that *could* have been that of the young woman who'd interviewed me earlier in the day in the guise of Kristi Powell. I dutifully recorded their names and any other pertinent information that was listed, intending to cross-check the information against other Cabot Cove rolls to see what might have become of them. With Doris Ann's help, I could probably complete much of that process right there in the library, but it was too late to bother her with such things, and there was always tomorrow.

"Anything I can do for you, Jessica?" Doris Ann asked me, suddenly over my shoulder.

"Is it closing time already?"

"Twenty minutes ago"—she nodded—"but I've got some more inventorying and cataloging to finish up, so you're welcome to stay."

"Thank you. And as for your offer . . ." As my voice trailed off I handed her the list I'd made. "If you can provide any notion of what's become of these girls, all Cabot Cove High graduates, I'd be even more grateful to you than normal."

"What are you looking for?"

"Anything that stands out," I told Doris Ann. "Anomalies. Oh," I added as an afterthought, "if any of them went on to become writers or at least tried."

Doris Ann looked at the list, then back at me. "Does this have something to do with a case you're working on?"

"You know, I'm not sure." Something else occurred to me. "You don't keep Appleton High School yearbooks anywhere about?"

"No, but I think they're online."

They were indeed. And I went back through seven years of the older ones with nary a result. I was pushing too hard through the fatigue that had caught me in its clutches. As a result, I stopped jotting down the names of potential candidates because one face bled into another until all of them and none of them could have grown up to be the young woman who interviewed me. I resolved to take a fresh look at the same faces in the morning, either at the library again or on my own computer in my suite at Hill House.

After managing the bike ride back there with the brisk fall air doing its utmost to revive me, I turned on my computer with exactly that intention in mind until another thought struck me. For a book I'd written a few years back called *The Dead Man Sang*, I'd done considerable research into facial-recognition software. I'd even downloaded a rather professional program to better acquaint myself with the process to make proper use of it.

I probably should have given into exhaustion, but I figured I'd just spend a few minutes utilizing the software to get the rudimentary details of the young woman's features down. Two hours later, I was still at it behind the computer and had managed to compile a sketch that looked reasonably like the young woman I'd spent an hour with at Mara's earlier in the day—the day before now. One more hour tapping away at the keyboard to hone the more intimate details of her face and get her glasses right left me with a more-than-passable likeness I was actually excited about, enough so that I just might take Seth Hazlitt up on his offer to make a field trip to Appleton that afternoon to show the computerized sketch around.

I didn't have a color printer. But the sheriff's department and the library both did, and I was so excited, I decided to e-mail the sketch to Mort immediately. Then I decided to call his cell instead.

"Do you know what time it is?" he greeted me groggily.

"Obviously not. I'm sorry, Mort. I must've gotten carried away."

"Who died?"

"Nobody yet," I said, and filled him in on what I'd been doing all night.

"You should go to sleep," he said curtly once I'd finished.

"That the best you can do?"

"It's the best I can do at one o'clock in the morning, Jessica."

"Deepest apologies for disrupting your beauty sleep, Mort. How can I make it up to you?"

"Really? How about something you avoided telling me in the office today?"

"Just name it."

I heard Mort yawn on the other end of the line. "That first murder case you got swept into, the one the impostor was so interested in, the one in Appleton twenty-five years ago."

"What about it?"

"I'd like to hear more."

Chapter Five

Twenty-five years ago . . .

Over my dead body.

"What was that, Jess?" Frank asked me.

He startled me so much, I almost fell out of my chair. I'd been hunched over a stack of papers and hadn't finished correcting a single one, unable to chase out of my head that phone call I'd overheard from outside Walter Reavis's office that afternoon. I'd scampered out of the school office without keeping the appointment we'd made to discuss his bringing me on full-time as Bill Gower's replacement. I'd been excited by that prospect all day, only to dash away so Walter wouldn't think I'd been eavesdropping on his conversation.

"Just thinking out loud," I managed, clearing my throat and having no idea what it was Frank thought I'd said.

Walter Reavis had a private life like everybody else, and I guess I must've caught him in an argument with his wife, maybe over one of their children, one of whom, his elder daughter, currently attended Appleton High—a junior, I thought. Or maybe the call had been with one of his children. He had another daughter, in elementary school, and a son who'd just entered the military.

"Well," Frank said, grinning, "if you can tear yourself away from your homework, I've got a surprise for you."

I noticed Grady already had his jacket on and was raring to go, and I recalled that hint Frank had given just after we'd finished breakfast. "Now? It's been a long day. Could this wait until tomorrow?"

Frank eased me out of my chair and up onto my feet. "No, my dear, it can't. That's why they call it a surprise. Come on—let's do this while we've still got light to burn."

I smiled, glad he'd lifted me up physically the way he'd done so often emotionally through this disappointment or that. Frank had been a war hero in the Air Force, hardly a stranger to adversity, and a man who knew how to put on a brave face for his men no matter what the situation was. It's one thing to spend a good part of your life in the military, quite another to see actual combat, and Frank had seen more than his share.

We'd met building sets for a play at the Appleton Theater a number of years back. Two single adults who might have appeared lonely to others, if not for the fact that we'd managed to build full lives for ourselves that were instantly enriched when we got together. A head of prematurely gray hair and a penchant for cardigan sweaters made Frank look older than he was. He had the bluest eyes of anyone I'd ever known, the kind of eyes real writers refer to as piercing. But they were warm and reassuring, a perfect complement to the smile he flashed early and often. I got the feeling his experience in the war had left him grateful for the things in life most of us take for granted, which made him the perfect foil for me since I was prone to fixating on the smallest things and lamenting laboriously on what wasn't right in my life.

I'd left college with so many dreams, and years later, when I'd first met Frank, I was at a stage where it seemed none of them was going to come true. I'd tried for many of those years to land a job with a major daily newspaper like the *Boston Globe*, but I couldn't land one even with the local Appleton paper or the New Hampshire daily based in the town where I settled briefly after graduating from college. That's why I'd been so looking forward to my meeting with Walter Reavis. Becoming a full-time teacher had never been my dream, but teaching was something I enjoyed, and that would afford me time to continue my passion for writing.

As Frank held my coat for me to stuff my arms into, I flashed back to the reaction of my students—well, still Bill Gower's students—to that story of mine I'd assigned them to read. If that wasn't confirmation enough I was lucky to be on the verge of landing a full-time teaching job, nothing was. Fate was funny that way, I mused again, given that my meeting with the high school principal had been scheduled for just a few hours after I'd been pronounced by a bunch of fifteen-year-olds a failure as a writer.

Of course, the girl named Missy had thought she was reading a mystery. Given that was my favorite genre to read, I guess my own preferred tastes had found their way into a story I fantasized about being published in *The New Yorker*.

"Where are we going?" I asked Frank as he snatched his car keys from the hook by the door. "I should be fixing dinner."

"There'll be time for that later. I want to see the look on your face."

"When?"

He winked at Grady, who winked back. "When we get there."

"Cabot Cove?" I said when, twenty minutes later, we cruised past the town limits along a road that rimmed the shoreline. "What kind of surprise have you got for me in Cabot Cove?"

Frank checked his watch, even though it would've been easier to check the dashboard clock. A habit that had become ingrained in him during the war, and this was the very watch he'd worn through its entire duration. Truth be told, I'm not sure I ever saw him take it off.

"You know when I talk, I slow down, and if I slow down, we'll miss our appointment. I don't want to be late."

"Frank?"

"What?"

"You're talking."

He glanced at the speedometer and saw he was slowing down well below the speed limit.

"Why don't you ever drive us, Aunt Jess?" Grady asked from the backseat.

"Because I don't have a license."

The boy rolled his eyes. "All grown-ups drive, Aunt Jess."

"You know," Frank chimed in, "you could let me teach you. You let me teach you how to fly an airplane."

"Yes, but that was different."

"How?"

"We had the sky all to ourselves."

"If you can get your pilot's license, my dear, you can get your driver's license."

"I have my bike, and you to drive me."

"I'm not always going to be around, Jess."

"Frank?"

"What?"

"You're slowing down again."

We wound our way through the outskirts of nearby Cabot Cove and through the rustic town center lined with shops that had been in business for generations. What a wonderful place to live this must be, something Frank and I had often ruminated about, even though the houses were well out of our price range. But now that I was on the verge of being hired full-time at Appleton High . . .

Perchance to dream, as Shakespeare wrote.

Even though he wasn't talking, Frank cruised the streets slowly, checking the signs carefully as if either lost or looking for one street in particular. The last of the light was burning from the sky when he jammed the brakes hard enough to jostle both Grady and me.

"Frank," I said in my scolding voice.

"Didn't want to miss our turn, Jess."

I looked up at the sign that reflected what little light remained of the day.

"Candlewood Lane?"

"Yup."

"That sounds familiar. . . ."

"Yup."

"We sat in our car staring at a house on Candlewood Lane for something like an hour once, didn't we?"

"Yup," he said, applying the brakes in more gingerly fashion this time.

"That house," I realized as he pulled up in front of the beautiful, stately white Victorian at 698.

"Yup," he said one last time. "It came up for sale, wouldn't you know?"

He and Grady bounded out of the car, leaving me in the front seat too weak-kneed from staring at the house to move. Frank had to practically lift me out, as a smiling woman with the blondest hair I'd ever seen approached from her car.

"Mr. Fletcher, I'm Eve Simpson from Cabot Cove Realty. I work for Harry Pierce. We spoke earlier"—then after casting me a quick smile—"several times."

"You sell her yet?" Frank asked, eyeing 698 Candlewood Lane.

"Not since lunchtime, no." Eve Simpson checked her watch, the kind of person already starting her next appointment while she was finishing yours. "Would you like to see the house?"

"That's what we came for," Frank said, while I remained tongue-tied, head over heels in love with the house already.

"Your timing is perfect, Mr. Fletcher. The owners have already relocated and are quite motivated to sell."

"How far are they willing to come down? Because we can't even come close to affording the asking price."

"Not even close? Not even in the ballpark?"

"Depends on the ballpark, Ms. Simpson."

In the backyard there was a swing that Grady set himself to play on beneath the spray of an outdoor floodlight, while Frank and I stood on the screened porch. Eve Simpson was nowhere to be found, having left us on our own as she placed a call on her mobile phone. Not many had what people also called cell phones, and judging by the number of times Eve said, "What?" or "I can't hear you," I could see why. I imagined myself with one of the newfangled things—me, who couldn't even manage the workings of a car.

Then again, I could fly a plane.

"We'll never be able to afford it, Frank."

"Do you trust me, Jessica?"

He lowered his voice dramatically—he had, after all, been a thespian before he'd turned his talents to set decorating and building. I'd been assigned painting duties at the Appleton Theater, and my work was so terrible that almost all of it had to be redone. I blamed my infatuation with Frank for distracting me, but I'm sure the theater company was glad to be rid of me for future productions.

"I've got a plan," he continued. "We can cash in a chunk of my military pension for the down payment."

"Frank—"

"Shush now, my dear. Don't you go arguing with me. You talked about this house for two days straight after we spotted it."

"It wasn't for sale then. I was just dreaming."

He reached over and ran a hand through my hair, then held his hand against my cheek. "I love that look on your face when you're dreaming."

"As in, asleep?"

He cupped my other cheek with his free hand and drew me in closer. "Everyone dreams when they sleep. Only the special ones dream when they're awake. I look at you drifting and wonder where you've gone off to."

"Sometimes I don't know myself. My mind starts to wander, and off I go with it."

"To places that are yours and yours alone. Let me make this place yours, too."

"Are you sure, Frank?"

"Never surer of anything in my life."

I glanced at Grady going higher and higher on the swing, climbing toward the heavens. "But can we afford it?"

"Absolutely not. So we'll find a way, just like we always do."

The clacking of heels announced the return of Eve Simpson.

"So," she said, mobile phone in hand, "what are we thinking?"

We lingered in the front yard for a time after Eve Simpson left for her next appointment. Grady was in the car listening to his favorite radio station, though we didn't expect so many songs to have come and gone while we stood there.

"She's a beauty, all right, *ayuh*?"

The voice came from a man in a sweater buttoned all the way up to his neck. He was approaching along the street near where it met the edge of the lawn, which seemed to extend forever.

"I delivered the boys who lived here, watched them grow up, and gave them their physicals for college. Three, one after the other."

He was a kindly-looking sort with salt-and-pepper hair and a belly protruding slightly over his belt. He hooked his thumbs into the pockets of his sweater, then raised one hand to take off his glasses.

"I can tell you who lives in every house now and who lived there before them. They all got a story to tell, most happy but some not." He cast his gaze on 698 Candlewood Lane. "This one's all happy since the time it was built ninety years ago. I could give you the whole history, if you want."

"Frank Fletcher," Frank said, extending his hand. "And this is my wife, Jessica."

"Seth Hazlitt," the friendly man greeted us, taking Frank's hand. "You folks have children?"

I was about to offer an explanation when Frank said simply, "Yes."

"Well, no better place to grow up than Cabot Cove. You look up 'quiet' in the dictionary, there's a picture of our town. Reason people move out from time to time, as a matter of fact, is nothing ever happens here. And as for crime, most folks I know don't even bother to lock their doors. We did have a murder here once, but nobody can say exactly when that was. You folks would be real happy here." He reached into his pocket and came out with a business card. "Put this somewhere you can always find it. Once you move in, you may require my services."

Frank checked the card. "Thank you, Doctor."

"That's Seth to my friends. And if you live in Cabot Cove, odds are you're my friend. All my patients are my friends—a fine thing until it comes to collecting the bills," he said, smiling. "I'll be leaving you folks to the house now. Don't say 'good-bye' to her when you leave. Say 'so long.'"

Grady honked the horn, which was Dr. Seth Hazlitt's cue to resume his evening constitutional and ours to head on home. In the car, I kept my gaze cocked backward through the darkness at 698 Candlewood Lane until Frank swung around the corner and the house vanished from sight. But I saw it every time I closed my eyes and could barely sleep that night, I was so excited over the prospect of our potentially buying it. I was concerned that, seeing how much I loved it, Frank would make the sale happen no matter what, and I resolved to insist that we exercise restraint and discipline going forward. Not that it would matter. Frank was as headstrong as I was when it came to his singular focus on a goal and pursuing that goal with relentless intensity until it had been achieved.

That said, I awoke the next morning never having felt better about the future. Grady had settled into his life with us, I was about to be brought on full-time at Appleton High, and in the near future, we might be the proud owners of a beautiful home in tony Cabot Cove. I could barely wait for Frank to drop me at school so I could meet up with Walter Reavis to explain away my "failure" to show up for our meeting and, I hoped, pick up our discussion about my future.

"Oh my, what's this?" Frank said as he braked the car well before our normal drop-off point.

I looked up from the stack of papers I'd been sorting through on my lap and saw a pair of Appleton police cars to go with a quartet of Maine State Police vehicles and a dark wagon with no markings.

"That's the coroner's wagon, Jess," Frank told me.

I bounded out of the car in the next moment, the stack of papers shed to the floor and my shoulder bag left behind. Thankfully, as was our custom, Frank had dropped Grady off at Appleton Elementary first, sparing us the need to explain to an eight-year-old what a coroner's wagon was.

I rushed up to the front of the school, where a number of my colleagues were milling about as students filed silently past them into the building. I'd never heard it so quiet at this time of the day, so quiet that the collective rumbling of the buses sounded more like a roar. I spotted Wilma Tisdale approaching me.

"Oh, Jessica," she said, hugging me lightly. "Did you hear?"

"It's Walter Reavis, isn't it?" I said, gazing inside the building, my voice full of dread.

Wilma nodded sadly. "He's—"

"Dead," I completed for her, picturing Walter found dead of a heart attack at his desk that morning in the wake of that argument I'd overheard him having over the phone the previous afternoon.

"Not just that," Wilma Tisdale told me. "He might have been murdered."

Chapter Six

The present

"We're going to have to finish this later, Jessica," Mort interrupted me over the phone.

I looked around the living room portion of my suite, reacquainting myself with the time and stunned at how late it had gotten.

"Sorry, Mort. I must've lost track of time. Again."

"It's not that. I just got a text. A body's been found. Looks like we've got a murder on our hands in the present, too."

"Who?"

"You're not going to believe this, Mrs. Fletcher: a woman who meets the description of the one who interviewed you yesterday morning."

He was right: I didn't believe it.

I was waiting outside Hill House when Mort picked me up in

his department-issue SUV. He was on the police radio for the entire drive to the outskirts of Cabot Cove and one of the few remaining scenic overlooks in the region. I'm not sure where the term originated or why town managers throughout Maine thought it would be a good idea to carve out wide swaths of road that resembled the truck weigh stations that still dot much of the East Coast highway system.

This particular scenic overlook didn't overlook much of anything anymore, given the lack of pruning and upkeep on the undeveloped land beneath the overlook that would have once been described as "rustic" but now might more aptly be labeled "crumbling." Two Cabot Cove cruisers, their lights flashing, were already on the scene, parked on either side of an older, and smaller, BMW.

"Nice car for a high school student," Mort said, frowning at me as if I were somehow to blame for not figuring out the ruse earlier.

"The young lady was already inside Mara's when I got there, and we left separately, so I never saw what she was driving. And let's not jump to conclusions until we're sure it's her."

One look inside the car told me it was. The young woman I knew as Kristi Powell had clearly been shot. Of all the murder victims I've come upon in my time, those killed with guns have always taken the greatest toll on me. I can't explain why exactly. I mean, murder is murder, the means not nearly as important as the act itself and finding justice for the victim. But there's something about the sudden finality of a gunshot, the brutality of it, not to mention the blood and the mess. In my books, a great number of murders are random acts, as opposed to premeditated ones. The killers respond on impulse and do something they'll have to spend the rest of their lives lying about and covering up. And beyond that, my experience, at least through research, has yielded the fact that the majority of gun murders are not acts of passion so much as acts of planning. Whoever this young woman really was, that was the kind of crime she'd fallen victim to tonight.

The driver's-side window was down, and the young woman's head rested on the windowsill, a neat bullet hole carved just above her right temple. Her body was twisted at an odd angle, as if she were reaching for something she never got the chance to grab. Her left hand dangled outside the car, and her right had flopped into her lap. Gazing into the car, I noticed on the floor a pair of glasses that I recognized as the ones she'd been wearing when we'd met at Mara's the day before.

The young woman who'd impersonated Kristi Powell was wearing different clothes than the ones I recalled from fifteen hours earlier, now the previous day: she was now wearing black tights, shapely boots, and a waist-length tapered leather jacket that I was certain bore the label of some fancy designer.

"Tell me what you're seeing, Mrs. F.," Mort said, using the pet name he'd given me in his early years as sheriff of Cabot Cove.

Maybe murder made him nostalgic.

"The killer was inside the car when he or she shot the victim," I told him.

Mort nodded, squeezing his hands into a pair of latex evidence gloves. "And you know this because . . ."

"The same way someone with twenty-five years in the NYPD does." I backed slightly away from the driver's-side window. "Had the victim not known her killer, or the murderer approached from this angle, she would've been shot in the opposite temple and slumped toward the passenger side of the car instead of toward the driver's window."

Mort nodded again. I couldn't tell whether he was a step ahead of or even with me in his thinking. "What else?"

"She's not wearing her seat belt. That tells me she took it off because she was waiting for someone to show up."

"Positioning of the car could be a giveaway to that, too, Mrs. F."

"Of course. Someone who makes a random stop to place a call, think, or whatever else normally parks nose in. The fact that the victim backed in against the fence there indicates this was a prearranged meeting, not a random encounter. She arrived first and was waiting and watching when the killer arrived. If the order had been reversed, she would have pulled in next to the killer's vehicle. No need to back in next to it."

"Good point," Mort said, looking down at the asphalt as if it might yield something through the chilly darkness. "I'll ask the forensic team from the Maine State Police to check for tire tracks."

"You may want to cordon the area off in the meantime."

He fingered his chin as if what I'd just suggested was some kind of epiphany. "You know, that's a smart idea. Too bad a cop with twenty-five years' experience in New York would never have thought of it."

I ignored his remark and circled round to the other side of the BMW, not bothering to suggest that Mort check the door for prints. "The killer shot her from the passenger seat. The victim saw the gun in time to turn away, maybe try to flee. That explains the odd angle of the entry wound."

"Couldn't she just as easily have been shot from outside the car?"

"I suppose. Only the window's closed now, and it wouldn't have been open then either because of the cold. And yanking a door open and shooting someone at the same time would be a difficult task for all but the most experienced gunmen. No, Mort," I said, turning back toward him, "whoever killed this woman wanted to be sure. I think that the forensics team will find powder burns that prove the bullet was fired from no more than two feet away."

"Want to know what I see, Mrs. F.?"

I had no idea why he'd taken to calling me that again. "Oh, did I leave something out, Sheriff?"

"A second bullet."

"*Second* bullet?"

Mort shone his flashlight toward the black upholstered ceiling on the driver's side above the victim. "You see this slight crease here? Looks to me like this was the first shot fired, but the victim managed to deflect the shooter's hand, sending the bullet askew."

"Maybe she thought she'd hurt the killer," I postulated, "at least enough to try to make a run for it instead of continuing the struggle. And that tells me it was a struggle against a stronger opponent, a struggle she didn't think she'd be able to win."

"A man, then."

"I was just about to say that."

"Sure, steal my thunder." Mort stepped away from the BMW, squeezing his chin and shining his flashlight about at nothing in particular. "So, somewhere around twelve hours after interviewing you," he continued, "a young woman who claimed to be a high school student winds up dead."

"Be nice if we could trace back where she'd been for those

twelve hours. She must've gone somewhere to change, and if we check the trunk, I wouldn't be surprised if we found an overnight bag of some kind."

"Meaning she may have checked into one of the gazillion motels within easy driving distance," Mort agreed. "I'll put my deputies on that as soon as we get some photos."

That made me think of the sketch I'd created of the young woman. As I looked at her face again, the likeness was incredible. Mort was shining his flashlight over the car again, first in the front seat and then in the back, until his beam stopped on the fashionable shoulder bag resting on the floor behind the driver's seat. I could picture the victim lifting it from the passenger seat and stowing it there when her killer arrived. In my mind, I saw it all unfold as if I'd been standing right there. What I didn't know was how much time had passed, or what the purpose of the meeting had been, before the fatal shot had been fired.

"No wallet or ID," Mort said, riffling gently through the contents of the bag with his evidence gloves.

"Belated attempt to make it look like a robbery, you think?"

"Could be. Or maybe some kind of tryst set up on one of those Internet sites gone wrong."

I nodded. "Keep us off the track for as long as possible."

Mort gave me a long stare. "You know what I'm thinking?"

"Of course, because I'm thinking the same thing: The young woman's murder and her interviewing me in the guise of a high school student must be connected."

"In which case, maybe this meeting was all about the victim telling the killer what she'd learned."

"Except she didn't learn anything she couldn't have found in a Google search. I didn't answer any of her questions about Walter Reavis's murder, but it sure seemed like she already had a clear notion of the level of my involvement in the investigation."

"You think that's important?"

"Only because very, very few people knew about it. So maybe, yes, because it seemed like our murder victim here knew more than she was saying about my part in bringing a killer to justice."

"Your first killer," Mort said, sounding whimsical. "Is that like your first boyfriend, your first paycheck, your first—"

"I get the idea, Mort," I said, cutting him off.

"Tell me again what she was most interested in. Make believe you haven't told me anything yet."

"You really are good at this," I told him.

"I have had some experience with murder, Mrs. Fletcher—not nearly as much as you, of course."

"The young woman wanted to know about the first murder I ever solved."

"Walter Reavis's?"

I nodded, recalling where I'd left off the story while talking to Mort on the phone and making a mental note so I'd recall at what point to pick up the story for him.

"But she didn't say why she was interested?"

"She didn't even tell me who she really was. And she asked me just enough pointed questions to keep me from growing overly suspicious."

"You thought she was a high school kid. Who gets suspicious about walking hormones with acne and cell phones?" He cast me a long look. "You see any possible connection between the murder of your school principal twenty-five years ago and this one tonight?"

"You mean this morning," I corrected him.

"Don't change the subject. We were talking about Appleton."

My hands went to my face. "Oh my . . ."

"Oh boy . . . I hate when you get that look."

"There was something I didn't tell you in the office, Mort."

"I remember."

"It's about that retirement party I've been invited to. I got the invitation only earlier today—yesterday, actually," I told him, recalling what had dawned on me earlier.

"So?"

"So yesterday was Tuesday, and it's Wednesday now. Who sends an invite with only a few days' notice before the day of a party?"

"Last-minute decision, you think?"

"I need to call Wilma Tisdale."

Mort gazed dramatically toward the sky. "Might want to wait until the sun's up, Mrs. F."

I rolled my eyes. "'Mrs. F.' again . . ."

Mort was looking back inside the car at the young woman who had impersonated Kristi Powell. "I'll lift her fingerprints, see if she's in the system. Who knows? We might get lucky."

"It wouldn't surprise me. I sincerely doubt this was the first time she stepped outside the lines."

"And in my experience people who get murdered during shady late-night rendezvous are no strangers to crime. At least there's some good news, Mrs. F."

"What's that?"

"Even though it's in my jurisdiction, this scenic overlook is technically located outside the Cabot Cove town limits. That means we don't have to add it to the murder tally."

* * *

There have been very few times in my life when I experienced firsthand the old phrase about being too tired to sleep. This was one of those times.

The sun was rising when Mort dropped me off back at Hill House. I drew all the blinds in the bedroom portion of my suite, making it as dark as I could, and climbed into bed, pretending it was closer to my normal turn-in hour. An hour later, with the sun sneaking through the cracks between the blinds, I gave up trying to sleep and turned on the television to one of the early-morning news shows.

Normally, that was the perfect recipe to help me drift off, but this wasn't a normal day or time. So much was racing through my mind, both from that day and the day before and from twenty-five years earlier, that I just couldn't slow down my thoughts.

I kept coming back to the young woman who'd impersonated a high school student to land an interview with me in the morning, only to be murdered that night. Given that I could no more easily control my imagination in real-life investigations than I can in fictional ones, I kept fixating on two questions: Who was this woman really, and what had she wanted to get out of me in the interview she'd conducted?

It was difficult for me to speculate on the first question, but not on the second, since the only area we covered that seemed off in tone consisted of the young woman I believed was Kristi Powell pushing me to tell her about the murder of Walter Reavis. She hadn't mentioned him by name or expressed any knowledge of the case's ultimate resolution but, as I looked back, it was clear that was what our interview had been all about, regardless of the pretext.

What if I had, in fact, unwittingly given up what she wanted? What if I'd considered whatever it was innocuous, but it was anything but that in the young woman's mind? Somewhere around twelve hours later, she'd been murdered, and I could no more dismiss the potential connection between that and our meeting than I could stop breathing.

I finally faded off to sleep, and woke up to different news anchors and a ringing cell phone.

"Is this my wake-up call?" I greeted Mort, seeing his name light up on my caller ID.

"You might call it that, Mrs. F. . . ."

"Uh-oh . . ."

"Turns out, our murder victim was indeed in the system. Her name is Ginny Genaway, age thirty-three, from neighboring New Hampshire."

I couldn't believe what I'd just heard. "Thirty-three? And I took her for a high school student? I need to have my eyes checked."

"It's her name you should be paying attention to, not her age."

"Why, Mort?"

"Because Genaway was her married name. Her birth name was Reavis. That principal murdered in Appleton twenty-five years ago was her father."

Chapter Seven

For a second, I thought I was still dreaming. In dreams, after all, time is skewed, lacking all sense of meaning. That was what this felt like: the past and the present, separated by twenty-five years, colliding.

"You fall back asleep, Mrs. F.?"

"I'm trying to pretend I never woke up."

"I thought you'd be excited."

"'Baffled' would be a better way to put it. How old did you say she was, Mort?"

"Er, let's see. I had it written down right . . . Here it is—thirty-three."

Meaning Ginny Reavis had been eight years old when her father was murdered. Come to think of it, I seemed to recall her being in Grady's class at Appleton Elementary. Now she'd been murdered, too. Like father, like daughter. She had done her absolute best to look like a high school student when we'd met the day before, but the fact that she wore her hair in that bun should have been a dead giveaway that something was awry.

"You ever cross paths with her while you were working in Appleton?" I heard Mort ask me.

"Not even once. Walter Reavis was divorced and had pretty much moved on, though I seem to recall his kids much preferring him to their mother."

"How many kids did he have?"

"Three. An older daughter named Lisa Joy, who attended Appleton High, and a son I met very briefly at the funeral in his full-dress uniform. He was a Marine, just like you and Adele. But he wasn't as fortunate. As I recall, he was killed on his first deployment to the Middle East. A roadside bomb."

"Ouch," Mort said. "That's the one thing we didn't have in Vietnam."

"Good thing tours there and with the NYPD prepared you for life in Cabot Cove."

He started to chuckle but it ended as a snort. "And I thought I was moving here for the quiet life. The first year I was sheriff, there were five murders in town—remember?"

"I'm too busy pondering the one from last night."

"Care to guess my next question, Jessica?"

"You'd like to know why the daughter of my former principal would bother impersonating someone to get me to talk to her."

"You must be psychic."

I switched the phone from my left hand to my right. "There are police departments that make regular use of psychics, Mort."

"The last thing we need in Cabot Cove when I can predict the future as well as any of them."

"Really, Mort? Why don't you tell me what's showing in your crystal ball?"

"Murder. What else? Up for a field trip to New Hampshire, Mrs. Fletcher?"

"New Hampshire?"

"Manchester, specifically. Home of Ginny Genaway, born Ginny Reavis."

Mort said he had some loose ends to tie up regarding the young woman's murder before we could head south. Considering he was dealing with the coroner, waiting on the ballistics report in addition to the report from the state police crime scene unit, and trying to track down and inform the victim's next of kin of the murder, those loose ends amounted to an entire rope. Meanwhile, I called Doris Ann at the Cabot Cove Library to tell her she could break off her research into what became of the Cabot Cove High coeds who resembled my interviewer from the day before, since the interviewer's true identity had now been revealed. Sadly.

I'd already been driving myself crazy working out how all this tied together and how Ginny Reavis's murder might have been connected to her father's a generation before. She'd been too young to have figured into the investigation, bringing me back to the other mystery here—that being how it was I'd received the invitation to Wilma Tisdale's retirement party here in Cabot Cove yesterday, just four days before it was scheduled for, this coming Saturday. As near as I could figure, that book signing where I'd last seen her must've been about ten years ago. That meant it was likely for either *Murder in White* or *The Killer Called Collect.*

It's funny how I've come to measure time not so much in years as in books. I'm sure I'm not alone among writers as far as that proclivity is concerned, and it's one of the reasons so many of us are described as "ageless," and that I don't think I've ever met one who ever uttered the word "retirement."

The invitation included the number at which to RSVP. I didn't need to read it off the invite, because I'd studied the fancy lettering so much, I'd memorized it. I lifted my cell phone and pressed out the numbers before I could change my mind.

"Hello," a happy-sounding voice greeted me.

"I'm calling for Wilma Tisdale."

"This is Wilma Tisdale," I heard in a singsongy voice I didn't recognize at all.

"Wilma, this is Jessica Fletcher."

"Why, Mrs. Fletcher, what a pleasant surprise!"

"Jessica, please."

She chuckled. "Well, I've never been on a first-name basis with a celebrity before."

"You still haven't. It's just me, your former teaching colleague, and I've called to RSVP for your party on Saturday."

Wilma cleared her throat once and then again. "Jessica, how lovely that you're able to come!"

"I have to admit that holding it right here in my backyard had something to do with it. I'm on deadline for my next book and I can hardly spare the time to breathe. But it will be great to see some old friends. And you couldn't have chosen a better venue than the Cabot Cove Country Club."

"Of course," Wilma said, as if her mind was somewhere else. "That's what I've heard."

"How many people are you expecting?"

"Oh, you know, around sixty or seventy, I should think. You'll probably know about half of them."

"My, I hope I'll be able to remember them all."

"They'll certainly remember you, Jessica."

I thought she was referring to the success I'd managed as a writer after moving to Cabot Cove. But her tone suggested something else, bringing me back to the murder of Walter Reavis.

"I wonder if I might ask you something related to Walter Reavis, Wilma."

"Of course. Be warned, though, my memory isn't what it used to be."

"Is anyone's? Anyway, do you recall ever meeting Walter's daughter Ginny? She would've been around eight at the time of his murder."

"No, not her. But I did know the other two a bit, since his elder daughter was still at the high school and his son had graduated a few years before. Then he went off to the Middle East and . . ."

"Yes, how terrible."

"Some families are cursed, Jessica, don't you think?"

First, Mort mentioning psychics and now Wilma Tisdale raising curses—maybe I really was still sleeping. . . .

"Why'd you ask me about Walter Reavis's daughter, by the way?"

I wasn't about to lie to Wilma, but it wasn't the right time to tell her the truth either. "It's a long story. Why don't I share it with you on Saturday? I'll make sure to get to the party early."

"And is there a plus one in the life of America's favorite mystery writer?"

"Just my imagination, which does tend to take on a life of its own."

"You have that to thank for your career, I suppose. You know, my memory may not be what it once was, but I still remember you clacking away on that typewriter whenever you had a free period."

"I published barely anything I wrote on that old thing. The ribbon must've been cursed."

"See, I told you, Jessica."

The moment I hung up, I realized that something had seemed off about our conversation, but I couldn't put my finger on what. My husband, Frank, used to say, "Sometimes you have to look closer at what you are hearing." My talk with Wilma Tisdale made me realize for the first time what he'd meant by that confusing sentiment. There was definitely something unspoken in her words, but I couldn't "see" *what* for the life of me.

As soon as the call ended, I felt guilty about not sharing the news about Ginny Genaway, born Ginny Reavis, having been murdered the previous night. Wilma might turn on the television and learn about it; she'd know instantly that I had held the information back from her. I'd go from being the only celebrity with whom she was on a first-name basis to a snob and a liar. I wondered if I might even end up disinvited from her retirement party.

I would've actually been looking forward to seeing so many of those from another phase of my life, if the circumstances had been different—both now and twenty-five years ago. My biggest reservation was that such reunions have the effect of making us feel just as we were when all of us were last together. In my case, that meant with Frank still alive at one of the happiest and most exciting times of my life, when anything seemed possible. I thought about the night Frank drove Grady and me to Cabot Cove, when I'd laid eyes on 698 Candlewood Lane for the last time before we made it ours.

I'm not saying I was happier then, but in the battle of the past versus the present, the past will win out every time. We exaggerate the things we think made us ever so happy, blowing them wildly out of proportion. It was doubly difficult for me because my memories of that time were particularly intense, given that there hadn't been a lot of years left when the three of us would be together. Grady had already left our household to go back to his mother before Frank's death, and I was afraid Saturday night's festivities would remind me of what it had been like to come home to find someone else always there.

Then again, maybe "festivities" was the wrong word to refer to Wilma Tisdale's upcoming retirement party. If my suspicions, my instincts, were correct, and Ginny Reavis's murder last night was somehow connected to her father's twenty-five years ago, then some of the guests just might have information that could help me. Maybe I should dispense with the formalities, risk the gossip, and make Sheriff Mort Metzger my plus one. And I might have if I wasn't afraid he'd lapse into calling me "Mrs. F." again at the party.

While I waited for his call to finalize our plans to head to New Hampshire, I was struck again by something that felt amiss in my phone call with Wilma Tisdale. It wasn't anything specific, so much as a feeling that she was holding something back, something she stopped short of telling me. Another reason, I suppose, why I should be looking forward to Saturday night.

* * *

"You forgot to tell me what Ginny Genaway was fingerprinted for," I said to Mort as soon as he picked me up just past noon.

"No, I didn't. I just wanted to have all the details before I did, so I could answer all your questions."

"How are those details coming?"

"Slowly. Ginny Genaway was arrested for assault, but never stood trial after the victim dropped all charges."

I tried to reconcile that with the girl I'd mistaken for a high school student the day before. "Who was the victim, Mort? Who'd she assault?"

Mort didn't answer me right away, seeming to enjoy having answers that I lacked. "We're headed to meet him now, Jessica. It's better you see for yourself."

"I thought Ginny Reavis lived in Manchester," I said, when Mort followed the signs for Concord, New Hampshire, instead.

"It's Ginny Genaway, and we're making a stop here first. By the way, one of my deputies found the motel where she'd checked in earlier in the day and then checked out before heading to that scenic overlook. She must have used it just to kill time between meeting you and meeting her killer."

"Just a place to change her clothes, pretty much," I elaborated. "Get out of the disguise she'd used to convince me she was a high school student."

"When was the last time you had your eyes checked, Jessica?"

"Have you seen how young women look these days, Mort?"

"Adele would have my head if I even thought about it."

I gazed out the windshield. "Okay, so now we're headed to meet the person Ginny Genaway, formerly Reavis, assaulted, but who then dropped the charges, you seemed to enjoy telling me a few minutes ago." I gazed across the front seat of Mort's SUV. "You're being uncharacteristically cryptic today, Sheriff."

"Well, Mrs. F.," he said, casting me a sidelong smile, "I'm just enjoying being a step ahead of you for a change."

"Did I miss something here?"

"How about the name Vic Genaway?"

"What about it?"

"Doesn't ring any bells?"

"Should it?"

Mort gestured out the windshield at a sign on the side of the road.

"Oh," I said, starting to realize what he meant.

The sign announced the exit for the New Hampshire State Prison for Men, a sprawling facility of interconnected institutional buildings that sat in a lush, green, bucolic sprawl of land in the Merrimack Valley. I seemed to remember from research for a past book that it housed around twelve hundred inmates, all men since women incarcerated by the state were housed in a separate, dedicated facility.

From a distance, it might have been an apartment complex, until the twelve-foot steel fence, topped by twisty razor wire, came into view. The buildings initially appeared to be made of rustic red brick, but up close, I could see they were formed of painted concrete. I'd say the purpose was to make the inmates feel more at home than they would surrounded by institutional drab gray concrete slabs. But inmates didn't get to view their domain from the outside very much.

"Okay, Mort, I'll bite," I said as he slid onto the side road accessing the prison. "Why the pit stop?"

He grinned.

"Stop that."

"What?"

"Smiling."

"I'm not allowed to be happy?"

"Not when it's at my expense."

He looked across the seat at me. "How's it feel, Jessica?"

"What?" I asked now.

"Not knowing something. Being in the dark. Playing catch-up."

"Is this a multiple-choice question?"

"No, all of the above. I just want to savor this moment as long as I can."

"Okay." I settled back in my seat. "We're going to see this Vic Genaway."

"Ding," Mort chimed, doing his best imitation of a bell sound.

"He's the former Ginny Reavis's husband."

"Ding, ding."

"And the man she assaulted."

"Ding, ding, ding!"

"Care to tell me what Vic Genaway is in prison for?"

"Your specialty, Mrs. F."

"Murder . . ."

Mort nodded. "You sure his name doesn't ring any bells?"

"You know I don't get out much, Mort."

"But you love to watch movies. What's your favorite one featuring the mob?"

"*The Godfather*, of course."

Mort looked at me as if I'd made his point for him. "Substitute Boston for New York. That's all you need to know about Vic Genaway."

Chapter Eight

As we pulled onto the prison grounds, Mort explained that Vic Genaway was a high-ranking member of the Boston mafia, current head of the former Angiulo mob. The state of New Hampshire had made a case for conspiracy against him, thanks to a man the police there had dead to rights for murdering a liquor board employee. In New Hampshire all liquor stores were owned and operated by the state, bringing in huge revenues and helping to offset the lack of a state income tax. According to Mort, the Boston mob had enjoyed an "in" on the supply chain and distribution channel for some years, until a certain official either reneged on, or tried to renegotiate, the terms. The mob's means of renegotiation, under the direction of Vic Genaway, was to dispense the most serious of punishments for the man's indiscretions, while setting an example for whoever assumed his position.

My mind was wandering when Mort got to the part about the

killing itself. But I did get my focus back in time to hear about him figuring it must've been one of the hit men who'd done the actual deed who'd fingered Genaway as the man who gave the order. Since Genaway was much higher on the food chain, New Hampshire authorities would have jumped at the chance to put him away instead, while putting the informant into witness protection.

"But you're not sure about that," I surmised.

"The informant? No. Genaway pleaded out, so the case never went to trial, and the informant never had to testify. He's probably working at a Home Depot in Boise or someplace as we speak."

We were passed through security into the maximum-security wing of the prison, where we both checked our phones and Mort checked his gun. Then a guard escorted us to an interview room normally used for conferences between inmates and their attorneys. We waited five minutes before a key jangled in the lock and the door opened to allow another guard, who reminded me of my fisherman friend Ethan, to escort Vic Genaway inside.

I noticed Genaway's hands were strung together with a chain manacled to either wrist, a picture right out of an old B movie on the late show. He wore a prison outfit of a khaki shirt and matching khaki pants, the shirt a tight fit across his broad chest. He held his furtive eyes low, holding on to something resembling the upper hand by not so much as acknowledging our presence. Even when the guard sat him down, Genaway continued to act as if we weren't there at all. Speaking of Ethan, Genaway had the raw, scarred, and calloused hands of a fisherman. He had the look of a thug who'd climbed his way up on the docks, working the rackets and longshoremen's unions before climbing the ladder to the top of the mafia cadre.

The thing that struck me most about Genaway, though, was the difference in age between him and the former Ginny Reavis; she'd been thirty-three, while I had her husband pegged as early to mid-fifties. And it wasn't like Genaway was going to win any trophies for his looks, even discounting the inherent deterioration in appearance prison stretches were known to result in virtually overnight.

"How you doing, Vic?" Mort asked him.

Genaway looked at him. "Who's asking?" Then he looked down again.

"Sheriff Mort Metzger of Cabot Cove, Maine."

"I don't know anybody in Cabot Cove, Maine."

"We think your wife did."

Genaway looked up at that, concern flaring briefly across his features. He had a thick mane of silvery hair flecked with black and the typically sallow skin tone of an inmate who barely saw the sun. I haven't visited a lot of prisons, but when I have, I've been struck by their uniformity: the same sights, the same sounds, the same lighting, and the same smells.

Especially the smells.

I'd call it generally a combination of must, mold, and stale perspiration, all adding up to what I deemed to be hopelessness. That scent of hopelessness hung in the air, just as it hung on the person of each inmate, permeating the clothes and baked into the skin too deeply for any shower to relieve.

"You listening to me, Vic?"

Genaway turned his gaze on me, while addressing Mort. "What's my wife got to do with anything?"

"I'm afraid I've got some bad news for you, Vic. Your wife is dead."

Genaway smiled, pretending the situation was under his control. "What kind of game you playing, Sheriff?"

"No game. Ginny was murdered last night, shot once in the head in a way I'm sure you're familiar with," Mort said in a tone and a demeanor that must have been part and parcel of his twenty-five-year career with the New York Police Department. "Since it happened in my jurisdiction, I thought we'd come down to deliver the news personally."

"Who's 'we,' Sheriff? You and Miss Marple here?"

"'Miss Marple'?" I repeated.

Genaway held his steely gaze on me longer. "I recognize you from the prison library. I work there. You'll be happy to know you're real popular between these walls. Fresh stack of your books to reshelve every week. Not the newer ones, just the old ones. We get them used, hand-me-downs from other libraries."

"Perhaps I could arrange to send some of my latest titles down."

"Yeah." Genaway snickered, a man no longer able to recognize a simple kind gesture. "Don't knock yourself out over it or anything." He looked back toward Mort. "I don't believe your crap about Ginny. I don't know what kind of game you're running here, Sheriff, but play it somewhere else."

Mort reached into the pocket of his uniform jacket and came out with a crime scene photo of Ginny Genaway taken inside the BMW. He slid it across the table, holding his stare on her husband the whole time. "Sorry, Vic."

Genaway gave the picture a quick glance, then looked back up, lost in that transitional moment before an awful truth finally sinks to the bone. "What is this? What happened?" he said, his eyes glued to the picture now.

"We were hoping you could tell us that."

Genaway's stare, cold and hooded, fastened on me. "What's she doing down here? Why tote her along?"

"She met your wife yesterday."

"She can speak for herself. Can't you, Fletch?"

"Fletch was a character from a series of mysteries by Gregory Mcdonald, Mr. Genaway."

"And now it's your nickname, too."

"I met your wife yesterday," I told him. "She came to interview me in the guise of a newspaper reporter," I said, leaving out the high school part. "I was one of the last people to see her alive."

"You plan on solving her murder?"

"That's the sheriff's job, Mr. Genaway."

"You got your own rep in that regard, Fletch."

For some reason, I wasn't intimidated by him at all. "Why did Ginny assault you?"

"I dropped those charges, like it didn't happen."

"But it did happen, didn't it?"

"And what makes that your business, lady?"

"The fact that she was murdered last night, and I'm sure you want to do everything you can to help Sheriff Metzger find her killer."

Genaway's eyes misted up, a brief crack showing in his concrete veneer before he quickly recovered his tired bravado. But his voice turned softer, losing the edge based on the illusion he was the one in charge here.

"You said she interviewed you, Fletch? What'd she want to know?"

"I think she was poking around to find out about her father's murder."

"The high school principal? So why ask you?"

"Because I taught at the school," I told him, leaving it there.

Genaway shook his head. "What do you make of that? Father gets whacked and, a bunch of years later, his daughter. I mean, what are the odds?"

"Slim to none, Vic," Mort said. "That's why we wanted to see you in person."

"As long as you don't think for one second I had anything to do with this, Sheriff."

"Well, there was that assault beef she was charged on. She clean your clock that bad?" Mort said, pushing Genaway; he was all the way back in NYPD mode now.

The remark had been aimed at getting a rise out of Genaway but all he did was smile sadly. "That whole mess was over kids."

"Don't tell me," I said. "She wanted them, and you didn't."

"Wrong, Fletch. It was the exact opposite. Ginny might've made herself up all prim and proper for your interview, but let me tell you, she was no angel. You ask me, that's why she bothered giving a lug like me the time of day. I think she had daddy issues and don't think she ever really got over losing her father the way she did. Mine died in prison, and I might well end up following in his footsteps, just like Ginny did hers. What's the word for that?"

"Irony," I said.

"Yeah, that's it. Irony. I first met her in a bar I owned, a place I wouldn't try convincing you was an upscale establishment. I got grown kids from my first marriage, who never talk to me, and a pair of ex-wives living as far from me as the map allows. I figured Ginny was my chance at giving it a shot again. Young, beautiful woman like that—I figured I'd be doing her a favor, but she wouldn't even give me the time of day on the subject of having kids. You want to know why she came at me with a golf club in front of the whole dining room at our country club? Because I'd just told her if she didn't want kids, maybe she'd made the wrong choice in husbands and needed to reconsider her living options." A trace of mist returned to his eyes. "I'll give her credit for sticking with me all the way through the trial after I got arrested on that murder beef. It was me that insisted we get the divorce done before I went to prison."

"We checked the visitors' log, Mr. Genaway," I told him. "Your wife hasn't been to visit you since you were incarcerated here."

"People move on. It happens."

Something changed in Genaway's expression. He no longer had to hide his sadness and vulnerability, because they were both gone. And in their place was the cold, assured stare more typical of the man he'd been before he was imprisoned.

"You go about your way looking for Ginny's killer, Fletch. But when you or somebody else nails the bastard, him making it to trial would be the eighth wonder of the world. If I wasn't stuck in here, I'd do the deed myself. But there'll be others waiting in line to do the guy."

"You really think it's wise to share that kind of information in front of me, Vic?" Mort asked him.

Genaway leaned back and started to cross his arms, until the wrist chains stopped him in mideffort. "I'm already doing life, Sheriff. I can't die in this hole twice."

"That man was right out of *The Sopranos*," Mort said, once we were back in his SUV.

"I wouldn't know. I never watched the show. Too violent for my tastes."

"You should do a stint with the NYPD, Mrs. F."

"I was actually thinking about joining the Marines."

"I'll write you a recommendation."

"Where to now?"

"Manchester, and I mean it this time."

A Manchester detective met us outside the 875 Elm Street apartment complex, located in the heart of the city's downtown district, where Ginny had moved after leaving Vic Genaway in the wake of the golf club attack at their country club.

The building manager maintained an office on the premises and used his passkey to open the door to Ginny Genaway's luxury two-bedroom apartment. At first glance, it wasn't hard to figure why the complex boasted a reputation as Manchester's finest. It featured sparkling granite countertops, stainless steel appliances, a lavish open-concept kitchen with a sprawling breakfast bar, and oversized windows that featured expansive views of the city. The bedrooms were similarly oversized, and no expense had been spared with the fixtures or finish work, making me wish I'd hired this complex's contractor to handle the rebuilding of my beloved home at 698 Candlewood Lane.

The furnishings were obviously a work in progress, but it was still clear to me that Vic Genaway was picking up the tab despite his estrangement from Ginny in the wake of her attack on him with a golf club. The fact that it was clear he still had feelings for Ginny told me he'd made arrangements that would allow her to maintain her lifestyle even after he went to prison in the wake of the divorce he claimed he'd insisted upon. Genaway was the kind of man who was old-school like that, his gruff, tough-guy demeanor belying the romantic who'd ended up falling in love with a much younger woman.

According to the building manager, Ginny had been living here for nine months, which jibed perfectly with when she'd taken a golf club to her now former husband. Vic had been imprisoned for about half that time, and I found myself surprised she hadn't spent more time, and money, decorating the place, which remained sparsely furnished at best with just the bare minimum of furniture, as if Ginny hadn't planned on staying there all that much longer.

I was hoping the apartment might offer some clue as to what had brought her to Cabot Cove yesterday, particularly to seek me out. Something left in plain sight or easy to find that would tell me what accounted for the timing, given that I didn't think our interview the day before had been based on a whim.

The first thing I noticed in her bedroom was a framed eight-by-ten family picture on her bureau that was likely the last ever taken of Ginny with her father. It was of just Walter Reavis and the three kids and looked to have been taken at a restaurant by a server or someone who happened to be sitting at the next table. Seeing Walter happy, smiling, and alive was a welcome respite from the rekindled memories of his murder. The latter had too often been how I'd remembered him, especially lately. But this was the real Walter, and spying him with his three kids in a photograph taken just weeks or maybe even days before he was killed cast his mentorship of, and belief in, me in the light it deserved. My memories of Walter Reavis were skewed by the manner of his death and especially by what the subsequent investigation revealed about him, and the memories that had just risen to the surface felt much better.

I was able to identify Ginny in the picture immediately, because I knew she was Walter's youngest. The son who'd later die in service to his country in the Middle East was the eldest child, pictured here as a teenage boy looking as if he'd rather be somewhere else. Walter's elder daughter, a junior at Appleton High at the time, was a gangly girl with glasses and frizzy hair. I seemed to remember she almost never smiled, perpetually glum and morose.

"What about Ginny's mother, Walter's ex-wife?" I asked Mort.

"She lives in Cape Elizabeth. I've got her address. We could make a stop there on the way home."

"I don't have any other pressing appointments."

"Besides your retirement party on Saturday, that is."

"It's not my retirement party, Mort."

"You know what I mean."

"I'm sensitive about such things."

"I don't blame you," Mort nodded. "Look no further than how retirement worked out for me."

We conducted a scattershot, piecemeal search of the apartment, not sure of what we were really looking for. The only other things of interest we found were a few recent copies of the *Cabot Cove Gazette* lying around. That suggested Ginny had made other trips to town of late, not just to interview me in the guise of a high school student, and left me wondering what her source of fascination with our town might be.

Of the six copies of the paper she'd kept, the oldest went back just over five months.

It had been four months prior to that when she'd attacked her ex-husband. She'd developed an apparent fascination with a town to which she had no obvious connection, and this had occurred around the same time the divorce was finalized and her ex-husband, Vic, was incarcerated.

Was there a connection there perhaps? And what was it about Cabot Cove that had commanded her interest? Physical copies of the paper were sold in a very small radius, meaning Ginny was making regular trips to the proximity of our town for reasons yet unknown that might well have led to her death.

Were those reasons somehow connected to the interview she'd conducted with me under such patently false pretenses? Was there something in our conversation that might provide more hints as to the identity of her killer, someone she both knew and had set up a meeting with for later that night? I didn't believe for one minute that her visit the day before had been random. Something had clearly sparked the timing, and the only other connection I had right now was Wilma Tisdale's retirement party, which didn't appear to be much of a connection at all.

I waited until we'd completed our initial, cursory check of Ginny Genaway's last residence and were back in Mort's SUV before raising any of this with him.

"Looks like we've got plenty to talk about on the way to Cape Elizabeth, Mrs. F.," he said after I'd laid out a portion of my thinking. "And I think you may be right about Walter Reavis's murder twenty-five years ago having some connection to his daughter's last night." He glanced at me across the seat, as he started his engine. "I think you'd better tell me what happened next at Appleton High, how that murder became the first one you ever solved."

Chapter Nine

Twenty-five years ago . . .

"Not just that," Wilma Tisdale told me. "He may have been murdered."

Wilma didn't know much more, just that the school secretary, Alma Potts, had found the body and called 911. Something she'd seen had been the cause of the murder rumors, which, based on the hefty police presence and the fact that Appleton PD had called in the state police, must have been well-founded.

I felt like I was in a fog, chilled by the notion that I might very well have been the last person to see Walter alive. Except I hadn't seen him. I'd only *heard* him at the tail end of that argument, which had finished with Walter pronouncing, "Over my dead body."

Well . . .

I had to report what I'd heard to the state and local police. It would be left to them to learn who the principal of Appleton High had been arguing with, and that person, I assumed, would be someone they'd want to speak with immediately.

As a crime scene, the main office had been shut off from the rest of the school and guarded by a uniformed Appleton police officer I recognized as Tom Jennings. I spotted Alma Potts at work behind her desk, no doubt manning the phones, which I knew would be ringing off the hook all day.

"A terrible thing, Mrs. Fletcher," Tom greeted me as I approached.

"Tom, I have information I need to pass on to the officer in charge of the case."

"Between you and me, ma'am, I don't even know who that is right now, although I'm guessing it would be the Appleton detective assigned to the case."

"I didn't even know Appleton had a detective."

Jennings didn't quite move out of the way. "So, this information . . ."

"Mr. Reavis and I were supposed to meet yesterday afternoon. But when I got to the office, I overheard him arguing with someone. I'm almost positive it was over the phone."

Jennings's mouth dropped. His gaze narrowed on me, as if it took a few seconds for the information I'd imparted to sink in.

"Stay here, Mrs. Fletcher. I'll get somebody."

"Thanks, Tom."

I watched him enter the main office and disappear down the short hallway at the end of which lay Walter Reavis's office. He was gone only a few moments, before the office door opened anew and Tom Jennings emerged with a shorter man, slightly paunchy, with friendly doe eyes, a harried demeanor, and a sports jacket that had seen better days. He wore his police badge dangling by a chain from his neck, and it was accidentally flipped around so that it was facing his shirt. He looked haggard, anxious, and for some reason, I thought, happy to be away from where Walter's body had been found.

"Detective, this is Jessica Fletcher," Tom Jennings said by way of introduction. "She lives in Appleton and teaches here at the school."

"*Substitute* teaches," I elaborated.

The detective brushed his tweed sports jacket back and jammed his hands into his pockets. "The deputy here tells me you've got some information pertaining to Walter Reavis's death that may be helpful to us," he said.

"I believe so, Detective . . ."

"Tupper, ma'am. Amos Tupper."

I took his extended hand as I looked slightly down at Detective Tupper. Because I'm a smidge over five feet eight, it was something I was used to.

"I knew Walter Reavis from the lodge." Tupper sighed. "A wonderful man and a great educator. Not a good day for Appleton, Mrs. Fletcher, not a good day for Appleton at all. Now, Officer Jennings tells me you may be the closest thing we have to a witness."

"How did Mr. Reavis die, Detective?"

"He appears to have fallen and hit his head."

"You called in the state police for an accident?"

"We're just being super diligent. Make that hypervigilant. We don't have a lot of experience with such things in Appleton, Mrs.

Fletcher. Figured the state police would be able to weigh in with more expertise."

"I believe that's wise," I agreed as officers came and went past us.

"So, if you don't mind, I'd like to go over what you recall from yesterday afternoon," Tupper said, feeling about his pockets. "Hold on a sec. . . ."

"Your lapel pocket, Detective."

"Huh?"

I reached out and plucked a memo pad from his sports jacket.

"Will you look at that?" he said, taking the pad. "I feel like a chicken with its head cut off today." He lowered his voice. "Can I confess something to you, Mrs. Fletcher?"

"Of course, Detective."

Lower still. "This is my first murder investigation—potential murder investigation, anyway."

"It's certainly a rare occurrence in Appleton."

"Now, as to what you recall from yesterday . . ."

Detective Tupper listened intently to everything I had to say, and jotted down the most pertinent facts on his memo pad.

"Can you think of anything else?" he asked when I was finished.

"Like what?"

"You said that you had seen Mr. Reavis earlier in the day. How would you describe his demeanor at that time?"

"Nothing stands out, nothing out of the ordinary, except for that phone call I can't get out of my mind."

He made a note of that and pocketed his memo pad, seeming to think of something else. "Do you think you could do me a favor, Mrs. Fletcher?"

"Of course."

"Mr. Reavis's secretary found the body, but never formally identified it. She was pretty shaken up, and I don't want to bother her again. Would you mind identifying the body for us?"

I felt my insides tighten, but I nodded anyway. "It's something that has to be done."

Tupper looked appreciative of my obliging his request and started to lead me inside the office. "Say, you didn't tell me what your meeting with Mr. Reavis was supposed to be about."

I thought I had, but let it go. "He wanted to talk about bringing me on to replace a teacher who's likely going to be out for the rest of the year. Right now, I'm full-time but only as a substitute."

"Well, now, how can a substitute be full-time?"

"There's always some teacher out, and I'm the first to cover. And on those rare days when everyone's accounted for, the school finds other work for me."

"I see. Well, we'd best get this over and done with so you can get to that work."

Walter Reavis's body lay crumpled at an odd angle on the floor, its contours visible through the plastic crime scene sheet currently covering it. I was grateful for that, since it spared me seeing a friend and colleague in such a state without any time to prepare myself. I've never considered myself to have weak knees or a weak stomach. Beneath that sheet, though, was the corpse of a man who'd believed in me and championed my fledgling career as a teacher. Walter saw something in me, a potential that no one else had. I went about my business as a substitute in as unobtrusive and professional a manner as I could. But the fact remained that even fellow teachers didn't pay our kind much respect, given that the common perception was that there must have been a reason why I wasn't a full teacher.

I caught the state police officers snickering at Detective Tupper's presence in the principal's office. They exchanged a few whispered words and poorly suppressed chuckles, clearly disparaging him.

"You boys mind giving us the room?" Tupper asked them.

He watched them leave the office and didn't speak again until he was sure they were out of earshot. "Don't pay them any heed, Mrs. Fletcher. They don't respect me much and aren't keen on my investigative skills."

"I'm sorry to hear that, Detective. Their judgment must be severely lacking."

"Well, the truth is, they may be right when it comes to a murder investigation, but they don't place a lot of stock in the fact that I've closed every case I've been assigned so far."

"I must confess that I didn't even know Appleton maintained a detective squad."

"I am the squad, Mrs. Fletcher, and also the town's official detective. Town selectmen approved the position in this year's budget, and truth be told, I was the only one who applied for the job, fresh out of traffic detail. Investigated more than my share of accidents and made my ticket quota every month, but nothing prepared me for this."

"Then perhaps I can help."

"You have investigative experience?"

"None at all, but I found out yesterday I may have a future as a mystery writer," I said, recalling that sophomore student's critique of my story, which wasn't a mystery at all.

"Well, that counts as experience in my book."

Tupper moved to the plastic crime scene sheet covering the body of Walter Reavis and drew it back, turning toward me so as not to have to look at the corpse himself. "Can you identify this man, Mrs. Fletcher?"

"I can't see his face, Detective. It's turned the other way."

"Well, I'll be," he said, frowning at his oversight. "Being that we don't want to disturb the body, would you mind coming closer?"

"Not at all."

Actually, I was shaking like a leaf. I'd never seen a dead body before, much less the corpse of someone I knew, and knew well. Walter looked as though he might have been sleeping, if it hadn't been for the nasty gash on his forehead and the blood puddled beneath his head. I was grateful the drawn blinds shut out the light of the sun, keeping Walter's face cloaked by shadows.

"State police haven't ruled out murder yet, but I pretty much have."

"Oh? Why's that?"

Detective Tupper pointed to a pair of yellow evidence flags affixed to the edge of the desk, between which rested what was clearly a blood smear. "As I see it, he slipped and hit his head. Let me show you something, Mrs. Fletcher."

I followed him around to the back of Walter Reavis's desk. Before sliding open the bottom drawer, Tupper looked toward the doorway to make sure the state policemen were nowhere to be seen.

"Take a gander."

I moved into the spot he'd vacated and spotted a bottle of gin, half empty.

"At the lodge," Tupper explained, "when we got to relaxing,

Walter would say sometimes he needed a quick pop to help him get through the day. Now, I'm not one to pass judgment, and you may be thinking that as an officer of the law, I should've reported him, but the information was passed in an informal setting between friends. I figured I owed him sealed lips on the subject." Tupper frowned again, obviously his default expression. "Thinking on that now, maybe I made a mistake."

I waited for him to go on.

"Maybe Walter would still be alive if I'd spoken up."

"You believe he started drinking after that unpleasant phone call, then slipped and fell."

"And banged his head right there," Tupper said, pointing toward that blood smear between the two evidence flags. "If I were a betting man, and I'm not, I'd wager the autopsy report will come back with a high blood alcohol level."

I checked the positioning of Walter Reavis's body again. "This is the way he was found?"

"The body hasn't been moved an inch, as far as I know. Everything in the office is exactly as it was when we got here."

Now I wished we could open the blinds to let in more light so I could see better. "I'm no expert, Detective, but the gash on his head doesn't appear to match the contours of that desk edge, at least not exactly."

Tupper put on his reading glasses to check the spot again, then took them right off when he realized they weren't helping. "Yes, ma'am, I see your point. Wonder how the MSP missed that," he said, referring to the Maine State Police.

"They probably wouldn't have much longer, not once the crime scene technicians have a go at the place. I think we're looking for a potential weapon with a sharper and more concentrated edge. Also, when someone falls forward and bangs his head," I said, imitating that motion on another section of the desk, "the natural reflex is for the head to pop back straight upward. Impact strong enough to be fatal would've had to be flush, which means he could have been walking, or stumbling, for the door when he heard the phone ring. He started back toward his desk and slipped, and then the desk broke his fall."

"Makes sense, Mrs. Fletcher."

"Except that means he would have approached the desk on this angle to grab the phone from this side," I said, again simulating the action. "And if that were the case, approaching the only way he really could have, he would have fallen to the left, not to the right, after impact."

"Well, I'll be," Amos Tupper said, scratching his chin.

"It's a possibility, Detective. Another, connected possibility is that the killer wanted to make it look like an accident, so after the fact he smeared some of Walter Reavis's blood right there," I finished, pointing to the dried blood smear on the lip of the desk.

"Then what killed him?"

I swept my gaze about the office, focusing on the shelves and various keepsakes on display. "I'd look for an object that meets the general contours of the wound on Mr. Reavis's forehead." My eyes locked on one of the shelves. "Like that trophy up there or that paperweight with the stone dollar bill."

Tupper's gaze followed mine. "'The buck keeps going,'" he read out loud, squinting. "Seems likely the killer would've taken it with him, though, doesn't it?"

"Maybe. But then he, or she, would've had to find a way to dispose of it or risk being caught with it in his, or her, possession. The killer probably thought the ruse was sufficient, might have even been counting on the fact that someone investigating would know about that gin bottle."

"I was the only one on the force who knew about that, Mrs. Fletcher."

"You're also the only detective in Appleton and thus certain to catch the case."

"And given that plenty in town don't think I could catch a cold, the killer figured I wouldn't notice anything awry."

"The murder weapon's still here, Detective. I'd bet on it. Unless . . ."

Amos Tupper looked at me like he was hanging on my every word. "'Unless,'" he repeated.

"Unless the killer brought the weapon with him."

"You think they had an appointment or something, Mrs. Fletcher?"

"I don't know about an appointment, but I keep coming back to that heated phone call I overheard. Maybe the killer came over straightaway unannounced to continue the argument in person. Does the school have any security cameras that might show us something?"

"I'll check," Tupper said, making a note in his memo pad after touching the ballpoint to his tongue for some reason. "And I'll be certain to make sure that the crime scene team checks every object that isn't nailed down for blood residue, since the killer would have almost surely wiped down the murder weapon." Tupper nodded to himself, his sleepy eyes showing a bit more life. "Mystery writer, you say . . ."

"Just according to one of my students."

"Well, I'd say you'd make a pretty darn fine detective."

"Thank you, but I think I'll stick to teaching."

"Well, if you ever change your mind . . ." He looked taller as he moved for the door, with something of a spring in his step. "Now then, I'd better go tell those state police boys that their initial findings require some tweaking. If you turn out to be right, I guess I won't seem so dumb to them anymore."

"You mean, if *we* turn out to be right, Detective."

He led me toward the door. "Mrs. Fletcher, I believe you and I make a great team."

"Why, thank you, Detective."

He looked shy all of a sudden, like a boy trying to ask a girl to dance. "Would you mind if I contacted you to keep you informed of our progress?"

"Not at all. I'd appreciate it, in fact. Let's just hope we don't have to make a habit of this."

Chapter Ten

The present

"Amos Tupper was a *detective*?"

I nodded. "He was indeed, Mort."

"Now I've heard everything."

"You say that a lot when we work together."

"I know. For good reason. I can see why you're such a successful author, Jessica, given that you never seem to repeat yourself." He looked at me, as if needing more convincing about at least one part of the story I'd just told him. "*Detective* Amos Tupper? Really?"

Amos, of course, had gone on to become sheriff of Cabot Cove, taking the job just before Frank's passing and remaining in it for a number of years before turning the reins over to Mort Metzger. Having tired of police work after twenty years on the job, he'd left the Appleton police department shortly after Walter Reavis's murderer was brought to justice. He drove a bus for a time before growing bored and applying for the sheriff's job in Cabot Cove, once it came open, never imagining that the one murder he'd investigated during his time in Appleton was just a warm-up for what he would face in Cabot Cove.

"Returning to the present," Mort said, "Ginny's mother went back to using her maiden name of Demerest after the divorce. Madeline Demerest, but she goes by Maddie."

"Should we call ahead to tell her we're coming?"

"And spoil all the fun of surprising her?" Mort challenged me. "We used to have a saying in New York: If they don't know you're coming, they can't be ready for you."

"This isn't Manhattan," I reminded him.

"Last time I checked, Jessica, murder was murder. And it just so happens, Maddie Demerest never leaves her home, because her work *is* her home."

"Can you be more specific?"

Mort smiled. "I think I'd rather keep you in suspense again. Give you a taste of your own medicine."

"Ever hear of the Portland Head Lighthouse?" Mort asked me as we crossed the New Hampshire–Maine border just past the Portsmouth travel circle.

"The one in Fort Williams Park commissioned by George Washington himself?"

"Can't put anything over on you, can I?"

"I've lived in New England for most of my life and Maine for the bulk of it, Mort. But what does Maddie Demerest have to do with the Portland Head Lighthouse?"

Mort explained that the still-active light and fog signals were actually maintained by the Coast Guard these days, leaving the mother of the late Ginny Genaway to manage the rest of the complex. And one of the fringe benefits of managing the popular tourist attraction—which comprised an actual working lighthouse, a museum, and a gift shop—was an apartment carved out of the current Keepers' Quarters, built in 1891. Upgrades and improvements to the facility had been frequent in the years since its construction, such maintenance crucial to keeping the lighthouse fully functional and vital as ever in steering boats away from the rocky Maine coastline, especially in fog. The facility had continued to operate toward that end after being fully automated in August 1989. So although Maddie Demerest had lived at the facility for three years now, she had nothing to do with its continuing operation beyond her tour guide, museum director, and gift shop duties.

"Does she know about her daughter?" I asked Mort as the point containing the lighthouse came within view.

"State police paid her a visit up close and personal this morning. At last check she was still on the premises, tours canceled and the museum closed for the day."

"MSP happen to inquire about her whereabouts last night, Mort?"

"Ever the suspicious one, aren't you?"

I shrugged. "It's my nature."

"Mine, too. I thought that would change when I moved to Cabot Cove, but old habits die hard."

"Good thing, given that spike in the murder rate that accompanied your arrival."

"You're blaming me for that?"

"If the shoe fits . . ."

Mort slowed his SUV as we approached the entrance to the Portland Head Lighthouse parking lot, which was understandably deserted, except for a single Maine State Police cruiser. "You know, I think you're right about Amos Tupper, Jessica. He must not have been as dumb as everyone thinks; he was smart enough not to tell me what being sheriff of Cabot Cove was really like."

We parked and climbed out of his SUV. The MSP officer left behind to watch over Maddie Demerest must have spotted us, because he approached across the parking lot, hitching up his gun belt.

"Sheriff Mort Metzger from Cabot Cove, Officer," Mort said by way of introduction. "And this is Jessica Fletcher."

The officer nodded my way before turning all of his attention to Mort. "Cabot Cove being where the murder of this woman's daughter took place."

"Within our jurisdiction, anyway," Mort corrected. "Is she able to talk?"

"She's not sedated or anything, if that's what you mean, and I haven't seen any alcohol in evidence. So, other than shock and grief, she's definitely able. We offered to take her to the coroner's office, your town, or anywhere else. It seemed strange she didn't want to go."

"According to reports, she and the victim have been estranged for some time," Mort told him. "I couldn't tell you the last time they saw each other or even spoke."

"Living so close to each other, with her daughter down in New Hampshire and all?"

Mort frowned. "Yeah. Go figure."

"Let me tell Ms. Demerest you're here."

*   *   *

The first thing I realized about Maddie Demerest, mother of Ginny Genaway, was that she was a smoker. I detected the telltale odor as soon as we climbed the interior stairs of the building—which had once served as the lightkeeper's quarters in its entirety—toward her apartment. The smell got stronger the higher we climbed, and when Maddie responded to Mort's knock on her door with a cigarette in her hand, it wasn't hard to figure out why.

Mort took off his cap. "Ma'am, I'm Sheriff Mort Metzger from Cabot Cove. I'm terribly sorry for your loss."

The woman stole a glance at me, as if wondering what I was doing there, before fixing her gaze on Mort. "You're the one who found the body."

"Not me, Ms. Demerest. One of my officers. He noticed her car parked alone at this rest stop."

Scenic overlook, I almost corrected Mort before stopping myself.

"But Mrs. Fletcher here," Mort continued, gesturing toward me, "was probably the last person to see her alive."

"Besides her killer, you mean," Maddie Demerest managed, brushing away some tears she seemed surprised were there.

She uttered a sigh that drifted off with the smoke from her latest drag. Maddie must've been in her late fifties or early sixties, but her thin frame and slovenly appearance made her look at least ten years older.

"Why don't we move this inside?" I suggested. "I could fix us some tea or coffee while you speak with Sheriff Metzger."

She opened the door all the way. "I don't want any of either.

What I could use is a stiff drink, except I gave it up years ago. I thought it would help me reconnect with the one kid I had left, but sometimes things are too broken to glue back together."

I kept my eyes fastened on Maddie as I stepped with Mort through the door. "We're aware of your losing your son in the Middle East, but you have another daughter, don't you?" I asked, recalling the photo from Ginny's apartment in Manchester.

"My older daughter, Lisa Joy." She nodded. "Left this part of the country for someplace in the South, if you can believe that, as soon as she could after her father's death. Last I heard, she was teaching somewhere in Alabama." She took another deep drag of the cigarette and coughed out the smoke, retching. "Following in her father's footsteps," she added after getting her breath back. "Strange, given that she hated him as much as she hated me."

"Your older daughter was a junior at Appleton High at the time of your ex-husband's murder—is that correct?" I asked.

She looked at me oddly, the smoke from her cigarette wafting up between us. "Who are you, again?"

"Jessica Fletcher, Ms. Demerest."

Mort cleared his throat. "I thought bringing a woman along would be a good idea."

"Which doesn't explain what you're doing here either, Sheriff. If you came to inform me of my daughter's death, you're several hours too late."

"I thought you might know something that can help us find her killer."

"Ms. Demerest," I picked up, "it's been my experience that oftentimes relatives and others close to victims of violent crime know something without necessarily being aware of it until it's revealed in the process of a conversation."

"Your experience? But you're not here as a cop, just a woman—isn't that right?"

"Mrs. Fletcher has assisted numerous investigations in Cabot Cove as well as in many other locations," Mort interjected by way of explanation.

A brief flash of recognition struck Maddie Demerest's expression. "Oh, I remember now. You taught at Walter's school. You were working with that detective who was investigating his murder for the Appleton police. You ended up becoming a mystery writer, rich and famous now because that investigation set you on your way."

I let her remark pass. This woman had lost her son to a roadside bomb and a daughter to estrangement. I didn't yet know the depth of her estrangement from Ginny, whether it reached the level it had with Lisa Joy. I guess it didn't matter at this point. Madeline Demerest was a sad woman who'd tried to drown herself in booze and was now charring her insides with cigarette smoke. Her appearance indicated she was long past caring, and I wondered how she'd managed to weather three years there giving tours of the lighthouse, which meant smiling a lot, no easy task for her by any estimation.

"When was the last time you spoke to your daughter?" Mort asked her.

"What's it matter now?"

"I was hoping she may have given some indication of what brought her to Cabot Cove, ma'am," Mort persisted.

"Not to me, she didn't, Sheriff. I have no idea of what you're talking about. You're making me regret even letting you in."

I took a step sideways, partially positioning myself between them. "Why don't we sit down in your parlor over there? Or, better yet, the kitchen. I could make you that tea."

"I'll stand if you don't mind, Mrs. Fletcher. I don't want the two of you getting comfortable."

"I had coffee with your daughter Ginny yesterday. We met on the pretext of an interview for the local high school's newspaper she claimed to be a reporter for."

"And you believed her?"

"She did look the part, yes."

Maddie Demerest lit a fresh cigarette and dropped the lighter back into the pocket of the shapeless sweater she was wearing, which draped over her narrow, bony shoulders. "What did she want from you exactly?"

"I can't tell you because I'm not sure, not exactly. But she seemed interested mostly in her father's murder."

"After all these years?"

"I've been asking myself that question ever since learning she wasn't who she claimed to be, Ms. Demerest."

She narrowed her gaze on me. "You were at his funeral, my ex-husband's. I remember seeing you there. You introduced yourself to me."

"I'm sorry I don't remember. Would you mind if I asked you a question?"

"We're both standing here."

"How would you describe your daughter Ginny's relationship with her father?" I asked, changing the subject.

"As our youngest, she missed him terribly. I think he got a great deal right with her that didn't necessarily happen with Lisa Joy and Gavin, our son."

"According to Ginny's ex-husband—"

"You've been to see that hoodlum?" Maddie Demerest interrupted, her features flaring. "That criminal who took advantage of her?"

"I don't think she saw it that way, Ms. Demerest."

Maddie looked away from me and back toward Mort. "Are we finished here, Sheriff?"

"I believe we are, ma'am. I would like to reach out to your other daughter, though. Do you have a contact number for Lisa Joy down in Alabama?"

"I never did. I couldn't even tell you if she lives there anymore. I can't let myself care, Sheriff. If I do, I'll start drinking again. The one thing I've accomplished in all these years, the one good thing, was climbing on the wagon. Would you like to know how I got this job?"

Maddie looked back at me and I nodded.

"I was planning on jumping out of the light tower. But I wasn't sure it was high enough, and I didn't want to get it wrong, the way I'd gotten so many other things wrong. So I applied for this job instead. Fitting in a strange way, given that Lisa Joy had been obsessed with lighthouses. She used to paint them, build models, collect photographs. And now I've been living in one for, oh, the last three years. What do you make of that, Mrs. Fletcher?"

Just then I noticed a framed photograph of her with all three of her children. Since her son was in his Marine uniform, I assumed it was one of the last taken before he was killed by a roadside bomb and her older daughter left home for good.

"Do you think we could borrow that, Maddie?" I asked her.

She handed me the whole frame without giving it a thought. "Here you go. Knock yourself out."

I think Mort had had about as much as he could take. "Thank

you for your time, ma'am," he said, fitting his sheriff's hat back on as he angled back toward the door. "We'd best get going now."

"Aren't you going to promise that you'll catch my daughter's killer?"

"I can promise I'll do everything I can."

The woman nodded, her gaze so distant that she didn't even seem to be in the room anymore. "That's the problem with *everything*, Sheriff: It's seldom enough."

We sat in silence inside Mort's SUV for a few moments before heading back to Cabot Cove. The last of the day's light was bleeding from the sky and it would be night before we got there.

"Remember that Cadillac you used to drive, Mort?"

"The red Eldorado? How could I forget?"

"You know, you never once gave me a ride in it."

"Maybe I didn't want to make Adele jealous."

"I didn't think you were going to last, Mort. I was afraid Cabot Cove wasn't the retirement you'd been hoping for."

"It wasn't—not at first, anyway. But after the war and the NYPD, I realized too much peace and quiet would have driven me up the wall."

"And how do you feel now?"

"Like I would've been better off with the wall," Mort said, stopping just short of a smile.

I watched him check an e-mail message that had just come, using his fingers to make whatever he was reading bigger on the screen.

"Ballistics report just came in," he said, still eyeing the message. "The bullet that killed Ginny Genaway was a nine millimeter.

Powder burns on the passenger-side headrest confirm the shooter was seated in the passenger seat when he shot her to death."

"Just like we figured."

Mort nodded. "Right. All we've got to do now is figure out who pulled the trigger."

Chapter Eleven

Seth is waiting for us at Mara's," Mort continued, gunning his engine after reading another e-mail. "He says he has big news to share."

"It's only big news if it helps us solve the case."

"Patience, Mrs. F.," Mort said.

"We need to find Ginny's older sister, Lisa Joy, Mort."

"Even her mother doesn't know where she is."

"Madeline Demerest doesn't impress me as someone with a lot of initiative left in her tank."

"Good thing you have enough for her and ten other people, then. But her elder daughter appears to be someone who doesn't want to be found."

"For starters, we know she was teaching in Alabama."

"Do we, Jessica? Pardon me for not taking that woman at her word."

"No one drops off the map for good these days," I reminded

him, and took from my bag the photograph Maddie Demerest had given us. "And at least now we've got her picture."

"Sure, from when she was in high school in braces and pigtails."

"No braces or pigtails, Mort," I told him.

Mort had a minor emergency he had to attend to, thanks to a call he'd just received, so he dropped me off and I went inside Mara's to meet Seth Hazlitt ahead of him. He was seated at the same table in the luncheonette as yesterday and pretty much every other day. Someone else was also at the table, but I didn't recognize Cabot Cove High School principal Jen Sweeney until she turned around at my approach.

"Mrs. Fletcher," she greeted me, rising politely, "how nice to see you again."

"You, too, Ms. Sweeney."

"I was just discussing Career Day with Dr. Hazlitt. He's agreed to be our keynote speaker this year."

"Well," I told her, "the good doctor is never at a loss for words."

"Look who's talking," Seth groused. "And I promise to make it better than that snooze fest Mrs. Fletcher delivered last year."

"You'd best figure on the day running long," I warned Jen Sweeney. "I've heard him speak, and he tends to get a tad long-winded."

"That's only because I have a lot of important things to say. You'll see, Ms. Sweeney, *ayuh*."

She looked toward me. "I trust we can count on your participation again, Mrs. Fletcher."

"Of course," I told her. "Wouldn't miss it for the world. I hope the real Kristi Powell signs up for one of my presentations."

"I'll do my best to see that she does."

"Tell her I cover journalism, too, and how to transition to fiction writing, particularly novels."

"I think she'll find that most interesting. I know you influenced a great many young writers in your time teaching at the school. Some of their books share the local-author shelf with yours."

"Just as they did in my house. I'm going to order fresh copies, and they're going to be the first things I put back on the shelves as soon as I move back in."

She looked up at me, the admiration stretched across her expression clearly genuine. "On the chance you ever consider giving teaching a whirl again, Mrs. Fletcher . . ."

"That means so much to me, Ms. Sweeney. But it's been so long, I think I'm best off just sticking to Career Day presentations."

"Nonsense. You could reach students whose interest in most subjects doesn't amount to a hill of beans these days. Believe me—I know."

"I'm sure you do, being on the front lines every day."

Jen Sweeney pushed her chair back and stood up again. "Please forgive me for intruding on whatever plans you all made," she said to both Seth and me.

"Pie and coffee don't qualify as a plan," Seth told her. "They qualify as survival."

But his evening, as opposed to afternoon, slice of pie was long gone, and he was into what looked to be his third cup of coffee, judging by the number of stray Splenda wrappers soaking in the saucer. Mort passed Jen Sweeney and tipped his cap to her on his way through the door. Under Seth's caustic stare, he took the chair she'd just vacated.

"Took you long enough," Cabot Cove's favorite doctor and resident curmudgeon said by way of greeting. "Normally, I'm getting ready for bed right now."

"It's only eight o'clock, Seth."

"I start getting ready for bed early," he said, casting me a faux-derisive stare. "The coroner sent over Ginny Genaway's complete medical history with her autopsy report. And there's something in it you may find interesting: She was under a psychiatrist's care."

"Got a name for that psychiatrist?"

"Yes, and I already took the liberty of dropping him an e-mail."

"A little forward, wouldn't you say, Doc?"

"No more than you making me the medical officer of record for Cabot Cove. That's what the address label said. It would've been nice if you'd shared the news with me, Mort, that I'd been blessed with such a prestigious title, especially given that I'm not the only physician in Cabot Cove now."

"Don't go all high and mighty on me, Doc. I couldn't remember the names of the others, so you were my first and only choice."

"Should I be flattered?"

"What did the psychiatrist say when you reached him?" I said, breaking into their exchange.

"E-mailed me back that he couldn't break doctor-client privilege."

"It doesn't extend beyond death," Mort reminded him.

"Which might explain why he said to have local law enforcement contact him directly. I told him I was acting in an official capacity and made an appointment to see him on your behalf." Seth looked my way. "I didn't mention that you'd be coming along on Friday, too, Jess."

"I haven't been invited yet."

"Consider yourself invited, then, unless you're busy Friday."

"I think I can squeeze this into my schedule."

Mort checked the pie selections on the menu. "Where's the psychiatrist located?"

"Brookline, Massachusetts. Beacon Street, to be more precise."

"A long drive for nothing, if he hasn't got anything worthwhile to say," Mort groused. "Glad it's you and Mrs. F. handling this part of the investigation."

"Why's he calling you 'Mrs. F.' again?" Seth asked.

"It brings back happy memories of the days before Mort realized what he was getting into here," I told him.

"Speaking of memories, Doc," Mort said, folding his arms before him on the table, "did you know Amos Tupper was a detective in Appleton before putting on his Cabot Cove sheriff's badge?"

"No, I don't believe I did."

"Good. Jessica can tell you all about it on that drive to Brookline."

Seth scratched his fork over the plate to scrape up the remaining scraps of his strawberry-rhubarb pie. "Maybe it is a waste of time."

"Why don't I just ride my bicycle?" I snapped at them both. "If I leave now, I might make it by early next week."

"How'd you like to be a sheriff's deputy for the day?" Mort asked me. "That way, we can make it official."

"You're just worried that I'll be able to get more out of this psychiatrist than you."

"Why should this case be different from all the others?"

Mort had some catching up to do at the office, so Seth drove me back to Hill House in one of his ancient Volvos. He bought one after another, usually every three years, always used, each model somehow seeming older than the one that preceded it. His pat explanation for this was that he preferred cars as old as he was—until they broke down, that is.

I'd barely gotten settled inside my suite when a knock fell on my door. I opened it, stupidly without checking the peephole, to find standing there a pair of men I'd never seen before in my life.

"Could we have a word with you, Mrs. Fletcher?"

"That depends on who you are."

The two men looked at each other, turning their heads in perfectly synchronized fashion like puppets controlled with the same string.

"Vic Genaway sent us," the original speaker said, and I had the distinct sense he'd be the one doing all the talking.

"That doesn't tell me who you are."

"Yes, it does," the man said. "Mr. Genaway sent us up here to keep tabs on the investigation into his wife's murder, lend our assistance if it comes to that."

"What's that mean, 'lending your assistance'?"

"If it comes to that," the man repeated as if I'd grasp his meaning more clearly the second time. "Mr. Genaway only wants to make sure that justice is done, Mrs. Fletcher. Hey, you're a mystery writer, aren't you?"

"Yes, I am."

"My wife loves mysteries. You think you could sign a book for her? I don't have one with me now but . . ."

"I've got some books on hand. Why don't you gentlemen come inside?"

They looked at each other again, as if surprised I'd invited them in. I noticed that the man who'd done the talking left the door open just a crack, as if to reassure me I had nothing to fear from them, which I'd managed to conclude already. Men like this, when they intend to do you harm, don't normally knock on the door.

I picked up a copy of my most recent hardcover from the coffee table in the living room portion of my Hill House suite, sat down on the couch, and readied a pen.

"And whom should I make it out to?"

"Norma—that's my wife."

I started in on the inscription. "And what's your name?"

"Joe. But don't include me. It's for my wife. She's going to be thrilled. Wait until I tell her I met you. What's your real name, anyway?"

"Jessica Fletcher."

"You don't have a fake one you write under?"

I handed Joe the book so he could see the name displayed above the title. "I write under 'J. B. Fletcher.' The *B* stands for Beatrice."

He held the book as if it were a precious gem. "She's gonna be tickled pink. So excited she might just drop dead."

I tried to stop my mouth from dropping.

"That was a joke, Mrs. Fletcher."

"Oh, of course," I said, forcing a chuckle.

"We're staying at a motel just outside of town," Joe told me, exchanging a glance with his silent partner. "I'll give you my cell number, in case you need to reach us."

"And why would I need to reach you, Joe?"

He picked up the pen I'd used to inscribe the book for his wife and he jotted down on the top of a Hill House memo pad a number with a 617 area code, used in Boston.

"You never know when something might come up," he told me.

"Like what?"

"Like something you'd need to reach us about."

"That's what Mr. Genaway sent you down here to do? Nothing more?"

"Not right away, anyway."

"I'm not sure I know what you mean."

Joe looked at me, his eyes not blinking. "Yes, you do, Mrs. Fletcher. Mr. Genaway just wants to make sure that whoever killed Mrs. Genaway pays for it."

"I believe that's the job of the courts."

"Sure. But sometimes the law isn't up to the task, so Mr. Genaway sent somebody who is."

"And you expect me to keep you informed about our progress on the case—is that it?"

"At this point, Mr. Genaway wants to make sure you stay safe so you can bring his ex-wife's killer to justice."

"Like I said, that's the sheriff's job, Joe, along with the state police."

"Mr. Genaway doesn't trust them, ma'am. He trusts you. Our instructions were to get acquainted and let you know we're around." Joe started to backpedal for the door with a copy of my latest book tucked under his arm, his silent partner falling into step alongside him. "So, you got my number. You need it, use it. Don't hesitate."

"You think I'm really in danger?"

"Mr. Genaway does."

"Why on earth?"

"He didn't say, and I didn't ask. A word of friendly advice, though: Mr. Genaway is usually right about this kind of thing. And don't say it's his imagination, 'cause, believe me, he hasn't got one. If he thinks you're in danger, it's a safe bet he got word about something. That's why he sent us—insurance against that *something*."

I speed walked to the door, eager to be rid of my guests. "Please thank Mr. Genaway for his concern next time you talk to him, Joe. And assure him I'm doing everything I can to find out who killed his ex-wife."

Joe cast me a sidelong smile. "He already knows that, Mrs. Fletcher. You have a good night now."

He smiled again from the hallway, just before I eased the door closed.

Maybe the incident should have left me scared, at least rattled, but it hadn't. I knew Vic Genaway meant me no harm, just as I knew he'd dispatched these men to Cabot Cove because of how much he'd truly loved his ex-wife. I'd caught a glimpse of that when he'd discussed the argument they'd had that led to their ultimate estrangement after Ginny had struck him with a golf club. I could imagine how helpless he felt, a man used to wielding all sorts of power cooped up in a jail cell. I felt truly bad for him, though I couldn't explain why exactly.

I checked the peephole to make sure my new friends were gone and then pulled out my old phone directory, which I'd filled up in the days before cell phones became the fashion. I was late coming to that technology, just as I had been late coming to computers, flat-screen televisions, and pretty much every other new form of technology available. I thumbed the address book to the *T*s and pressed a number into my phone, hoping it hadn't been changed.

"Hello," a familiar voice I hadn't heard in a very long time said, telling me the number hadn't changed.

"How are things in Kentucky, Amos?"

"Why, Jessica Fletcher!" said Amos Tupper. "As I live and breathe! It's wonderful to hear your voice."

"Yours, too," I told him. "I can't tell you how much."

"You managed to run Mort Metzger off yet?"

"Not quite. But you'll be happy to hear he curses you out every single day for retiring."

"I've been doing some constable work out in these parts. Nothing like the old days in Cabot Cove, though."

"I wouldn't expect it would be, Amos."

"Anyways, I wanted you to know I've been keeping my nose in it, in case you need my advice on a current case."

"I do indeed, but on an old case, not a new one: the murder of Walter Reavis."

"Well, I'll be, our very first murder investigation, Mrs. Fletcher. That was a time, wasn't it?"

"Yes, it was."

"Say, you remember that time we took the bus to that police convention where you were supposed to be the featured speaker?"

"Only to be waylaid by murder when a storm washed out the road and we were stranded at that diner."

"Waylaid by murder . . . Make a nice title for a book, wouldn't it?"

"It would indeed."

"Say, how about the case where we—"

"I was calling about the Reavis murder, Amos."

He sighed. "Sorry, Mrs. Fletcher. Living with my daughter and her family's not exactly a recipe for stimulating conversation. And Maine's got Kentucky beat six ways to Sunday, for sure. Remind me next time I retire to move near a coastline. It just doesn't feel right being landlocked like this and—" He stopped himself suddenly, as if he'd yanked his words back with a leash. "Sorry, Mrs. Fletcher. I get to rambling on, it takes a lot more than a washed-out road to get me to stop."

"I understand, and I miss you, too. The truth is, Mort Metzger doesn't value my assistance nearly as much as you did."

"Really?"

"No, but I thought I'd say it to make you feel good."

We shared a laugh, and I plopped into a chair to continue our conversation.

"So, what is it I can do for you, Mrs. Fletcher? What is it about a twenty-five-year-old murder case that's got you calling out of the blue?"

"Another murder," I told him. "Walter Reavis's younger daughter."

"You don't say. How can I help?"

"Well, Amos, I'm a little cloudy on some details. I was hoping I could tell you what I remember, and that you could correct anything I've got wrong."

"Be glad to. My memory's not what it used to be, but when it comes to murder, my mind's like a steel trap. So what is it you'd like to tell me?"

Chapter Twelve

Twenty-five years ago . . .

"You were right, Mrs. Fletcher!"

"Detective Tupper, is that you?" I said, holding to my ear the newfangled cordless phone we'd just bought.

"Yes, yes! About that trophy on the shelf in Principal Reavis's office, I mean. We found blood on the statue part that's a match for Walter Reavis's blood. It was the murder weapon, for sure, and I'm the one who found it!" Amos Tupper said, sounding almost giddy.

It had been nearly thirty-six hours since I'd identified Walter Reavis's body for him. I'd been correcting papers at the kitchen table, and now I stood up, shocked that my intuition had been correct. Walter Reavis's funeral was the following day; school was scheduled to be in session only in the morning in order to let interested faculty and students attend.

"What about fingerprints, Detective?"

"Wiped mostly clean, but we were able to pull a partial print of someone who's not in the criminal database. My guess is the killer forgot to wipe the part of the trophy he must have been holding when he wiped the rest of it down. The killer tried to do the same with the blood, but there were enough traces to positively identify it as belonging to the victim, even before it turned out the head of the figurine was a perfect match for the fatal head wound."

"How about that?" I said, deciding not to leave it there. "What about that phone call I overheard only Mr. Reavis's end of? Were you able to trace the number?"

"Not yet. The phone company is balking at releasing the information. Legal issues and such, privacy or something."

"There's always something. But I'd like to see the look on the faces of those state police officers who were making fun of you now that you've been able to prove definitively that it was murder." I could picture Amos Tupper smiling from ear to ear.

"What should we do next?" he asked.

"I've been thinking about that," I told him. "How are your interviews going with potential witnesses?"

"Well, based on the timeline we've been able to put together, only between four and six people we know of for sure were in the building at the time he was killed: two janitors, three teachers, and one student."

"What was the student doing there?" I wondered.

"He was waiting for a ride."

"So he could have been outside at the time of the murder. He could have seen the vehicle the killer was driving."

"That's what I thought," Amos Tupper told me. "He was actually inside the building standing by the door at the far end of the building. So he wouldn't have had a clear view of the other end, where the office was located."

"Too bad. Did anything at all stand out in the rest of your interviews with the witnesses?"

"Nothing particularly, no. Nobody heard or saw anything out of place. A few of them left through the front door and did mention the lights in the office were turned off, to the best of their recollection."

"That's interesting."

"And one of them tried the door and found it locked."

"Also interesting. You might want to check Mr. Reavis's keys."

"His keys?"

"Yes, because if all of them are accounted for, then the killer would have to be someone with a key to the office. If one of Mr. Reavis's keys was missing, it would have to be someone who knew which particular key to pinch."

"Hold on while I write this down, Mrs. Fletcher."

"Take your time."

"Say, have you ever done this before?"

"Done what?"

"An investigation—murder, in particular."

I laughed. "Not unless you include playing along with my favorite television mysteries."

"Bet you're pretty good at that, if helping me out is any indication."

"Walter Reavis was very good to me, Detective. I want to see his killer brought to justice."

I heard the crackle of paper being scrunched up.

"I wrote this down wrong. I'm going to start again, about the keys. I'll check right away. I imagine they'd be among his personal effects."

"Or in his top right-hand desk drawer. That's where he kept them when he was in his office because there were so many and he hated the weight of them in his pocket."

I could hear Tupper scribbling down fresh notes to replace the ones he'd discarded.

"Anything else you can think of, Mrs. Fletcher?"

"What time did the witnesses who noticed the office lights were off leave the building?"

"Both said it was around five o'clock."

I didn't know what I was looking for and realized I should have been writing all this down, too. "What about the witness who tried the office door and found it locked?"

"The lights were still on at that point. And it was earlier, closer to four thirty."

I tried to make sense of all this. The conversation I'd overheard had happened around three forty-five, which left plenty of time for a killer to complete his or her work in the timeline Amos Tupper had managed to assemble. I pictured Walter Reavis locking the door to the main office when his murderer arrived, then the murderer shutting off the lights, exiting the office, and locking the door again once the deed was done.

"That phone call I overheard would have been just past a quarter to four, Detective," I reminded him. "That means the killer arrived sometime between then and four thirty."

"So it does."

"You can see what I'm getting at."

"I can?"

"It's not just who was in the building closer to five o'clock or so. We need to expand that out to around four, on the chance somebody saw something, anything, that might provide some hint of whom Principal Reavis was meeting with."

"Why didn't I think of that?" Amos Tupper sighed.

"And there's something else, Detective. Maybe there were sports teams or field trips returning to the building in that same time frame. You should be able to get a list from Alma Potts, the school secretary. The transportation log would be the easiest vehicle for that."

"'Trans-por-ta-tion log,'" Tupper said slowly as he wrote that down.

"Yes."

"Wow, this opens a whole bunch of new doors for me. Would you mind if I called you back to get your thoughts after I follow some of this up?"

"Not at all," I told him.

"Oh, and there's something else. The coroner found an object clutched in Walter Reavis's hand: a tiny gold football made of some kind of composite material."

I tried to picture how the football that the figurine must've been holding had ended up in Walter Reavis's grasp, but tabled my thinking on that topic for now.

"I did uncover something else in the course of the interviews I've been conducting," Amos Tupper said, sounding like he had to force the words out. "Apparently, there were some rumors about Walter Reavis getting cozy with some female faculty members over the years."

"That's news to me."

"Like I said, it's just rumors, but I heard it from several different people. Not that they were sure, and I haven't confirmed any of this independently, but if it's true . . ."

"Something that needs to be checked out, Detective."

"You're not mad?"

"Why would I be mad?"

"It's just that I know you liked Walter, and it feels wrong to disparage a man after his death."

"Not when you're trying to catch whoever killed him," I said.

"You really believe that?"

"I wouldn't have said it if I didn't."

"I'm starting to think we make a great team, Mrs. Fletcher."

I helped Grady with his homework, but I couldn't get my mind off my conversation with Amos Tupper, nor had I been able to stop thinking about Walter Reavis's murder since the moment I'd gotten the awful news from Wilma Tisdale in the parking lot.

What left me truly unsettled was the fact that I'd been in the office not long before he was killed. Maybe if I had stayed and kept our appointment, he'd be alive today. It was even possible that the killer would have shown up and then left when he realized that Walter wasn't alone.

After all, it seemed obvious that Walter Reavis's murder had not been premeditated; otherwise, why would the killer have used a trophy as a weapon? No, if it had been planned out in advance, the killer would've almost certainly brought the murder weapon with him—or her. This was a crime of passion, as they say, that might never have happened if my overhearing that heated argument over the phone hadn't chased me away.

Still, Appleton High's principal had been struck from the front, facing his killer. Yet there was no evidence he had made any effort to defend himself, nor was there any evidence of a struggle inside the office. No upturned furniture or broken fixtures, nothing like that. I tried to envision a scenario where Walter Reavis could've been struck from the front without putting up any resistance. He was a reasonably young man, bigger than average, and in decent shape. Not an easy patsy, and I could only assume he'd somehow not seen the blow coming.

But how can you be taken by surprise by a strike coming from the front?

I considered the wound: a jagged gash from the top of his forehead all the way to his brow. A strike like that could have been wielded only in some form of overhead blow struck by someone taller than Walter. It was the only explanation that made sense, and I resolved to mention it to Detective Tupper the next time we spoke.

"Aunt Jessica?" I heard Grady say.

"Yes, Grady?"

"You said you'd help me."

"And so I am."

"No, you're not," the boy said in a whiny voice. "You aren't paying attention."

"You're right," I said, squeezing his shoulder, "so I'm not. How about we take a break and have some hot chocolate?"

"Okay!"

"I just have one phone call to make while we wait for the water to boil."

"Don't know why I didn't realize that myself, Mrs. Fletcher," Amos Tupper said after I'd passed on the conclusion that had just occurred to me.

"I'm sure you would have, Detective. Or it almost certainly would have been included in the forensics report once that's submitted."

"How tall you figure the killer was?"

"Well, I'm five eight, and Principal Reavis was at least two, and probably three, inches taller than I. So I'd say our killer is no less than six feet one or six feet two."

"I'm five six on a good day or when I wear my heavy shoes."

I nodded, even though he couldn't see me. "It's not much, but it does almost surely eliminate one entire group of suspects."

"And what group would that be, Mrs. Fletcher?"

"Women, Detective," I told him as the kettle began to whistle.

"What's eating you, Jessica?" Frank asked, peering over his copy of the day's *Portland Press Herald* as the late-evening news played softly on the television before us.

"Walter Reavis's death. I've been wondering what happens to that full-time job now that he's gone, and I feel terrible for thinking like that."

"Ahem," he said, clearing his throat dramatically.

"What was that, Frank?"

"My way of saying you're not telling the truth." He laid the newspaper down in his lap. "I've never known you to think of yourself, especially in view of a tragedy like this. Nice try, though."

I sighed, then settled myself with a deep breath. "It's—well, I've never known anyone who was murdered before."

"Very few people have, given that murder is as rare as it is. Thankfully."

"You saw more than your share of death in the war."

"I did, indeed. But nothing that anybody ever stood trial for or that required an investigation. And in war, both sides are equally guilty, aren't they, each trying to kill the other? No, this is quite different, and nothing I experienced can be of any particular help to you."

"It's the unfairness of it all that bothers me more than anything else. I mean, who speaks for Walter Reavis? One minute he was alive and running a high school, and the next minute he was dead, no more than a lab experiment for men who never met him to poke, prod, and measure."

"Hmmmmm, this really is bothering you. . . ."

"In a way nothing ever has before. Who speaks for the dead, Frank?"

"That sounds like the title of a book."

"Really? I just made it up. Did I tell you one of my students thinks I should try my hand at writing mysteries?"

"You let a class read one of your stories, didn't you?" he asked, trepidation riding his voice.

"I did, indeed."

"And?"

"They hated it. Mostly."

"Mostly?"

"There was a girl who thought it would make a great mystery."

"Nothing wrong with a good mystery in my mind," Frank said, picking up his newspaper again.

"Except *The New Yorker* doesn't publish mysteries. Neither does *The Atlantic* or *Harper's* or even *The Saturday Evening Post*."

"What about *Collier's*?"

"Out of business for years."

"Well, cross them off the list, then."

Walter Reavis's funeral was the following day. I'd heard his ex-wife, Madeline, reluctantly handled the arrangements, since there was no one else to do so. I met her briefly outside the church and hovered near the front of the cortege at the burial site to watch her with two of her children. I couldn't recall the name of his younger daughter as I watched Madeline try to grasp her hand only to be rebuffed by the little girl, who didn't look to be more than eight or so. The Reavises' son had come in his full-dress Marine uniform, remaining at attention through the entire ceremony. Their older daughter, who was a junior at the high school and whose name I seemed to recall was Lisa or something, had skipped the entire funeral for reasons I wasn't aware of.

I excused myself profusely as I changed positions among the mourners surrounding the grave site, wanting an angle that would let me get a look at as many of those in attendance as possible. I caught Amos Tupper standing unobtrusively in the back. We noticed each other but exchanged only a nod. I knew Amos was there for the same reason I'd changed positions: in the hope of spotting something awry or amiss, someone or something that stood out. The facts we'd assembled so far certainly suggested Walter Reavis had known his killer, which meant that killer was almost surely among us now, perhaps even sobbing like so many of those gathered for the burial were.

Frank had volunteered to accompany me and seemed a bit put off when I told him not to bother. I wondered if he realized I didn't want him to catch me snooping, eyeballing the grieving crowd instead of simply grieving myself. I focused on men who stood more than six feet tall, of whom there were plenty. Many of the students in attendance were crying and some of the faculty, too. Walter didn't have much of a family beyond his ex-wife and children, one of whom hadn't even bothered to show up. There should have been more to bid their final farewells to a man who'd touched so many lives and been such an integral part of the community.

I found my way over to Amos Tupper after the service concluded; he had his thumbs tucked into the pockets of his suit.

"Spot anyone of interest, Mrs. Fletcher?"

"Not a one, Detective."

"Yeah," he sighed, "me neither. Guess I was hoping someone would throw himself on the coffin and confess."

"That doesn't even happen on television."

"First time for everything, though, right?"

The murder of Walter Reavis continued to consume me. Each day left me with less focus on anything else. The vice principal, Jim Dirkson, was appointed interim principal and the assistant principal, Beverly Leander, was promoted to take his position. I didn't know either very well, and to both I was no more than a substitute. I'd never be able to approach either about the last thing Walter Reavis and I had discussed, specifically my taking over for Bill Gower, especially our new acting principal, who held substitutes in generally the same esteem as he did students. Beyond that, he had been passed over for the principal job originally when the school board voted to appoint Walter instead of him, but he had remained as vice principal out of what he claimed was loyalty to the system.

Meanwhile, the roads I'd directed Amos Tupper down had led nowhere. By all accounts, no groups had been out of the building that day. Tupper, to his credit, had created a mess of a document that filled most of his memo pad, with a page devoted to each teacher. He had circled the time he or she had left the building the day of the murder, and torn out the nine pages belonging to those who'd left the building after me and thus before the killer's arrival. In order to create a more accurate timeline and perhaps collect additional clues, he had glued all nine pages to a poster board. But the glue didn't hold, and he had to start all over again.

That phone call I'd overheard, meanwhile, had still led nowhere. The phone company wasn't cooperating, leaving Amos Tupper at his wits' end and bearing the blame from the Appleton PD.

A colleague dropped me home that Friday, four days after the murder, to find Frank seated at our kitchen table with a vase full of roses sitting before him.

"What are those for?"

"We're celebrating."

"Celebrating what?"

"Our new house in Cabot Cove, at six ninety-eight Candlewood Lane."

My knees literally went weak. "Did I just hear you right?"

Frank rose, grinning as broadly as I'd ever seen him. "You only live once, Jess."

I practically leaped into his arms, never happier in my life. I didn't ask him how much we'd paid or how he'd managed the down payment. We'd have to sell our house, of course, but that wasn't about to stop us. Nothing was going to stop us.

I'm not sure what was better: the excitement I was feeling or getting a respite from my obsessing over Walter Reavis's murder. I couldn't think of anything I'd rather do in that moment than move out of Appleton, and to beautiful Cabot Cove, no less.

"There's more," Frank said, after finally breaking our embrace. "Turns out, that real estate agent Eve Simpson knows the Cabot Cove High School principal."

"I got the feeling that Eve Simpson knows everyone, Frank."

"But she sold the principal his house. She'll make the introduction anytime you're ready."

"Is this really happening?" I asked him.

"It's like flying, Jessica. Sometimes you've got to aim for the stars."

Our phone rang, and I snatched the receiver to my ear.

"Mrs. Fletcher!" the voice of Amos Tupper broke in before I'd completed my greeting.

"Detective?"

"You were right again, Mrs. Fletcher. Everything you said turned out to be right. I just arrested Walter Reavis's murderer!"

Chapter Thirteen

The present

I'd spoken for so long, I'd drained my phone battery and had to stop to plug it in.

"How am I doing so far, Amos?" I asked the former detective and sheriff of Cabot Cove.

"Just fine, Mrs. Fletcher. Your recollection's right as rain. You brought things to mind I haven't thought about in a whole lot of time, but that's exactly the way I remember it. I get a little fuzzy after that, though."

"No problem, Amos. That's all I need for now."

"I didn't use to get this fuzzy about things," he said, unable to disguise the sadness, maybe mixed with fear, in his voice. "Talking to you has made me feel sharp as a tack again. Reminds me how much I miss Cabot Cove. My mind's not fuzzy on that at all."

"You were a great sheriff, Amos."

"You really think so?"

"Yes, yes, I do."

"We did have our times, didn't we?"

"We sure did."

"And how are things there now? What are you up to these days?"

"I'm investigating a murder."

"So things haven't changed, in other words."

"Do they ever?"

"Not for me anymore. But I've been keeping up with your books. And I've found myself another writer who holds a decent candle to you."

"Who's that?"

"Shakespeare."

"You're reading Shakespeare, Amos? How wonderful."

"Well, you did recommend him a while back, and I've finally got the time to give him a whirl. Can't always make sense of what he's saying, but I'm hooked, I tell you. My favorite so far is *Richard the Third*, because he's short like me."

"That's one of my favorites, too," I told him, meaning it.

"So, how is it you still have any time left to solve murders when you're so busy writing?"

"It often seems like more the opposite is true, Amos."

"Are you able to tell me why the murder of Walter Reavis has become so important again after so many years?"

"His daughter's murder is the one I'm working on now."

"No!"

"Yes, I'm afraid."

"Which one, the older or the younger?"

"The younger."

"I can't remember meeting either one of them. That fuzzy head of mine, like I was telling you."

"I may need to check in about any new developments that arise, Amos. Can I call you again to make sure I've got my facts from the past straight?"

"Of course, Mrs. Fletcher, anytime. Anything I can do to help put another murderer away—well, let's just say it brings back happy memories."

I stopped short of criticizing his unusual statement.

"That didn't come out right, did it?"

"I understood what you meant," I told him.

"It's mostly true, because of how much I enjoyed those times the fates threw us together on a case. That time the man was murdered on the bus, did we ever make it to Portland for the conference?"

"No, it was too late. But I won the big television they were raffling off anyway. Remember that?"

"Sure, I do! I had my eye on that."

"I remember. People miss you around here, Amos."

"Really?"

"Mort isn't a Mainer or a New Englander. He'll never win people over the way you did."

"That makes me feel good, Mrs. Fletcher. I wonder if I made a mistake by leaving when I did."

I don't think Amos Tupper would have fared very well in the "new" Cabot Cove. He was a small-town sheriff, not necessarily the right fit for a town that was not nearly as small as it used to be, especially during the summer months.

"Anyways, I still get the *Gazette* delivered by mail. Usually comes a week late, and that's good enough for me, though I suppose it's online now, too."

Amos mentioning the *Cabot Cove Gazette* made me recall

those copies of it Mort and I had found in Ginny Genaway's New Hampshire apartment, the oldest issue going back just over five months. I still hadn't figured out what had triggered her sudden interest in Cabot Cove around that time, but I had a sense that it was important—a sense that there was something in that timeline that might lead me straight to her killer.

It never ceases to amaze me how the rigors of investigating an actual murder hold so many similarities to the challenges of conjuring a fictional one. It's uncanny how similar my thinking and my mind-set were in pursuit of either. I guess that the part of my brain that always comes up with the answers I need in my books is the same part that steers me in the right direction in reality.

"Nothing much changes, does it, Mrs. Fletcher?" Amos finished.

"Not the things that matter the most, no, but that doesn't stop them from trying."

"I had some visitors, Mort," I said, negotiating the cord of my still-charging phone. "From Boston."

"Friends of Vic Genaway, no doubt. Did they threaten or intimidate you in any way? Because if they did—"

"I signed a book for one of them—his wife, actually."

"So what'd they want, besides a free copy?"

"To be kept informed of things."

"Of course, so they're in a position to exact their own brand of justice on the killer once we find him."

"I actually think it's more to make sure that justice is done."

"What's that mean exactly, Jessica?"

"That Joe and his friend will leave us alone and stay out of our way, unless we don't have enough to arrest the killer."

"'Joe and his friend'?"

"I didn't get the other guy's name. Any updates on Lisa Joy Reavis, Mort?"

"My fingers are numb from typing in her name so often."

"I suppose I should take that as a no. And maybe you should consider using cut and paste."

I could hear keys clacking even now, and I pictured Mort listening to me on speakerphone while he hunted and pecked away. "I think maybe somebody cut Lisa Joy Reavis and pasted her somewhere else entirely."

"That's what we need to find out."

And I wasn't about to sit back and wait for Mort to get it done. He had an entire sheriff's department to run, on top of trying to solve a murder. Besides, finding people who've made a concerted effort to disappear is an art form in itself, so I called one particular artist.

"This is Harry McGraw," I heard a familiar, craggy voice greet me after I dialed a number long committed to memory. "I can't come to the phone right now, so please leave a message on my answering machine at the beep. . . . Beep!"

"Stop it, Harry," I said to the best private investigator, and one of the best investigators period, I'd ever encountered.

"Hey, can't blame me for running to the hills every time your number comes up. What gave me away?"

"Well, first off, you made the 'beep' sound yourself. And nobody calls them answering machines anymore."

"I do."

"You're hardly in the majority."

"I'm a majority of one, Jessica. And you'll have to talk to my accountant before enlisting my services now."

"And why's that?"

"He seems to have a problem with what he calls 'my shoddy paperwork.'"

"You don't do any paperwork."

"That's what I told him, my dear, but then the discussion came around to billing."

"Which you don't do either."

"He wanted to know my top clients, in terms of hours. I mentioned you and—wouldn't you know it?—he asked to see invoices."

"Which you don't generate."

"He fired me. I didn't know an accountant could fire a client."

"How many times have you tried to fire me, Harry?"

"But I'm a private detective. We're allowed to do that. Says so in the handbook."

"That would be the private detective's handbook?"

"It didn't say. Now, what do you need me to do that I won't be sending you an invoice for?"

I laid it all out to him in as much detail as I thought proper, rehashing the timeline of Ginny Genaway's last day alive, spent in Cabot Cove, as best I could.

"So Lisa Joy Reavis is her sister's name."

"Used to be. The fact that she's dropped off the map can only mean she changed her identity and did so in a very sophisticated way."

"I'm talking legal here. See, there're all sorts of ways to change your identity, and all of them can keep somebody from seeing anything awry on the surface. Below the surface is something else entirely. When people change who they are, they tend to leave shadows of who they used to be. That's how I find missing persons who don't want to be found, by following those shadows."

"Are we on the clock now?"

"My watch cost five bucks on the street, and the timer came broken." Harry hesitated for a few moments. "You said Lisa Joy Reavis taught in Alabama for a time?"

"I have it on good authority, yes."

"What about after?"

"There is no 'after.' That's why I called you."

"With a name that's no longer active for a woman who hasn't been seen in, what, maybe fifteen years?"

I tried to do the calculations quickly in my mind, but gave up. "Something like that."

"Anything else you can tell me about her?"

"I'm afraid not, Harry."

"Par for the course, then. I'll try not to disappoint you, like I always do."

"You never disappoint me," I insisted.

"Right. That explains why you tip me so well."

"I can't tip on top of a bill I never get."

"Always the formalities with you, Jess. Do you at least have a picture of Lisa Joy Reavis you can send me?"

I thought of the snapshot her mother had given me, in which

Lisa Joy appeared as a miserable-looking teenager with her siblings, both of whom were now dead. Given all that, I wasn't sure I'd ever heard a less appropriate name than "Lisa Joy."

"I can scan and e-mail one to you, Harry," I told him.

"Why don't you just e-mail it?"

"I have to scan it first."

"You could fax it."

"What's your fax number?"

"I don't remember. I never use it."

"Check your e-mail in ten minutes, Harry."

I got the signal that another call was coming in and saw it was from Mort.

"I got your message. What's up?"

"We need to pay a return visit to Vic Genaway, Mort. What's your schedule look like tomorrow?"

Vic Genaway was waiting in the interview room when we arrived at New Hampshire State Prison for Men the next morning. No chains were attached to his wrists this time, and his hands were cupped casually behind his head. He was smirking at me, acting as if Mort wasn't there at all.

"I heard you met the boys, Fletch."

"I left a bag of my books with the guard at the entrance, Mr. Genaway. He wouldn't let me give them to you personally."

"No, they figure I might use the pages as weapons. You know," he said, finally regarding Mort in a derisive fashion, "death by paper cut."

"I did meet the men you sent to Cabot Cove," I told him.

"Behaving themselves, are they?"

"Perfect gentlemen, from my perspective, although Joe did all the talking."

Genaway nodded. "Yeah, Nails doesn't talk much."

"Nails, Mr. Genaway?"

His smirk returned. "You don't want to know how he got that nickname, believe me. And why don't you just call me Vic, since this is your second visit in two days?"

"I'll stick with Mr. Genaway, if you don't mind."

"Hey, whatever floats your boat, Fletch."

Mort leaned forward next to me, signaling he was taking the floor. "I thought we had good faith between us, Vic, this tragedy you suffered and all with your wife. But then you left some important things out the first time we came to see you." He shook his head. "I thought you wanted to help us find your ex-wife's killer."

"I do. Why do you think I sent Joe and Nails to town?"

"Would you mind if I asked you another question about Ginny, Mr. Genaway?" I said, stepping in.

"Knock yourself out."

"After she left you," I resumed, getting to the point of this visit, "did you have men like Joe and Nails keep tabs on her?" I finished as politely as I could manage.

"From time to time, sure. For her own protection, you understand, Fletch, on account of I've made a few enemies over the years."

"No," Mort said curtly, "really?"

I leaned over the table a bit to put myself between him and Vic Genaway. "So whoever you had watching her from time to time would have been aware of her comings and goings. Where she went and whom she talked to when she got there."

"More or less," Genaway answered, eyeing me suspiciously. "Why?"

Mort let me keep the floor. "Because those comings and goings may provide a clue as to what brought her to Cabot Cove, who killed her, and why."

He nodded, smiling tightly before that gesture dissolved into a smirk. "I can see why the flatfoot there brought you along for the ride."

The remark had clearly been meant to get a rise out of Mort, but he smirked back at Vic Genaway.

"I gave the job of watching my ex-wife to Joe and Nails on account of I trust them. You want to know where Ginny's been keeping herself since our little spat, especially since I've been inside, they're the guys to talk to. You need Joe's number?"

"He already gave it to me. One more thing, Mr. Genaway. Do you have any notion as to the source of Ginny's interest in Cabot Cove?"

He shrugged. "The fact that she even had any is news to me." His expression became as cold as I'd seen it yet. "You ever have a character like me in any of your books, Fletch?"

"Not exactly, no."

"Then," Vic Genaway told me, as if Mort wasn't even in the room, "prepare to learn something."

Chapter Fourteen

Joe and Nails were staying just outside of town at the Oceanview Motel, which was five miles from the coast and boasted no view of the ocean. It was the only establishment with its own coffee shop in the area, which I thought at least partially accounted for their choosing to stay there. And sure enough, I found them inside at a table in the back with mugs of coffee before, and an ashtray centered between, them. Each was smoking a cigarette, and the smell hung over the table like a cloud, even though smoking in restaurants had been illegal for years. Maybe the two of them were having a late lunch, since it was just after two in the afternoon.

"Hey, Mrs. Fletcher," Joe said, rising from his chair when he saw me approaching.

Nails followed suit. Grudgingly. Then sat back down as fast as he had risen.

"Care to join us?" Joe continued.

"You know you're breaking the law."

Joe glanced down toward his belt, as if to look for a pistol. Then he noticed the Cabot Cove Sheriff's Department SUV parked outside, with Mort behind the wheel working his cell phone. "We're not carrying."

"I was talking about the cigarettes."

Joe held up the ashtray. "That's why we carry our own with us. Comes in handy."

Joe glanced out the window again, Nails following his gaze but letting his hold out the window when Joe turned back to me.

"That your friend the sheriff?"

"I asked him to let me talk to you alone."

"Probably smart to keep yokel law enforcement at arm's length."

"Sheriff Metzger spent twenty-five years with the New York Police Department. He was a Marine and fought in Vietnam before that."

Joe joined Nails in gazing out the window. "I'll keep that in mind."

"Good idea."

"Such a polished investigator, and yet he's waiting in the car."

"I told him you'd be more helpful if I came in by myself."

"You were right, Mrs. Fletcher," Joe said. "You want to join us?"

"I don't smoke."

"I was talking about for a coffee." He stamped out his cigarette in their traveling ashtray, Nails following suit again. "See, now we're not breaking the law anymore." Joe smirked, looking toward Mort's SUV again.

"So you're not," I agreed, and sat down in the chair next to Nails, casting him a smile that must not have registered.

"Boss told us you'd be stopping by."

"He has access to a phone in prison?"

Joe smirked again. "This is the boss we're talking about."

"Did he tell you why I'd be stopping by, Joe?"

"Not beyond the fact that it had something to do with Mrs. Genaway. May she rest in peace."

He crossed himself, with Nails mirroring him yet again.

"Mr. Genaway, the boss, mentioned you'd been following his ex-wife for some time."

"You mean *watching* her. And it was for her own good."

"He mentioned that, too."

"Boss told us to help you in any way we could."

I pushed my chair in farther under the table. A server came over, looking surprised that I'd joined the only other customers in the place, and I ordered a tea.

"I was curious where she was spending her time the past, say, month or so," I said after the server had taken her leave.

"Nowhere special or out of the ordinary, for the most part."

"What about *not* for the most part?"

"If you're talking outside her routine, I'd say a trip she made to Appleton. Right, Nails?"

Nails didn't respond while I processed what Joe had just told me.

"Appleton, *Maine*?"

"Is there another?"

"Not that I know of."

"Me either. That's why I asked." Joe narrowed his gaze on me, sending a thin chill up my spine. "The look on your face says you think that might be important."

"It's the town where she grew up. Her father was the principal of the high school in Appleton when she was a little girl. He was murdered in his office."

Nails perked up a bit at mention of the word "murder."

Joe looked like he missed the cigarette he'd just pressed out. "Wait. Mrs. Genaway's father was *murdered*?"

"You didn't know?"

"Boss never told us. I guess he didn't think it was important."

"With good reason. It was twenty-five years ago. But she must've had some reason for going to Appleton. . . . When was it exactly?"

Joe pulled a notebook from a pocket he had wedged it into. He wet his fingers and flipped pages until he came to the one he was looking for. "Six days ago—no, that's not counting today," he corrected himself. "Make that seven. Yeah, seven."

I did the math, and something occurred to me that I placed on the back burner for now. "What did Mrs. Genaway do while she was in Appleton, Joe?"

"She wasn't there for the sights. I can tell you that much. She stopped at the newspaper office and several other places, like she was looking for something. Oh, and she stopped off and talked to some people. I wrote down the addresses for the boss if you'd like them."

"I would, indeed." I paused long enough to meet Joe's stare, forgetting Nails was sitting there next to me. "You weren't really following Mrs. Genaway to protect her, were you?"

"Yeah, we were protecting her from herself. Make sure she didn't do something that would upset the boss. You know, Mrs. Fletcher."

I didn't, but I nodded anyway.

"You think whatever she found out in Appleton is what brought her to Cabot Cove?" he asked me.

"I'm not sure, Joe. The time frame would seem to suggest that, and maybe I'll have a better idea once I learn whom she spoke to in Appleton and what exactly she was looking for there."

He weighed my words, not looking too impressed by my intentions. "People go back to the scene of the crime—could be they're chasing ghosts. Hey, maybe she was looking for her father's killer."

"Her father's killer has been in jail for almost twenty-five years. Whatever brought her to Appleton, it wasn't about solving his murder."

"And who did solve it? Was it you, Mrs. Fletcher?"

I ignored his question, my gaze fastened on his open notebook. "Those addresses, Joe."

Instead of copying them down, he tore the sheet out altogether. "Knock yourself out," he said, handing it to me.

I climbed back into Mort's SUV, noticing he'd hitched his holster outside his department-issue jacket.

He followed my gaze. "Hey, once a Marine, always a Marine. Excuse me for not trusting your newfound friends."

"Whether I trust them or not, it turns out they may have served our investigation well," I said, and handed him the slip of paper with the addresses that Ginny Genaway had visited in Appleton.

"What's this?"

"Apparently, Ginny made a trip to Appleton the week before she was murdered. Those are the addresses she made stops at."

Mort regarded them with his professional gaze. "Your new friends tell you that?"

"Apparently, they were tailing her for their boss."

"Pity the man who crosses Vic Genaway. . . ."

"I was hoping you could get me the names associated with these," I told him, "as in who lives at the addresses."

"I figured that out all on my own, Mrs. F."

I was starting to get used to his calling me that again. "How's Adele, by the way?" I asked, referring to Mort's wife.

"I didn't tell you she's taken an administrative position with the Reserves?"

"Once a Marine, always a Marine, right?"

His eyes met mine across the seat. "I wish you'd keep that in mind when you're driving me crazy." Mort fired up the engine while I fished my phone from my bag. "Anybody I know?" he asked me.

"Playing a hunch about one of those stops Ginny Genaway made."

I checked my phone for recent calls and redialed the number I'd used to call in my RSVP for Wilma Tisdale's retirement party at the Cabot Cove Country Club.

"Hello," her already familiar voice greeted me.

"Wilma, it's Jessica Fletcher."

"Jessica! We don't hear from each other in twenty-five years, and now twice in two days!"

"That's why I'm calling, Wilma. I need to ask you some frank questions. I hope you don't mind."

"Of course not," she said after a pause just long enough to tell me my suspicions that something was off here were well-founded. “I’m an old, soon-to-be retired schoolteacher. What could I possibly have to hide?”

“Did you hear about the murder here a couple nights back?”

“The woman shot at the rest stop?”

“Scenic overlook, actually, but yes. It was our old principal Walter Reavis’s younger daughter.”

My statement was greeted with silence, broken only by Wilma Tisdale’s rapid breathing.

“Are you there, Wilma? Are you all right?”

“Er, yes. I’m just having trouble processing this. After all these years, it brings it all back, doesn’t it? I haven’t thought about that poor girl since her father’s murder.”

“You mean, until last week, don’t you?”

More silence and this time I kept talking after turning on the speaker so Mort could hear both sides of the conversation.

“Ginny Reavis, now Ginny Genaway, came to see you last week, didn’t she, Wilma?” I said, playing my hunch that Wilma Tisdale’s was one of the addresses where Ginny had stopped in Appleton as witnessed by Joe and Nails on her ex-husband’s orders.

“How did you know?”

“You’re aware of who her husband is.”

“She mentioned a bit about him.”

“He had men following her. I just spoke with them.”

“They’re in Cabot Cove?”

“Close by. She came to see you last Wednesday. My invitation to your retirement party must’ve been mailed either Thursday or Friday, perhaps even over the weekend. I think you decided to invite me because you wanted to talk about Ginny’s visit, and you thought the party you'd already scheduled for right here in Cabot Cove would provide the perfect opportunity."

Wilma didn't bother confirming or denying my assertion.

"You should know," I continued, "that Ginny interviewed me, pretending to be a high school student, the day she was murdered. She wanted to know all about my first murder investigation, and we both know what that was."

"She didn't look like a high school student when I saw her, Jessica."

"In retrospect, I must've seen what I expected to. I suspect she would've made a pretty good actress, given how well she played the part. What did she want from you, Wilma?"

"Information about her older sister, Lisa Joy, whose life was apparently anything but joyful."

"Explaining why she left home and never came back. So, what made Ginny come to you?"

"Did you know I tutored Lisa Joy?" Wilma asked me.

"No."

"All through middle school, and high school, too, right up until her father's murder, when she seemed to lose interest in everything. Besides her parents, I probably knew her better than anyone. Moody all the time and depressed a good portion of it. I can count on my fingers the times I saw her smile. Today, she'd be a prime candidate for antidepressants, but they weren't being as widely prescribed in those days, especially to children."

"That's not the subject at hand today," I said. "I believe Ginny came to Appleton looking for something, and I think she thought you could help her."

"Well, I . . ."

I could hear her choking up on the other end of the line. "It's okay, Wilma. There's no way you could have known what was going to happen, and you shouldn't think for one minute that whatever you told her had anything to do with her death."

"I didn't tell her anything, Jessica. I couldn't."

"Why?"

"Because she had gotten it in her head that her older sister had murdered her father."

"She thinks you caught the wrong person," Wilma finished as I locked stares with Mort and wondered what he made of such an assertion, not at all grounded in the facts of the case.

"That makes no sense," I reminded her. "The real killer confessed to the crime."

"Ginny didn't believe that. She was convinced Lisa Joy Reavis was the real killer. She pumped me for everything I could remember about the days following her father's death. She was especially interested in what you'd shared with me and what I'd observed. You're right about the invitation. I should've invited you anyway, but it had been so long, and what would a famous person like you want with a party at a club we could only afford because it's off season?"

"I'm not famous, Wilma. I'm just a mystery writer and, like you, a former teacher. I would have loved to come under any circumstances, and I'm looking forward to seeing you and all the rest of my old friends from Appleton."

"But you never came back to visit after you moved to Cabot Cove. We thought you'd moved on, forgotten us."

"After Frank's death . . ." I said, listening to my own voice trail off. "Well, let's just say everything changed. It was only a couple of years after we'd moved here. I'd landed a full-time job teaching at Cabot Cove High. Things couldn't have been better until he got sick."

"I'm sorry for even bringing it up," she said, her voice cracking over the speaker.

"You were kind enough to come to the funeral, Wilma. And you're right. I should've done a better job of keeping in touch. But for me Appleton and the murder of Walter Reavis were linked inextricably. Then I started writing, and it was like my whole life started over again. Can you remember anything else Ginny asked you about, some of the specifics perhaps?"

"Not much, because I really wasn't able to help her. I think, more than anything, she wanted me to confirm that her sister was capable of such a thing."

"And did you? *Do* you believe she was?"

"Of murder? My stars, how would I know? I was a teacher and the girl's tutor, not her psychiatrist."

"Ginny came to you first, Wilma. She made three other stops after leaving your house, one being the high school. My guess is you provided the addresses for the other two."

"Jim Dirkson, the man who replaced Walter as principal, was one."

"He's still in Appleton?"

"Retired a few years back and still living in the same house. Plays a lot of golf these days when the seasons allow."

"Who was the other person?"

"Tyler Benjamin."

"He's still in town?"

"Moved back a few years ago."

"He'd be . . ." I did the math in my head. "He'd be in his early forties now."

"He still talks about you, Jessica, what might have happened to him if it wasn't for you. He never contacted you when he returned?"

"I'm sure he'd prefer to forget everyone associated with such a terrible time for him, including me, and who can blame him?"

I heard Wilma take a deep breath. "I heard that detective you worked with became sheriff of Cabot Cove."

"Amos Tupper," I said with a nod, even though she couldn't see me. "He retired a few years back."

"What's his replacement like?"

"Old, crotchety, and prone to taking naps behind his desk in the middle of the day," I said, looking at Mort, who waved a reproaching finger at me.

"Why now, Jessica?" Wilma asked. "Why after all these years did Ginny Reavis come to believe her older sister was a killer?"

"That's what I intend to find out," I told her. "But don't worry, Wilma. I promise it won't spoil the party on Saturday."

After we'd said our good-byes for now, I looked back at Mort.

"'Old, crotchety, and prone to taking naps behind his desk' in the afternoon . . . Really?"

"I didn't say that."

"Yes, you did."

"No, I said 'prone to taking naps in the middle of the day,' not the afternoon."

"Thanks for the clarification," he said, shaking his head. "Why do I think the murder of this high school principal twenty-five years ago and the murder of Ginny Genaway the other night are stuck together like peanut butter to the roof of my mouth?"

"You call that a simile, Mort?"

"Never mind what I call it. I think it's time you told me more about the murder of Walter Reavis, Mrs. Fletcher."

Chapter Fifteen

Twenty-five years ago . . .

You were right again, Mrs. Fletcher. Everything you said turned out to be right. I just arrested Walter Reavis's murderer!

The suspect, I realized as Detective Tupper continued, was not a jealous husband or a woman scorned, as those rumors about Walter may have suggested, but a student at Appleton High. Specifically, a football player with behavior issues named Tyler Benjamin. Walter had expelled Tyler for threatening a teacher, a decision supported by the superintendent and the school board. It was his third, and most serious, transgression of the fall, and it was determined that he was too much of a risk, a ticking time bomb, to remain in the building.

I knew Tyler from one of Bill Gower's English classes. He was a handsome young man with strong looks that were both haunting and brooding. He had played linebacker and running back on the football team, all state in both positions, and had been on the verge of deciding between multiple scholarship offers from colleges. Of course, being expelled destroyed all those opportunities.

I'd never had a problem with him, in class or otherwise. He wasn't a very good student, but he handed in his assignments on time and was diligent in studying for tests, even though he never managed higher than a B minus.

"Tyler Benjamin blamed Principal Reavis for ruining his life, Jessica," Amos Tupper was saying. "His expulsion meant he was banned from school grounds, but Jim Dirkson reportedly saw him lurking about when he was about to drive off just short of five o'clock."

"Is 'lurking about' the way he described it?"

"Yes, ma'am. It was starting to get dark, and Dirkson says it looked like Tyler was hiding behind the corner of the building, like the kid was waiting for him to leave."

"Did Dirkson explain why he just let Tyler go and didn't approach him?"

"He said he intended to write it up first thing the next morning. The truth is, Mrs. Fletcher, I believe he was scared to confront Tyler Benjamin, and from what I've heard about the kid, I don't blame him. Which brings me to the murder weapon."

Something about the narrative Detective Tupper had provided didn't sit right with me. Something felt off, but I kept listening instead of pondering further.

"That partial print we found on the trophy that wasn't in the system? Tyler Benjamin's was a perfect match."

"Do you recall what kind of trophy it was, Detective?"

"I remember the football that we found clutched in the victim's hand."

"It was the district championship trophy from this season."

"Yes. I was at the game. Right around Veterans Day, as I recall, just before the boy was expelled."

"So it stands to reason that it would've been presented to Tyler as team captain. So of course his fingerprints would be on it."

"Well, I suppose that's possible," Tupper said after a pause.

"Would it be possible for me to speak with the young man, Detective?"

"I don't think the chief would approve of that."

"Do we have to tell him?"

"No," Tupper said hesitantly, "not necessarily."

"I was one of the boy's teachers, you know."

Tupper sighed, and for some reason, I could picture him shaking his head. "No bad kids in the world in your mind, are there, Mrs. Fletcher?"

"I'm sure there are plenty. I'm just not sure Tyler Benjamin is one of them. I'd like to see the boy, Detective, and I think we need to have a talk with Jim Dirkson as well," I said. What I couldn't quite grasp before had crystalized in my mind.

"The acting principal? Why?"

"He claims to have spotted Tyler Benjamin lurking in the parking lot when he was leaving the building, right?"

"Yes, ma'am."

"Then how is it he wasn't in his own office when I was waiting to see Walter Reavis?"

I guess I didn't want to believe Tyler Benjamin was a killer. In the minds of many teachers, there's no such thing as a truly bad kid. We want to believe they can all be redeemed if people like us put in the time. Of course, sometimes kids go bad in spite of the best efforts of their parents, teachers, and coaches. Sometimes it's unavoidable.

Had Walter Reavis paid the ultimate price for that oversight?

Amos Tupper called me back just after noon the following day to let me know that the chief of the Appleton police had left early for the day, freeing up an opportunity for me to speak with Tyler. Frank was out giving flying lessons, Saturday being his busiest day. So, not wanting to inconvenience anyone, I decided to ride my bicycle over to the police station. Grady was at a friend's house and I made sure to call to make sure they could keep him until I was back home.

Of the many things Frank and I enjoyed doing together, fishing and bike riding were at the top of the list. We normally wouldn't have done either with Thanksgiving breathing down our necks and the early bite of the Maine winter that came with that. But that day was unseasonably warm, the air crisp and clean with almost no wind to speak of, and I found myself full of energy as I pedaled across town, careful of the traffic.

I can't say exactly why I've never gotten a driver's license. The explanation has shifted over the years, as I've sought the answer for myself. There was no catastrophic incident, no near-death experience either with me as a passenger or while I was learning how to drive. I think it comes down to the fact that I simply didn't enjoy the process. It wasn't like I felt a panic attack coming every time I tried to get behind the wheel. It was more like once seated there, I lost all desire to be anywhere else and thus drive there. The old saying that it's not the destination but the journey didn't apply to me, at least when I was doing the driving.

People who know me well find it strange that I have a pilot's license and not a driver's license. I personally don't.

Tyler Benjamin looked terrified as we walked into the single interview room at the Appleton police station. It was actually the coffee room, but limited space required it to maintain multiple uses. And given the crime rate there in town, it got far more use for coffee than it did for interrogations or interviews. As a result, the single Formica table, which looked as if it had been lifted from the high school cafeteria, was circular instead of rectangular. Around the table were five chairs that also appeared identical to the ones at Appleton High.

Tyler Benjamin sat at that table, hands and lips both trembling. Tom Jennings, the same uniformed officer who'd been guarding the main office when I arrived at school the morning Walter Reavis's body had been found, stood against the wall with his arms crossed. He took our entry as his cue to leave. I saw the cuffs lashed to Tyler's wrists and wanted to cry—something he had clearly been doing, judging by the tearstains down both cheeks. He wore an Appleton High hooded sweatshirt and was trembling visibly. His long, dark hair was damp at the edges and his deep-set eyes appeared more scared than brooding today. He looked at me and tried to smile but failed.

"Hey, Mrs. Fletcher," he said, his voice cracking.

Amos Tupper and I took chairs across from and on either side of him; as usual, I was unable to hold my tongue when I saw something I felt was wrong.

"Does he really need to be handcuffed, Detective? Can we take the cuffs off?"

"I'm afraid not, Mrs. Fletcher." Tupper frowned. "It's department policy."

"There aren't enough arrests here for this town to have a policy," I said, not meaning to snap at him.

"I didn't do it, Mrs. Fletcher," Tyler said, near tears. "I swear. I didn't do it. . . ."

His voice drifted off, as if he were speaking from someplace else, anywhere else in his mind, I imagined.

"I know I shouldn't have been there," he resumed. "I knew I was breaking the rules of my expulsion, but I couldn't help it. I had to talk to Mr. Reavis. I made a mistake. I know I was wrong, but I thought if I tried apologizing again . . ." Once more, emotion choked off his words.

"What did Mr. Reavis say when you tried to apologize and plead your case to him again?"

"That's just it, Mrs. Fletcher. It's like I tried to tell the detective. I never got the chance because I never saw him."

"You know you can have a lawyer present, Tyler," I advised. "You don't have to talk to us."

"I don't want a lawyer here because I didn't do anything. I don't understand why everyone thinks I did. Somebody's lying."

Detective Tupper frowned, obviously having heard that claim when he took the boy's statement.

"The guy—the lawyer my parents made me talk to—told me not to talk to the police. But you're not the police."

"True enough."

"You were always nice to me, Mrs. Fletcher," Tyler said, preferring to address me. "Not all teachers treated me like you did. I think I scared them."

At that moment, I had no idea why more of the faculty didn't see this boy the way I saw him. Looking across the table, I certainly didn't see a killer, but what did I know about such things?

"In the statement he gave Detective Tupper, Mr. Dirkson claims he saw you in the parking lot," I said. "He described you as 'lurking.'"

"'Lurking'?"

"That's what he said."

"It's a lie, Mrs. Fletcher."

"You weren't in the parking lot?"

"Yes, but that's not where he saw me. He saw me when I knocked on the door to the office. Mr. Reavis's car was still parked in the space reserved for the principal, so I knew he must be there, but the door was locked. So I knocked, and he answered."

"Mr. Reavis?"

"No, Mr. Dirkson."

"Wait," I said, thrown by this. "You're saying Mr. Dirkson opened the door when you knocked."

"More like banged. Nobody responded when I knocked. I was ready to break the door down—that's how much I wanted to tell Mr. Reavis how sorry I was and ask him if there was anything I could do, anything at all, to make him, you know, change the expulsion to a suspension or something."

I turned to Amos Tupper and got the sense he was hearing this version of things for the first time, that Tyler had left it out of his statement. Given how he must have felt after being arrested, I couldn't blame him for either neglecting to mention that or forgetting about it altogether.

"If I can't play football in college, I don't know what I'm going to do," Tyler added, sniffling.

"What time would this have been, Tyler?" I asked him.

"When?"

"When you came to the school, when you knocked on the door?"

"I thought Mr. Reavis would be alone in the office, especially when I saw Ms. Potts leaving."

"Alma Potts? Mr. Reavis's secretary?" I asked, recalling that Alma had been out sick the day of Walter Reavis's murder.

"Yes, I watched her driving away."

"Her or her car, son?" Detective Tupper asked him.

"Who else would have been driving her car?"

"Just answer the question."

"I recognized her behind the wheel. Just a glimpse, but that was enough."

"Did you see the license plate number?"

The boy shrugged, his big shoulders slumping. "No."

"So the car might've just looked like hers, right?"

"Well," he told Amos Tupper, "it was white like hers. Oh, and it backfired."

"Backfired?"

"You know, like a gunshot. I thought it was going to stall."

"Tyler," I started, "I need to ask you again what time this was."

He shook his head, his hair flopping about. "I don't know. I wasn't wearing my watch."

"Was it dark?"

"Oh, for sure. Ms. Potts's car had its lights on," he said, looking toward Tupper briefly. "That's why I only caught a glimpse of her. Yeah, it was definitely dark."

That meant it had to be after the sun went down, which would've been four thirty or so this time of year. I had left the office, after hearing Walter Reavis arguing with someone over the phone, around quarter to four, when there was still light left in the sky. The office door hadn't been locked, and I'd seen no sign of Jim Dirkson. I tried to remember whether the door to his office, located across the hall from Walter's, was open or closed, but I couldn't.

"What else did you see when Mr. Dirkson opened the office door, Tyler?"

"Er, nothing."

"Did you see Mr. Reavis?"

"No, Mrs. Fletcher, I didn't see anything. Just Mr. Dirkson. He wouldn't let me in. I lied and told him Mr. Reavis had asked me to stop by, but he told me to get out, that he was going to report me to the police for trespassing or something. He said I was going to jail. He never did like me. You know that."

Truth be told, I think our acting principal, Jim Dirkson, hated kids in general. Why he chose education as his profession, I'll never understand.

I looked at Tyler Benjamin and tried to reconcile my own experiences with the boy with the reputation for violence that had led directly to his expulsion. I couldn't help myself from taking our conversation in another direction.

"Tell me about this outburst you had in class, Tyler, the one that led to your expulsion."

His eyes moistened with tears. He swiped a sleeve to wipe them away, no easy task with his hands lashed together. When he responded, he kept his gaze angled downward, casting me an occasional furtive glance.

"Mr. MacMillan's got it in for me, Mrs. Fletcher. He told me to go to the office and see the principal, and I wouldn't go."

"Why did he tell you to leave class?"

"He doesn't like me."

"That's not a reason to tell a student to go to the office."

"I didn't do anything other than say something to the kid next to me when he was passing out a quiz—that's all. And he still sent me to the office, which meant I was going to get a zero. I couldn't just take that. I had to stand up to him. I think he was smiling when I was yelling at him because he knew he had me."

"Did you threaten Mr. MacMillan in any way?"

The boy shrugged his broad shoulders. "I don't know. I don't think so, but I don't remember everything I said. I guess it's possible."

"Did you explain all this to Mr. Reavis?"

"I saw Mr. Dirkson first. He's the one who told me I was going to get expelled over this. I saw Mr. Reavis later, but he said there was nothing he could do. His hands were tied, he said. It was in the school board's hands. Don't you get it, Mrs. Fletcher? If I was coming to school that day to hurt somebody, it wouldn't have been Mr. Reavis. It would have been Mr. Dirkson or Mr. MacMillan. I was coming to see Mr. Reavis to beg him for another chance. It wasn't like I hit anybody or something." The boy's eyes welled with water again, and this time he made no effort to swipe away the tears, which now poured down his cheeks. "I didn't do it, Mrs. Fletcher. I don't want to go to prison. They told me I could spend the rest of my life there."

"You're not going to prison, Tyler," I promised him.

"You're just a teacher. What can you do about it?"

I glanced at Amos Tupper and then back at the boy. "I can find the real killer."

Chapter Sixteen

The present

"You caught the real killer, right?" Mort asked me when I stopped my narrative there, the SUV still running.

I nodded. "Turned out, it—"

"No, don't tell me."

"I was just about to get to the best part."

"All right, tell me."

My phone rang before I could resume my tale, and HARRY lit up in the caller ID.

"Harry," I greeted him, on speaker.

"He's not available."

"You called me," I reminded him.

"Must have been a butt dial. Who is this?"

"What did you find out about Lisa Joy Reavis?"

"Who?"

"The topic you must be calling about."

"Oh, yeah. How about this? I'll let you know when I've got

something, and I'll make sure the next time you hear from me, it's not my butt placing the call."

"I'd appreciate that, Harry."

"But since I've got you on the line now, an update would seem to be in order," he told me. "The last confirmed whereabouts of one Lisa Joy Reavis were at Robert E. Lee Elementary School in Tuscaloosa, Alabama, home of the Crimson Tide. Prior to that she received her degree in education at the University of Virginia. One of my daughters got her degree in teaching, you know."

"I didn't, actually. You never told me, Harry."

"She didn't last long enough in the profession for me to. Kept getting laid off and ended up teaching at a Catholic school for less than you pay me."

"I don't pay you anything . . ."

"My point exactly."

". . . because you never send me a bill."

"I'm going to make an exception in this case. A hundred times my normal rate to make up for all the other work I've done for the great Jessica Fletcher."

"What is your normal rate?"

"I don't have one. Hey, is Mort there?"

I looked across the front seat of his SUV. "How'd you know?"

"I'm a detective. It's my business to know."

"You heard the car running, right?"

"I prefer to call it using my powers of deductive reasoning."

Mort rolled his eyes.

"Getting back to Lisa Joy Reavis . . ."

"Getting back to Lisa Joy Reavis," Harry McGraw picked up, "she took this job at Robert E. Lee Elementary in Tuscaloosa, where she remained for five years. By all accounts from the people I was able to track down, she was one of the most popular teachers in the building."

"Why do I think this story doesn't have a happy ending?"

"Because it doesn't. Lisa Joy Reavis died in a car accident the summer after her fifth year at Robert E. Lee Elementary. And wait for it. . . ."

"Don't tell me she . . ."

"That's right, my dear Jessica. Lisa Joy Reavis just might have been murdered, too."

Mort looked as stunned as I was.

"Is this based on factual evidence or that overactive imagination of yours?" I asked Harry.

"I don't have an overactive imagination. In fact, I don't have any imagination. It's why I never read your books."

"Thanks, Harry."

"You're welcome. Anyway, we're going back a bunch of years now, fourteen to be exact. There was one detail the detective on the case could never quite figure out. He just retired as chief of the Tuscaloosa Police Department, and I managed to track him down."

"Have I told you lately how good you are at this?"

"Not enough. Ever heard of Highway Four-thirty-one, Jess?"

"Since I never got my driver's license, I don't pay a lot of attention to highways, Harry."

"You should make an exception in this case, because it's right up your alley. Highway Four-thirty-one, aka the 'Highway to Hell,' is generally regarded as one of the most dangerous roads in the world, never mind just Alabama or even the country as a whole. It runs north to south along the eastern portion of the state, and Lisa Joy Reavis had the misfortune of being on it on a stormy night with even worse visibility than usual."

"Misfortune doesn't normally equal murder."

"A tire blowing out caused the crash. Remember I told you there was one detail that just-retired chief couldn't figure out?"

"You mean, what you shared not more than thirty seconds ago?"

"I've learned to take nothing for granted, my dear lady, just like the former police chief of Tuscaloosa, Alabama—specifically, the presence of butane on rubber samples lifted from the blown tire."

"Butane, as in lighter fluid?"

I pictured Harry nodding as he responded, "The very same. What the chief didn't know, but I was all too happy to inform him of, was what happens when you inject butane into a tire through the valve stem using a syringe."

"Don't tell me, Harry: The butane causes a blowout."

"Boy, I can't put anything over on you, can I? You should consider doing this kind of thing for a living. Say, have you ever considered becoming a writer?"

"Right now, I'm seriously considering hanging up."

"No, you aren't, because I haven't gotten to the best part yet: specifically, that the butane rolls around the inside of the tire until the rubber heats up sufficiently and then *boom*!"

"How hot are we talking, Harry?"

"Well, critical mass for that boom would be around a hundred and seventy-five degrees. At fifty miles per hour, after traveling twenty miles, the average tire temperature would be around a hundred and fifty. But since Ms. Reavis was driving an SUV with tires known to heat up faster and hotter, we're talking the perfect crime here."

"Except for that butane the former chief of police, then a detective, detected."

"Only trace amounts, nothing to base an investigation on for someone not used to that particular MO—that's detective speak for 'modus operandi,' or 'method of operation.'"

"I know what it means," I told him. "What I don't know is how you're so familiar with this particular MO."

"I solved another murder under similar circumstances back in the day."

"When was that?"

"My life BJ."

"What's that?"

"'Before Jessica.' In my life there's 'Before Jessica' and 'After Jessica' and nothing else."

"Should I be flattered?"

"You should pay your bills. Anyway, the body was burned beyond recognition. They identified Lisa Joy Reavis from a single fingerprint found on the rearview mirror."

"The mirror survived the fire?"

"I think I'll double my bill today for educational services provided. The back of a mirror, composed of either silver or aluminum, will oxidize in a fire but the glass itself, typically, won't melt unless temperatures exceed three thousand degrees. That's possible for the engine compartment, but not for the interior cabin. Surprised you never came across that in all that research you do for your books."

"Now that I think of it, Harry, I don't think I've ever researched anything to do with cars or driving."

"Your loss, my girl. Anyway, that former chief didn't know any more than you did until I informed him, too. I think I tempted him to see if he could get the case reopened."

Something struck me at that moment, courtesy of the conversation Mort and I had had with Madeline Demerest in Cape Elizabeth. "Lisa Joy's mother has no idea her daughter's dead. As next of kin, why was she never informed?"

"Can't say. Given what you told me about the state of this young woman's estrangement from her family, it could well be she didn't list any next of kin anywhere. So when she was killed, technically there was no one to inform."

"That makes a degree of sense, in a sad way."

"It makes perfect sense. Not to mention the lag in time between her print being lifted off that rearview mirror and run through the system."

"Wait. How was it that Lisa Joy Reavis was in the system?"

"A shoplifting beef while she was a college student in Virginia. She paid a small fine for what she claimed was a misunderstanding. The charges were dropped, but her prints stayed in the system."

I realized Mort and I would now have to deliver this news to Lisa Joy's mother, Maddie Demerest, and we'd have to do it in person.

"You know what this means," I said to Harry.

"No. What does it mean?"

"First, the father is murdered, then the older daughter in this staged car accident, and now the younger daughter."

"You're forgetting the oldest kid, that high school principal's son."

"No, I'm not, but he was killed while serving as a Marine in the Middle East."

"Come on, Jessica—where's your conspiratorial side? I'd say we're looking at a serial killer who targeted a single family. It's your dime, but I think I should do a deeper dive, into cousins, pets, domestic help, maybe even neighbors. With you involved, who knows how deep this might go?"

I cringed at his macabre sense of humor. "Harry, you're the only person I know who's adept at making light of murder."

"Working with you has given me a whole lot of experience in the subject, after all." He hesitated, his voice tightening when he resumed. "You really think all three murders here might be connected?"

"That was your theory, remember? For my part, I know Ginny Genaway, Walter Reavis's younger daughter, was sniffing around Appleton for clues about his death the week before she was murdered. And she had plenty of questions about her older sister."

"So there must be something to all this—that's what you're saying."

"How much would you charge me for you to make a trip to Tuscaloosa?"

"I could be on a plane in two hours," Harry McGraw said, in answer to my question, "if I can expense out a ticket to the Southeastern Conference Championship on Saturday, Alabama home against Georgia."

"I don't want to waste your time yet."

"But the game's the day after tomorrow, Jessica. Come on, give a guy a break."

"Roll tide, Harry!" I said, quoting the Alabama football team's favorite cheer.

"Not unless I'm in the stands," he groused.

"What are you smiling about?" I asked Mort, after I slid the phone back into my bag.

"The fact that this fourteen-year-old murder by butane is in someone else's jurisdiction, Mrs. F."

"Why did Ginny Genaway have copies of the *Cabot Cove Gazette* lying around her apartment, Mort?"

"You pull that question out of midair?"

"Mrs. F. did. And why did Ginny come to Appleton to poke around in her father's murder and her sister's potential part in it?"

"How am I supposed to know?"

"You are a trained investigator with twenty-five years on the NYPD."

"You'd think that would've prepared me for anything, wouldn't you?" Mort said, only half joking.

Mort dropped me at Mara's, where Seth Hazlitt was at his usual table inside, picking at salad for his afternoon snack.

"Finish your pie already, Seth?" I greeted him as I sat down, thirty minutes late at three thirty.

"Nope, skipping it for today."

"Really?"

"Skipping it for a while, truth be told, *ayuh*."

"What on earth for?"

"I stepped on the scale at the office this morning. Thought it was broken when I kept sliding the weight balance to the right. Turned out, it was: ten pounds in the wrong direction if you know what I mean."

"Ouch."

"My diet changed immediately to foods certain to be more in my favor," he said, pronouncing that last word "fava" in his typical Maine speak.

"When are you going to teach me to talk like a local, Seth?"

"When you're reborn as one, Jess. There are some things that come by birth that can't be taught. It just wouldn't sound familiar," he explained, pronouncing the last word in this sentence "familia."

"Maybe you should consider pitching a Babel for Maine speak—you know, like a foreign language."

"Speaking of which"—he frowned—"the way the rest of you talk sounds like a foreign language to those of us who know what words are supposed to sound like."

I realized something in that moment.

"Uh-oh," I heard Seth utter.

"What?"

"You've got that look, Jess."

"You say that to me a lot."

"Because you get that look *a lot*. The one that says, 'I just figured out who the murderer is.'"

I shook my head. "It's probably nothing this time, almost surely nothing."

Seth wasn't buying it. "Since when?"

"No, the likelihood that both of Walter Reavis's daughters were murdered has me playing pin the tail on the killer. I'm seeing shadows even in the dark."

"That supposed to be a metaphor? Because if it is, I'd seriously recommend you consider another line of work. Maybe take Principal Sweeney up on that offer to teach at the high school." He stopped and regarded me more closely. "There's that look again, Jessica."

"You picking me up tomorrow morning as scheduled?" I asked him, changing the subject.

"Bright and early. Ginny Genaway's psychiatrist, the good Dr. Sam Sackler, is expecting us. He's freed up an hour at eleven o'clock. Means there'll be time for you to buy me lunch at Frank Pepe's Pizzeria at the Chestnut Hill Mall afterward."

"What happened to your diet, Seth?"

He shook his head slowly to exaggerate the gesture. "Guess your book sales have hit a bad patch if you want to get out of paying that much."

Chapter Seventeen

I didn't know exactly what I expected to get out of Ginny Genaway's psychiatrist. Certainly, I wanted to get a notion of Ginny's general mental state recently, and hoped for a clue as to what exactly she was after in Cabot Cove that had spurred her to impersonate a high school student for our interview. Maybe Dr. Sackler would have some tidbit to provide about her older sister, Lisa Joy, now a potential murder victim as well.

My desire to see Dr. Sackler, though, was rooted in a single assumption: Since Ginny had clearly been acquainted with her killer, it was reasonable to believe that he or she had been mentioned somewhere in her sessions with the psychiatrist.

Dr. Sackler's office was located on the first floor of a tony brick Brookline brownstone on the corner of Beacon Street and St. Paul Street, the mailbox outside indicating his residence was on the second floor. That made me long for the renovations on my beloved home at 698 Candlewood Lane to be completed at last. I often did red-line edits of my manuscripts at the kitchen table, but I wrote in an upstairs study I'd lovingly furnished over the nearly twenty-five years I'd lived there. Originally, I was heartsick over losing so many of my cherished keepsakes to smoke and fire damage. But over the months, I'd come to embrace the challenge of starting from near scratch in making the study my retreat again. Many of those keepsakes—the ones I'd insisted on salvaging at great expense through a restoration company called TRDN, which specialized in such things—brought with them my sharpest memories of Frank, which grew even sharper when I was pounding away at my Apple keyboard.

I miss the nostalgic clack of the typewriter keys on my old Royal, though not the bother of having to retype entire manuscripts. Then there was the terror that came with completing a manuscript that was truly my only copy and taking it to be photocopied at the local storefront copy store because of the possibility that the building would burn down, destroying my just-completed book forever. That copy store had long since closed, replaced on Main Street first by a fruit shop and currently by a trendy women's clothier that had also bought the old drugstore next door. I used to have all the prescriptions that Seth Hazlitt wrote for me filled there, and I often whiled away at the soda fountain the minutes it took the pharmacist to finish the order, the soda fountain now living only in my memories as well.

I know it sounds crazy, but whatever was left of Frank's presence and aura hadn't seemed to accompany me to Hill House. Writing at the antique desk in the living room section of my suite felt like work, as if my muse wasn't there to make the pages and time speed by. More than anything, I wanted to return to 698

Candlewood Lane to get back to whatever remained of Frank. And having rekindled memories of that night Frank had taken Grady and me to meet Realtor Eve Simpson, and then of how he somehow managed to put the funds together to buy the house, left me more reflective and nostalgic than ever for the world stripped from me by smoke and flames.

I rang the bell to Dr. Sam Sackler's door. It rattled open, and a sprightly woman maybe half my age stood before me.

"You must be Jessica Fletcher. I've been expecting you."

I quickly got over my momentary surprise that Dr. Sackler was a woman.

"Thank you for seeing us, Dr. Sackler," I said, shooting Seth a glance.

I could tell by the way he looked at me that he hadn't been aware it was "Samantha" Sackler either.

"And you must be Dr. Hazlitt." She smiled, extending her hand. "It's always nice to meet a colleague."

"I'm hardly much when it comes to matters of the mind, ma'am."

"Don't sell yourself short. You've probably helped as many patients out of mental scrapes as you've treated scraped knees."

"Well, now that you put it that way . . ."

"Seth," I said, "once you're done patting yourself on the back, let's get started so we don't take up any more of Dr. Sackler's valuable time than necessary."

"I envy you your small-town practice, Doctor," she continued gushing to Seth in genuine fashion, "the last bastion of old-school medicine before we ended up where we are now."

"Doctor," Seth returned, "my motto is, if it was good enough when I first hung up my shingle, it's good enough now."

They shared a smile while I rolled my eyes.

"Should we talk in your office?" Seth asked Dr. Sackler.

"I'd rather we talk here in the parlor that doubles as my waiting room. There's something, well, that feels unseemly about having this kind of conversation in the same room where I see patients."

"And where you saw Ginny Genaway regularly," I said. "How long had you been treating her?"

"I checked her file this morning. I started treating her after she married Vic Genaway just over two years ago. She said it was his idea."

Seth and I sat down on the couch. Dr. Sackler took a chair and maneuvered it so it was centered between us. She crossed one leg and then tried the other side, searching for a comfort that plainly eluded her.

"I've been practicing psychiatry for ten years, Mrs. Fletcher, and this is the first time I've lost a patient to violence this way."

"By which you mean murder."

She nodded. "How do you live with it every day?"

"I don't. I only write about it."

"Isn't that the same thing?"

I shook my head. "When I'm writing about murder, I can turn if off when I turn off my computer. Not so when I'm investigating one in real life, which fortunately doesn't happen too often."

"Could've fooled me," Seth said under his breath before feigning a cough.

I shot him a disapproving glance. "We're most interested in your final sessions with Ginny, Dr. Sackler, the ones that would've occurred closest to her untimely demise."

"I'd love to help you, but Ginny canceled her last five appointments and then stopped scheduling new ones."

"Going back how long?"

"Right around six months. I was seeing her twice a week, you see. The last time I saw or spoke to her was her final appointment. When she first started seeing me, she was living with her husband around here. We were making great progress leading up to the move, and it's difficult to replicate the same rapport with another psychiatrist. Even after she moved to New Hampshire in the wake of the divorce, she considered it worth the drive."

Seth patted me on the knee and leaned forward. "Is it unusual for patients to end their treatment so abruptly, Doctor?"

"It is unusual but it still happens more than I would like."

"Dr. Sackler," I said, "we're trying to understand Ginny Genaway's mental state in the days leading up to her murder. Since you hadn't seen her for a while, we'll have to speak more generally. In your sessions with her, based on what you're comfortable sharing, did she ever indicate that she felt threatened in any way?"

"All my patients feel threatened in some way, Mrs. Fletcher. That's why they seek treatment."

"I was talking more in a physical way, if she feared for her life or anything like that."

Sackler thought for a few moments. "Ginny's issues were primarily related to her relationships with two men: her father, Walter Reavis, and husband, Vic Genaway. Sometimes she would even confuse the two, as if she found them emotionally interchangeable."

"'Emotionally interchangeable,'" I repeated. "That's an interesting term."

"You won't find it in any textbook, but I wrote a paper on it that received several awards. The basic tenet is the old trope of a young man looking to marry his mother or a young woman looking to marry her father."

"Not literally, of course, Doctor," Seth noted, needing to inject his two cents into the conversation.

"Of course not, but Ginny's case was rather unique," Samantha Sackler said, addressing him now more than me. "She enjoyed a very close relationship with her father as a little girl before his murder. Losing him left a void that led to a host of psychological problems through the rest of her childhood, extending well into young adulthood, including her college years and after. Did you know she was working as a server at a bar owned by her future husband?"

"Mr. Genaway mentioned that when we spoke to him, yes."

Sackler nodded. "You might say she developed an old-fashioned schoolgirl crush on him."

"Because he finally filled the void left by her father's murder all those years before," I surmised.

Sackler nodded. "The feeling was mutual, and they started dating, with Vic truly wining and dining her, making her feel safe in a way that nobody had been able to since her father's death. I'm not sure she ever truly loved him in the traditional sense, but she came to depend upon him, and oftentimes, that makes for an even more powerful attraction. I'm always clinically suspicious of relationships between superiors and subordinates because it suggests a level of dependence that was classic in this case, on Ginny's part."

"And then came the fight in the country club, when she took a golf club to her husband's head," I said.

Sackler looked toward Seth again. "Care to hazard a forensic diagnosis of what all that means, Doctor?"

"I'd say, Doctor," Seth replied, beaming, "that she replaced the dependence she had transferred from her father to her husband to someone else."

Sackler nodded. "Exactly! The psychological trauma left by her father's murder had rendered Ginny incapable of transferring emotion to more than one party at a time. It was the primary psychosis I was treating her for."

"In your work with Ginny," I started in again, "did she ever discuss other incidents where she resorted to violence?"

Sackler looked impressed by my question. "It was a tendency she fought continually. If you asked her mother, you'd find her to have been a little girl prone to temper tantrums and other means of lashing out in the wake of her father's death. That part of her never really grew up. In fact . . ."

"Yes, Doctor?" I prodded her.

"We're venturing a bit into the weeds here, and I'm hesitant to get into a topic we'd only begun to broach before Ginny ended her treatment."

"Which was . . ."

"Ginny was convinced she'd murdered her father."

"In the sense that she was responsible for his death," Dr. Sackler quickly elaborated.

"What would account for that?" Seth asked her.

"Guilt. It's common with children who've lost a parent, a means of displacing their grief, however misconceived. Picture the mind as a pane of glass. When it breaks, it's not a simple glue job so much as a patch followed by a new window pane to replace the broken one. In Ginny's case, the patch kept falling off, allowing the wind to blow through. So she patched the hole with guilt. When she finally sought me out, it was to replace that entire broken pane."

"In other words," I said, "she remained impetuous and impulsive long into adulthood."

"I often tell people, Mrs. Fletcher, that maintaining the heart of a child is a good thing, but maintaining the mind of a child is a recipe for psychological trauma."

"Did she ever mention her mother?" I asked Sackler, thinking of the slovenly woman I'd met at the Portland Head Lighthouse in Cape Elizabeth.

Dr. Sackler shook her head. "Barely at all. They had no relationship. The divorce left Ginny entirely in her father's camp, and things didn't improve one iota after his murder."

"What about her sister?" Seth chimed in. "The one who dropped off the family map entirely after high school? Did your patient ever speak about her?" he asked, not bothering to mention that Ginny had voiced to Wilma Tisdale the opinion that Lisa Joy had murdered their father, literally instead of just figuratively.

"Originally, there was a total disassociation in that regard. Out of sight, out of mind, would be the best way to put it—literally, in this case. But then something changed, and I mean out of nowhere."

"How so?"

"Ginny seemed to develop an obsession with Lisa Joy, constructing what appeared to be an elaborate fantasy that they were going to become close again, like sisters. Displacement again, I thought at first, since Lisa Joy had pretty much left Ginny's life at the same time her father did."

"Makes sense, *ayuh*," Seth acknowledged with a nod. "She couldn't have known about her older sister having perished in that car accident down Alabama way."

Sackler's eyes widened in surprise. "How horrible. When did this happen?"

"Fourteen years ago," I told her.

"And Ginny never knew?"

"I don't know how she could have. When did this obsession with Lisa Joy begin?" I continued.

"I'd have to check my notes to be specific, but just before Ginny broke off her treatment. That would have made it, oh, a week or two short of six months ago."

I tried to reconcile that timeline with what I'd learned in the wake of Ginny's murder. It jibed perfectly with the time she began reading the *Cabot Cove Gazette*, judging by the dates on the back issues Mort and I had found. Then last week she'd shown up in Appleton, asking questions about her sister before coming to Cabot Cove to pry information out of me about her father's murder.

"Is it possible Ginny suspected her older sister, Lisa Joy, of murdering their father?" I blurted out. "In the literal sense, I mean, not the figurative."

"That's an interesting thought, Mrs. Fletcher," Sackler noted. "Have you considered trying your hand at psychoanalysis?"

"I write fiction, Doctor, so you might say I do it for a living, only with people I make up."

"I can tell you one thing: Ginny didn't believe the police ever caught her father's real killer. So your theory is a sound one, but not appropriate in this case. No, Ginny concocted an entire fantasy scenario in which she might have a relationship with her sister—displacement again, since this coincided with the general time frame of her divorce from her husband, Vic, and his subsequent incarceration. As a matter of fact, I'd say those factors were the prime contributors to the new delusion she'd begun to foster. It represented a drastic setback in our therapy, and I expressed as much to her. I think that's why she stopped showing up for appointments and broke off her treatment. I think she may have done that because we'd begun to make real progress."

"Shouldn't that have been a positive thing?" I asked.

"Not in Ginny's case, Mrs. Fletcher. The condition she suffered from is the equivalent of digging a hole and filling it in. The vast majority of people fill in the holes that crop up in their lives when they first appear, while they're still small. But someone like Ginny waits for the hole to become a crater before grabbing a shovel. She doesn't really want to fill it in, because its existence defines her purpose in life. So her abandoning treatment at the time she did was the equivalent of preferring that the hole remain unfilled."

I leaned forward so Seth was positioned a bit behind me. "I'd like to get back to her obsession with her older sister, Lisa Joy, if we could. Are you certain it was a delusion?"

"I'm certain Ginny broke off treatment when I effectively suggested it was. Perhaps a mistake on my part, but I thought we were at a precarious point of her therapy, given the setback I was witnessing right before my eyes. I only wish that she'd known her sister was dead, since it would have prevented the delusion from forming."

I nodded, my thoughts falling together in my mind to assemble a fresh picture or to add to the one I'd already formed. I now had a clear idea of the timeline. How something had triggered Ginny's delusion about her late sister, Lisa Joy, around the very same time she began reading the *Cabot Cove Gazette*. Then just last week she showed up in Appleton to revisit the past ahead of interviewing me twelve hours before she was murdered. Those were the pieces I'd now managed to fit together, but the apparently completed puzzle revealed no discernible picture.

Which meant there were still pieces missing.

"In your final sessions with Ginny, Doctor," I started, "did she express any concerns that she was in danger or under some threat?"

"Not at all, Mrs. Fletcher. In fact, I don't think I'd ever seen her happier. With the split from her husband and all, it was as if she was embarking on a new beginning."

"Which came to an abrupt end," I couldn't help myself from saying.

"I'll have a salad, and you can have the large clam pizza," Seth said, regarding the Frank Pepe's Pizzeria menu after we'd been seated in the restaurant located inside the Chestnut Hill Mall ten minutes from Dr. Sackler's office.

"I can't eat a large pizza."

"Then I guess I'll have to help you, won't I? Be a shame to see good food go to waste. After we order, you can tell me the rest of the story."

"What story?"

"How you and Amos Tupper solved the murder of Walter Reavis over in Appleton."

Chapter Eighteen

Twenty-five years ago . . .

I glanced at Amos Tupper and then back at the boy. "I can find the real killer."

"Mighty big pickle you got yourself into there, Mrs. Fletcher," Amos Tupper told me after Patrolman Tom Jennings had come to take Tyler Benjamin back to his cell.

"I wouldn't have said it if I didn't mean it, Detective. And we're going to do it together."

Tupper frowned. "This coming from a substitute teacher."

"Well, now I guess I'm a substitute detective, too."

He seemed to take offense at that. "And who exactly would you be substituting for, Mrs. Fletcher?"

"I didn't mean it that way."

"It certainly sounded like you meant it that way."

I looked at him more closely. "Were you the one who arrested Tyler Benjamin?"

"After Jim Dirkson reported seeing him enter the building, given the boy's history with Principal Reavis, I had no choice."

"But Tyler's history is more with Vice Principal Dirkson, Detective. And according to the boy, Dirkson was inside the office, not outside the building."

"I'll admit that inconsistency in their stories did cross my mind."

"One of them is lying. I think we can assume that much. And what about the fact that Tyler also claimed he saw the school secretary, Alma Potts, driving out of the parking lot before he entered the building?"

"What about it?"

"Alma Potts was home sick that day. It explains the blinds."

"The blinds?"

I nodded. "Mr. Reavis liked having the sun at his back, which meant it was in the eyes of anyone he was meeting with, as they'd be seated in front of his desk. I experienced that firsthand at our meeting sixth period the day of the murder because Alma wasn't around to close them as she did every afternoon, even when it was cloudy. Force of habit, I guess."

Amos Tupper shook his head, trying to make sense of all the case's new wrinkles I'd brought up, motivated by my desire to help Tyler Benjamin, who I was convinced was not a murderer.

"Know what I think?" he asked as if reading my mind. "That this boy might have you fooled, Mrs. Fletcher. He could be one of those psycho sociopaths."

I didn't bother correcting his terminology.

"He's a student of yours, so the last thing you can picture is him taking a trophy to the skull of his principal."

"Except for one thing."

"What's that?"

"Did you notice Tyler wears his watch on his right wrist?"

"He wasn't wearing a watch, Mrs. Fletcher."

"But you could see the pale impression where he normally does. One of those sport watches, judging by the size of the face."

"You noticed that?" Tupper asked, scratching his head.

"You didn't? I thought it was obvious, along with something else."

The detective looked like he'd be happier if I didn't continue, but I did anyway.

"The gash that ran down Walter Reavis's brow from where the trophy first impacted with his skull was angled to the left. That angle suggests he was struck by a right-handed person, while this boy is clearly *left*-handed."

Tupper thought for a moment. "Maybe he's ambiguous."

"Ambiguous?"

"You know, able to use either hand. He is quite an athlete, after all."

"You mean 'ambidextrous.'"

He nodded. "Sure, that's what I said."

"Here's what I say, Detective: We need to have a little talk with both Alma Potts and Jim Dirkson so we can determine who's lying here and who's telling the truth."

Detective Tupper looked at me differently from the way he had through the course of the long week, almost like I was suddenly a stranger. "Maybe I should talk to these folks on my own."

"Oh."

"I don't mean anything by it, Mrs. Fletcher. It's just that at this stage of the case, maybe it's best to leave things to a trained professional."

"Well, that certainly does make sense."

"You don't mind?"

"Not at all. I was glad to be of service while I could, Detective."

"Given all we've been through, why don't you call me Amos?"

"Only if you call me Jessica . . . Amos."

He shook his head. "Sorry, ma'am. That wouldn't be professional since you're a civilian and all." He eyed me more closely. "You really don't think Tyler Benjamin is the killer?"

"No, Amos, I don't."

He frowned, regret spreading across his features. "Well, if you're right, Mrs. Fletcher, that means I put a teenage boy in jail for nothing. Doesn't say a lot for my detective skills, does it? If only life came with a redial button, right?"

"Well, I can't deny that." I hesitated, just long enough. "Of course . . ."

"What is it, Mrs. Fletcher?"

"Oh, it's probably nothing."

"*What?*"

"There's something we need to check out at the high school, Amos. First thing Monday morning."

Monday morning, the door to Walter Reavis's private office inside the main office was locked, with yellow crime scene tape still strung across the jamb.

"Now what are we supposed to do?" Amos Tupper said, shaking his head.

"Amos, you're the lead detective on the case. You have every right to enter the office where the victim was murdered."

"So I do." He beamed, as if a lightbulb had gone off. "Except the door's locked, and I don't have a key."

"Allow me, Detective."

I left him there and headed back to the front of the office, where Alma Potts manned the bridge from behind the school's reception counter at her perpetually cluttered desk.

"Do you have the key to Walter's office handy, Alma?" I asked her.

She started fishing through her top desk drawer, only to stop. "Terrible about Tyler Benjamin being arrested for the murder," she said, dabbing her eyes with a tissue, due more likely to the cold she was still fighting than to lingering sadness.

"Beyond terrible," I said.

"Do you believe he did it, Mrs. Fletcher?"

"What do I know, Alma?"

"Well, everyone's talking about how you're working with that Detective Topper."

"Tupper," I corrected her. "And I'm acting as a sounding board more than anything. We just came from seeing Tyler, actually."

"How's the boy doing?"

"How do you think?"

"I'm sorry," Alma Potts said. "It was a stupid question."

"No, it's me that's sorry, Alma, for being short with you. I know you worked for Walter ever since the two of you were at the middle school."

"He hired me. Can I tell you something, between us?" she asked, lowering her voice to a near whisper as she cast a glance beyond me to see if anyone else was there.

"Of course."

"I'm not looking forward to working for Jim Dirkson, Mrs. Fletcher. He may make a decent principal, but he's no Walter Reavis."

"Well, there's no guarantee he'll be appointed on a permanent basis, as opposed to interim."

Alma forced a smile. "Well, a girl can sure hope."

I lowered my voice to match hers. "Can I confide something in you, too, Alma?"

She perked up. "Of course, Mrs. Fletcher."

"Between you and me, Mr. Dirkson's name came up in the conversation Detective Tupper and I had with the Benjamin boy."

"Really? How?"

"Dirkson's statement was vital to the police arresting Tyler. Dirkson claims he spotted Tyler lurking about the parking lot when he was leaving the building. But Tyler claims Dirkson was in the office when the boy came to plead his case to Walter."

Alma's eyes widened, then practically bulged. "You don't think . . ."

"Of course not. I think Tyler's clearly lying and for good reason," I said, hoping Alma Potts bought into my lie.

"What reason is that, Mrs. Fletcher?"

"He claims he saw you driving out of the parking lot while he was waiting to enter the building. But you were out sick the day of the murder."

"Yes, with this nasty cold I can't shake. It's all over the building, you know."

"Indeed, I do. I've been downing vitamin C and washing my hands twenty times a day."

"That didn't work for me." Alma frowned.

"Any idea how Tyler could have been mistaken?"

"I drive a white sedan, and there're probably ten of those out in the parking lot right now, for starters. Not much, if anything, to distinguish them. And it would've been dark, wouldn't it, around the time of the murder? So I doubt very much he got a very good look."

"But I should inform Detective Tupper it definitely wasn't you," I said, casting myself as a third-party conduit to the police to increase my credibility.

"Please, if you don't mind."

"Not at all, Alma. He'll want to know if there was anyone at home with you who can corroborate your story."

Her expression scrunched up as she considered this. "Of course, I'm not sure of the exact time you're referring to. One of the twins might've been home," Alma said, referring to her teenage boy and girl, who attended another high school since the family didn't live in Appleton. "But I can't be sure off the top of my head."

"Of course not. Why would you be?"

"I wish I could be more specific, Mrs. Fletcher."

I started to back away from her desk. "I think what you mentioned about the number of white cars and the fact that it was dark more than explains what Tyler thinks he saw. But you've given me something else to follow up on: these white cars, specifically. If the boy did see a white car leaving the parking lot before he entered the building, perhaps we could put a list together of who owns the rest of them—you know, the other nine or so to go with yours."

"I might already have that somewhere on file. We update the list at the beginning of every school year for security reasons, don't we?"

"Since I don't drive, I guess I wouldn't know."

I smiled back at her and started to walk off.

"Mrs. Fletcher?" Alma called to me.

I stopped and turned back around. "Yes?"

She was holding a key dangling from a wooden key chain that looked like a hall pass. "You forgot the key to Mr. Reavis's office."

Amos Tupper stripped the crime scene tape down and inserted into the lock the key Alma Potts had provided.

"Did I tell you this was my first murder investigation?" he asked me before turning the key in the lock.

"You did, yes. A few days back."

He swallowed hard. "You believe in ghosts, Mrs. Fletcher?"

"I've never really given it much thought, Amos."

"Because a few times when I looked up or turned around inside this office, I could swear I glimpsed Mr. Reavis sitting behind his desk, looking at me and wondering what I was doing here."

"Next time, maybe he'll remain there long enough to tell us who killed him."

The office was shadowy, somber, drenched in semidarkness. Amos flipped on the lights, and immediately the room was bathed in overly bright light shining down from old-fashioned fluorescents that had somehow survived from one building renovation to the next. I looked down at the carpet and imagined Walter's body still lying in the place where I had identified it earlier in the week, and I got a chill up my spine thinking of what Amos Tupper had said about catching glimpses of the principal's ghost.

"Now, tell me about this hunch of yours, Mrs. Fletcher," he said.

"This office is currently in the exact condition it was in when Walter Reavis's body was discovered. Is that right?"

"Yes, definitely."

"Nobody moved a thing or altered it in any way?"

"Most certainly not. The state police—those officers who don't think much of me—secured it as soon as our own patrolman confirmed Mr. Reavis was dead."

"And he remembered not to touch anything?"

"According to his report in capital letters."

"What about this phone, Amos?" I said, moving around to the back of Walter Reavis's desk, careful not to move the chair lest I disturb the ghost Amos claimed to have spotted.

"The phone?"

"None of your officers or the state policemen would have placed a call from it, correct?"

"We're professionals, Mrs. Fletcher," he said as if offended. "Why is the phone so important, anyway?"

"Because of that heated conversation I overheard when I was standing at the door. It's possible, fifty-fifty, that Mr. Reavis placed that call."

"Okay," he said, joining me behind the desk.

"In which case," I continued, pointing toward a button marked REDIAL, "the last number dialed might well have been to the person he was arguing with."

"Only one way to find out who that might be, I suppose."

We looked at each other as if to determine how to proceed.

"Would you like to do the honors, ma'am?"

I reached down and pressed the SPEAKER key, followed by

REDIAL. Amos Tupper and I listened to the numbers being dialed out from the phone's memory, followed by a line ringing. It was answered after the fourth ring, and we were greeted briefly with dead air before an answering machine came on.

"Hi, you've reached the Dirkson residence. Please leave your name, number, and—"

Amos Tupper reached down and hit the SPEAKER button to end the call. "Looks like we need to have a talk with Appleton High's acting principal, Mrs. Fletcher."

Chapter Nineteen

The present

Our food arrived at our booth in Frank Pepe's in the Chestnut Hill Mall, and I took that as my cue to stop.

"Don't tell me you're going to stop there," Seth pleaded. "I don't want our pizza to get cold."

His eyes widened as he regarded it, looking like a kid on Christmas morning. "What'd you think of the psychiatrist?" he asked me as he reached for the nearest piece, only to pull his fingers back when it proved to be still too hot.

"She confirmed what's become clearer and clearer through the week, Seth: Ginny Genaway was a deeply unstable young woman."

"You think?"

"You're the doctor. What do you think?"

"I try to hold off making judgments on those I've never examined or, at least, been acquainted with. But I would tend to agree with your assessment."

"It's unlike you to couch your words like that, Seth."

"I'm trying to sound like a psychiatrist."

"You mean, like Sam Sackler."

"I looked into her a bit before we made the drive, Jess. She's considered one of the best in Boston."

"That makes her a fine doctor to emulate."

The pizza had cooled enough for Seth to peel off a slice angled to his side of the table, careful to keep it from shedding its considerable toppings.

"I'm thinking about making an appointment to see her myself," Seth said, going to work on his slice with a knife and fork. "Maybe she can help me stop getting involved in your investigations. I'm going to ask for the Jessica Fletcher discount, which she must have, given the number of people you've driven crazy over the years, *ayuh*. You drove poor Amos Tupper all the way to Kentucky."

"Did I mention that I spoke with him the other day?"

"No. How is the old coot?"

"He's just a few years older than you, Seth."

"Right, but he's a coot while I'm a curmudgeon, according to the good folks of Cabot Cove."

I finally lifted a slice of plain cheese from my half of the pizza. "Anyway, he sounds fine. Maybe a little bored out there, but fine."

"Think he misses Cabot Cove?"

"I know he misses being sheriff."

Seth lifted a second slice from the tray. "I'm still having trouble picturing him as a detective."

"So did the town of Appleton twenty-five years ago, but he proved them all wrong."

Seth blew on his slice of pizza to cool it down a bit more. "Let me ask you a question, Jess: Would he have ultimately solved the case without you?"

"I guess we'll never know, will we?" I said noncommittally.

"Then let me ask you another question: Where to next?"

"Manchester, Doctor," I said, imitating the way both he and Sackler had exaggerated the syllables. "To give Ginny Genaway's apartment another look."

The building manager was on-site again and he didn't even question my desire to take another look inside Ginny's apartment downtown at 875 Elm Street when we got there just before four o'clock, perhaps confusing me with a real police officer, given that I'd accompanied one there during my first visit.

"Rent's paid up for the next six months," he explained, "so I'm not in any rush to clean the place out. Take your time," he added, opening the door for Seth and me while giving no indication he intended to join us inside.

"So, what are we looking for?" Seth asked me after I'd closed the door behind us.

"I really have no idea. Something I didn't see when I was here with Mort."

"If you didn't see it the first time, how do you know what you're looking for now?"

"I'll know when I find it," I proclaimed halfheartedly.

But Seth was right. When you don't know what you're looking for, it's very hard to find it. I thought back to our conversation with Dr. Sackler, and focused on the timeline she'd more or less confirmed. Something had changed drastically in Ginny Genaway's life around six months ago, when she'd started breaking appointments with Sackler and developed a fascination with the *Cabot Cove Gazette* and, likely, Cabot Cove itself. Everything pointed to the likelihood that this had something to do with her late sister, her late father, or both. Everything I'd been able to uncover about her, starting with that interview she'd conducted with me under a false guise, suggested she was on the trail of something that Dr. Sackler might have revealed to us with a line she'd spoken almost as an afterthought.

I can tell you one thing: Ginny didn't believe the police ever caught her father's real killer.

If Ginny's suspicions were correct, that would mean my first murder investigation had sent the wrong person to jail, that I'd convinced myself, Amos Tupper, and an entire town that an innocent person was the guilty party. And that meant I now had another reason to get to the bottom of what Ginny had been after, which had likely led to her death.

What if Walter Reavis's killer had been released from prison, though? After twenty-five years, given the charge was murder in the second degree, it was more than possible the killer had gotten out, perhaps to pick up killing again. Since I was the one who'd caught the killer, you'd think I would have kept better tabs on things, but the truth was I'd resolved to do my best to put the entire experience behind me and never revisit it.

Having again found nothing of value to the case in any drawers or storage boxes, I had begun to wonder whether our search was truly futile when I glimpsed Seth tossing a piece of gum in the kitchen trash.

"Don't do that!" I yelled at him.

"What?"

"Throw your gum away!"

He looked at me dumbfounded. "What, you want me to swallow it?"

"No, I meant don't toss it in the trash."

"Where am I supposed to toss it?"

Instead of bickering with Seth further, I moved to the kitchen trash container, located under the sink, but found only his piece of gum inside, clinging to the liner about halfway down.

"You know, Jess, if book sales are down, I could spot you a few bucks so you don't have to go picking through other people's trash."

He followed me from the kitchen into the second bedroom, which Ginny Genaway had converted into a makeshift office. In there a smaller wastebasket was practically overflowing. I was able to discard the magazines quickly, then began straightening out a whole bunch of crumpled pages to view their contents.

If you really want to know somebody, check out their trash. . . . I forgot where I'd heard or read that pearl of wisdom, but it certainly was coming into play.

"Anything I can do to help?" Seth asked.

"I wish there were, Seth," I told him, moving to another crumpled sheet of paper. "But I can't tell you what to look for if I don't know myself."

"What about that?" he said, pointing to the wooden floor where a jagged piece of paper had been ripped but not crumpled.

My efforts might have toppled it from the wastebasket. But it could have been there all along. I could picture Ginny tearing a piece of paper in two, three, or four and then discarding the fragments, only to have them flutter to the floor unnoticed.

"What is it?" Seth asked, moving in over my shoulder.

"Here, take a look," I said, holding the jagged piece of paper up for him to see.

We regarded the large capitalized letters together:

AMED PRIN

Based on the nature of the tears, it was clear that something had been ripped off from the beginning and another fragment had been torn from the end.

"Make any sense to you, Seth?" I wondered since it didn't to me.

"Not a thing. Well, except for one thing."

"What's that?"

His eyes widened, his smile playing with me. "You mean this old coot may finally have something on the brilliant Jessica Fletcher?"

"I thought it was 'old curmudgeon,' and why don't you tell me what you see?"

"Look closer, Jess."

"I already did."

"Try again."

I obliged him, and was struck instantly by what I'd missed before. "It must be the Web version of the paper," I realized. "I only read the print edition."

"Either way," Seth said, "it's the *Cabot Cove Gazette* for sure. I'd recognize that font anywhere."

We fished through the trash, and our sorting process became more deliberate. Soon we found a similarly torn and also crumpled smaller fragment of what looked to be another part of the same headline, judging by the type size and face:

F THE Y

"No sense I can see here," Seth noted.

"Looks like we're missing one word that ends in *F* and another that begins with *Y*."

"As I said, no sense there."

I laid the two fragments side by side to see what they added up to:

AMED PRIN F THE Y

"Ring any bells, Seth?"

"You're the Scrabble champion."

"But you've been watching *Wheel of Fortune* for as long as I've known you."

"What, you want me to buy a vowel or something?"

I stared at the two fragments together until my vision began to blur and the letters were implanted in my brain to the point where I'd likely see them in my sleep.

AMED PRIN F THE Y

The newspaper's editor and owner, Evelyn Phillips, wasn't in when we called the office, so I left a message with my cell phone number for her to call me back immediately. If I'd been in town, it would've been a simple matter of heading over to the paper's offices on Main Street to check the *Gazette*'s files myself so as not to waste any more time. I was able to log on to the website on my phone right there in Ginny Genaway's apartment. But a search for AMED PRIN F THE Y yielded nothing the first time I searched and then something like five thousand hits when I tried various letters in front of AMED.

Meaning we were still at square one here.

That left me with no choice but to wait for Evelyn Phillips to call back, which meant I'd have to accommodate her questions about the state of the investigation into Ginny Genaway's murder.

"Well, at least we found *something* that made it worth the trip," Seth said, climbing into his old Volvo.

I was holding the fragments in my lap, unable to lift my gaze from them as if the rest of the newspaper headline was about to magically appear.

"I'll bet you a piece of pie at Mara's that the date on that issue goes back six months," Seth said, "just before Ginny Genaway started picking up hard copies of the *Gazette*."

"I thought you were on a diet."

"I am, but I'll make an exception if you're buying, *ayuh*."

"How about a side bet about when Evelyn Phillips will get back to us?"

"Ready to get on home, then?" Seth asked me, firing up the Volvo's engine.

After all these years, it still purred like a kitten. "You mind if we make another stop on the way?" I asked him.

"Where?"

"Cape Elizabeth. We need to tell Maddie Demerest that her older daughter is dead, Seth."

The museum was closed for the day by the time we got to Cape Elizabeth under cover of darkness that found the now-automated lighthouse's massive revolving light brightening the sky far over the waters of the Atlantic, steering ships away from the rocky shoreline as it had done for centuries. Rapping on the main door brought no result, so we tried around the side of the building where the entrance to the museum and residence portion of the facility lay. The door there wasn't just unlocked; it was open, having fallen prey to the stiff wind blowing off the ocean.

"Maybe we should call the police, Jess."

I was already through the door at that point, racing up the stairs to the apartment Maddie Demerest kept as a fringe benefit of conducting lighthouse tours and running the museum. I could see the door at the top of those stairs was open, too.

"Maddie?" I called. "It's Jessica Fletcher, Maddie."

Feeling my heart pounding against my rib cage, I raced through the doorway and froze. Because Maddie Demerest lay on the floor.

My first thought, as my heart continued to pound, was that she'd joined both her daughters and husband as a victim of foul play. Then I heard her moan softly just as Seth joined me inside the doorway, his hands sinking to his knees as he fought to get his breath back. When he spotted Maddie on the floor, he sprang into action. He checked her pulse and her breathing, and checked her pupils with a small penlight it had been his habit to carry for as long as I'd known him. She moaned again when he held one eyelid open and then the other.

She was slumped on the floor between the galley kitchen and the living space, where a television was playing softly. She had fallen on a patch of the floor that was still wet from a spill and banged her head, judging by the lump Seth detected.

Just then, Maddie Demerest's eyes fluttered open. "Am I dead?" she asked Seth.

"No."

"Then who are you?"

"This is Dr. Seth Hazlitt, Maddie, a friend of mine," I said, drawing the woman's gaze my way and opting to address her as I would someone I knew far better.

"Oh, Mrs. Belcher."

"It's Fletcher. But please, call me Jessica," I told her, just as I had during my last visit.

I moved to one side of Maddie Demerest while Seth took the other.

"Now, let's get you upright."

"I don't need your help."

But Maddie struggled to get to her feet and relented to let us guide her to the couch set directly before the television.

"Thank you. I'm not used to that, you know, saying 'thank you.' It feels kind of nice to have someone to say it to."

"I wish we were here under better circumstances," I said, sitting down on one side of Maddie, while Seth sat down on the other.

Maddie swallowed hard. "This is about my older daughter, Lisa Joy, isn't it?"

"How did you know?"

"Because I've been waiting for this visit for a long time, Mrs. Fletcher."

"Jessica," I corrected her. "It turns out Lisa Joy was killed in a car accident outside Tuscaloosa fourteen years ago."

Her eyes flickered, the only reaction I could spot. "So long ago . . . I guess I knew, at least suspected, but why wasn't I informed?"

"The car caught fire, Maddie," I told her. "The police had trouble identifying the body. And by the time they did, contacting next of kin must've fallen through the cracks."

Seth eased himself closer to the sofa arm to better regard Maddie. "You need to get that lump on your head checked out for a possible concussion. I can call the rescue squad if you like."

"I'm fine. Just the same headache I've had for as long as I can remember."

The sadness that permeated Maddie Demerest's very being was palpable. She was a woman who'd withdrawn from the world only to have it chase her back down in the wake of her younger daughter's murder and elder daughter's death.

"Can I ask you something about your daughter Ginny?" I asked her.

"As long as you don't expect much of an answer."

"Did you see her sometime between five and six months ago?"

"You asked me that last time you were here, didn't you?"

"Not in so many words."

"The answer's still the same. She wanted nothing to do with me, and I can't really blame her."

I decided to try another tack as Seth looked on, his expression held so tight, it looked as if his jowls were frozen in place. "Would you describe Ginny as being close to her older sister?"

"I would indeed, Mrs. Fletcher. She was devastated when Lisa Joy moved away to college and never came back. You might say she lost her father and her sister at the same time, or pretty close. Then her brother was killed in the Middle East. She was always far closer to Walter than she was to me. I already told you that, didn't I?"

"I believe you did. Were you aware Ginny was seeing a psychiatrist?"

She almost laughed. "Isn't everybody these days?"

"She broke off her treatments around six months ago, around the same time she seemed to develop a new fascination with her older sister."

"Did she know Lisa Joy was dead?"

"I don't know how she could have, Maddie. Ginny also developed a renewed interest in her father's murder."

Her eyes widened a bit. "Come to think of it, she called me around six months ago. Visited, too. I'd forgotten all about it, or maybe I thought I'd dreamed it. That happens sometimes. She had this crazy idea that the wrong person had been jailed for Walter's murder. She had gotten this notion in her head that Lisa Joy had done it."

I tried to recall why Amos Tupper and I had never interviewed Lisa Joy Reavis at the time of her father's murder. I guess we hadn't seen the need with the suspects we already had lined up.

I recalled those fragments of a headline from the *Cabot Cove Gazette* we'd found in Ginny's apartment. "Did Ginny mention what triggered this belief all of a sudden?"

"I don't think so. If she did, I don't remember."

"Do you remember anything else about those calls, maybe visits, from Ginny?"

"She thought I might be in danger."

"From whom?"

Maddie's expression turned quizzical. "You know, Jessica," she said, finally calling me by my first name, "she didn't say."

"Well," Seth said when we were back outside, "that went well."

"Whatever's going on here," I told him, "I think I'll know a lot more after tomorrow."

"What's tomorrow?"

"Wilma Tisdale's retirement party, Seth. And I think there's plenty the guest of honor hasn't told me yet."

Chapter Twenty

Evelyn Phillips had returned my call, but I'd been with Maddie Demerest, so I'd missed it. I tried her back and left another voice mail. She was always terrible about returning her messages, so I made sure to tell her this time that I needed to talk to her about Ginny Genaway's murder. Murder always stoked Evelyn's interest, and she wouldn't be able to resist a potential scoop.

Both Seth and I had been exhausted upon returning to Cabot Cove around eight o'clock, too tired even to eat. I don't even remember climbing into bed at Hill House. I checked my phone the next morning, but there were no messages from Evelyn Phillips, and I was starting to think ahead again to Wilma Tisdale's retirement party that night when Seth called.

"You're not going to believe it, Jessica," he greeted me.

"Why do so many of your calls begin with that line?"

"Because with you, there's always a lot nobody can believe. In this case, it's the fact that the *Cabot Cove Gazette* website is down, so I can't search the back issues for the rest of that headline. I was thinking of trying the library first thing tomorrow and taking a gander at the hard copies back in our general time frame."

"Don't bother, Seth. The library only keeps the hard copies for a month."

"I'm assuming you haven't reached Evelyn Phillips yet."

"You're assuming right."

"And since their offices are closed on the weekend, this may have to wait until Monday."

"We may not have until Monday," I told him. "I think this is all going to come to a head tonight at Wilma Tisdale's retirement party."

"What makes you say that?" Seth asked me.

"The fact that she didn't invite me until Ginny Genaway paid her a visit with a ton of questions about her late sister."

"Lisa Joy Reavis again," he said in a way that left me picturing him shaking his head. "All roads seem to lead back to that family. You know what I'm starting to think?"

"That Maddie Demerest, formerly Reavis, is the killer."

"Mind reader!"

"I had the same thought myself."

"Still entertaining it?"

"I never did, Seth—not seriously, anyway."

"Way to rain on an old man's parade."

"Did you notice anything about the parking lot when we got to the lighthouse earlier today?"

"No."

"Of course you didn't. Because there was nothing there, including cars, meaning Maddie doesn't own one, so how would she have gotten to that scenic overlook outside Cabot Cove?"

"I'm hanging up now, because I have nothing left to say."

"Good night, Seth."

I'd no sooner laid my cell phone down on the table than there was a knock on the door to my suite. I opened it to find Mort Metzger standing there.

"You opened the door without checking the peephole first," he said, taking off his hat as he entered. "What were you thinking?"

"You mean, because there's a murderer loose?"

He rolled his eyes. "Around these parts, there always seems to be a murderer loose. I think I should have retired to someplace quieter, like Afghanistan, Mrs. F."

"Ugggghhhhhh . . ."

"Bothers you, doesn't it?" Mort said with a smirk.

"What do I have to do to get you to stop?"

"Solve this case, because I don't have a single lead left, other than this retirement party you'll be attending."

"And how did you know I didn't check the peephole?"

Mort winked. "I have my ways. I'm a trained investigator, remember?"

"Really? I'll try to keep that in mind. And just so you know, if you do put in for work in Afghanistan, Amos Tupper is ready to claim his old job back."

He frowned. "He couldn't do any worse than I've been doing, with the blank I've drawn following up Ginny Genaway's murder."

"Nothing's panned out on your end?"

He shook his head. "The tire print we lifted from the space next to her BMW at that rest stop—"

"Scenic overlook," I interrupted to correct him.

"—is standard equipment on maybe a hundred different car models. The victim's prints were the only ones found in her car, and before you ask me, yes, we dusted the passenger-side door handle, both inside and out. Wiped clean."

"Anything more on the death of Lisa Joy Reavis?" I asked him, recalling the information that I'd passed on from Harry McGraw about butane being identified on the tire that had blown.

"If you're referring to the possibility that somebody caused that accident, and thus killed her, no. The police in Alabama had no reason to suspect foul play, so there're no evidence reports, or evidence itself, left at all to inspect. A dead end, Jessica."

"Not entirely, Mort. If Lisa Joy really was murdered, that makes three family members to go with a son killed in action overseas, which leaves only the mother alive."

"You make her for a suspect?"

I shrugged. "Seth and I found her passed out on her apartment floor. She's a mess, Mort, and if she'd killed her daughter at that rest stop—"

"Scenic overlook, you mean."

"—the stench of stale cigarettes would've made Ginny's car smell like a bar in the old days."

"Good point," he acknowledged. "But who does that leave us with?"

"Wild hunch?"

"I'm up for anything."

"Delve deeper into the death of Walter Reavis's son."

"The soldier awarded a posthumous Purple Heart and Medal of Valor?"

"I checked, Mort. It was a closed casket, so maybe, just maybe . . ."

"Yup, that's wild, all right."

"I'm fresh out of options."

"Don't tell me the famous J. B. Fletcher is stumped."

"J. B. Fletcher is never stumped, because she makes everything up. Jessica Fletcher, on the other hand . . ." I said, letting the rest of my thought drift.

"When you solved your first murder all those years ago in Appleton, was it this hard?"

"Not even close."

When yet another knock fell on my door just after Mort departed, I did check the peephole and found none other than Joe and Nails, operatives of Vic Genaway, standing there. I still opened it without hesitation.

"Thought we'd check in, Mrs. Fletcher," Joe said, speaking for both of them as always.

"I don't have any updates, Joe."

"I'm sure you would've contacted us if you had, right?"

"You give me too much credit. Even if my efforts prove successful, I imagine Ginny Genaway's killer will face the traditional justice system once he or she is caught. And it's not within my control to change that."

"You're not giving yourself enough credit. I'm halfway through another of your books. You've really got a knack for this stuff."

"As a fiction writer."

"And where exactly is the line between fiction and fact? Because in your case, they appear to be the same thing."

"Except my imagination can't conjure up Ginny's killer. Reality follows its own rules, for better or for worse."

I could tell from his expression that my remark had sailed right over Joe's head. "What'd you get out of the psychiatrist?"

"Are you watching me?" I asked him.

"Maybe it's Ginny's shrink we're watching. She's not one of Mr. Genaway's top ten favorites."

"Dr. Sackler can't be blamed for the problems she was trying to help Ginny resolve."

"I'm with Mr. Genaway when it comes to shrinks."

"They're certainly not for everyone, Joe."

I wondered in that moment if his next question might pertain to the visit Seth and I had paid to Ginny's apartment, where we'd found those newspaper headline fragments, but that part of our trip had seemed to escape his prying eyes.

"I notice psychiatrists have appeared in several of your books. You ever make one of them the killer?"

I nodded. "A number of years back, in *Ashes, Ashes, Fall Down Dead*."

"How's Ginny's shrink compare to that one?"

"A man instead of a woman, for one thing. And a clear motive for murder, for another."

"Know what I think, Mrs. Fletcher? I think you've got the killer sniffed out. You might not have all the clues you need yet, but you've got a solid notion for sure. Tell me I'm wrong."

"You're wrong."

He smirked. "Yeah, well, when you're ready to spill, Nails and I will be waiting. Meanwhile, we'll make sure no harm comes to you."

"That's not necessary."

"No? Was it some other writer who nearly got burned up with her house not too long ago and got shot at scaling the Cabot Cove bluffs not long after that?"

"I sincerely doubt anything like that will befall me this time."

"Don't be so sure of that, Mrs. Fletcher," Joe warned. "Whoever's out there doing the killing seems to be getting a genuine taste for it. That means you could be their next bite."

I have to admit I woke up Saturday morning feeling a bit of excitement over that evening's retirement party for Wilma Tisdale, as well as trepidation. I'd be seeing many of the guests, my colleagues at Appleton High, for the first time in twenty-five years. While my final days at the school had been dominated by the investigation into the murder of Walter Reavis, they had also been a wonderful time in my life. Frank had surprised me by purchasing 698 Candlewood Lane, and raising Grady might've been hard work at times, but having him around brought the kind of joy to our lives that only a child can bring.

After the accident that had killed Frank's brother, we felt duty bound to take the boy in when his mother's state of mind made raising a child impossible for a time. But he ended up enriching and fulfilling our lives in ways a childless couple like us could have scarcely imagined. So I found myself of two minds about tonight's party. On the one hand, I hoped to rekindle more pleasant memories of my time at the school, apart from the murder that had marked the end of my service there. On the other hand, though, I was convinced Wilma Tisdale had something more, even plenty more, she wanted to share with me.

I thought about what my former colleagues would look like after so many years and studied myself in the full-length mirror on my Hill House suite's bathroom door, wondering how I compared. Leaving nothing to chance, I made an appointment with

Loretta Speigel, owner of the local beauty salon and irreverent gossip, to have my hair done.

"Reunion party?" she quizzed two hours later as she went at my freshly washed locks with a pair of long scissors. "I'd love to be a fly on that wall."

"I'll probably be the only one you know there, Loretta."

"That's why I'd love to be a fly on the wall—just to see your face, for one thing. How your mouth drops when you see what's become of your old friends after so many years."

"I'm not sure how many of them I'd call friends. Even without being privy to the invite list, I can tell you there's not a single one I've kept in touch with."

"Hmmmmmmmm," Loretta reacted, giving me that look of hers. "That tells me Jessica Fletcher has an ulterior motive for going tonight."

"Now, what would make you think that?"

"Simple arithmetic, Jessica. I add the fact that everyone in town's talking about you digging into the murder of that mobster's wife to the fact that you're going to a retirement party for someone you barely know. That adds up to a clear connection."

"What else has the town been saying?"

"Well, there's been some talk about a couple of thugs out of Boston being spotted here and there, and some speculation that a full-fledged mob war may have spread to Cabot Cove of all places."

"Please assure everyone they have nothing to fear from bullets flying from rival gangs across Main Street, Loretta. Tell them that's not the case at all."

She leaned in closer to me. "Then what is the case, pray tell? You know you can trust me to keep a secret."

I was spared having to respond to that when Seth Hazlitt barged into the shop, instantly uncomfortable in a salon filled with all women. He spotted me in Loretta's chair and made a beeline my way, his gait stiff and careful.

"Come for a trim, Seth?" I greeted him.

"Never mind that," he said, straightening his khaki suit jacket with all eyes upon him. "The *Gazette*'s website is back up."

"That's good."

"No, Jess, that's bad. I spent the morning reviewing every page of every issue starting five months ago and going back all the way to six in search of that partial headline we pulled from the trash in the girl's apartment."

Loretta was standing behind the chair, her scissors dangling by her side. She hung on Seth's every word and urged him on with her gaze.

"Something on your mind, Loretta?" he snapped at her.

"I was just thinking that maybe it's time for you to consider a new hairstyle."

"Glad to let you know when I'm ready for one. Something works for forty years, why change it? You mind giving Mrs. Fletcher and me some space?"

Loretta stepped back two feet, maybe three.

"More space than that, Loretta."

She sneered and pranced off in a huff.

"Now," Seth said, picking up our conversation, "where was I?"

"Telling me what you didn't find on those digital copies of the *Gazette*."

"How does anyone read a newspaper on a computer?" Seth wondered, seemingly flummoxed by the process. "How does anyone read *anything* on a computer or on a phone or on one of those readers?"

"They're not my cup of tea either," I told him, "but I'm glad I'm in the minority. I'd hate to see my book sales if I wasn't."

"Maybe they'd just buy books instead, the way they used to, *ayuh.*"

"You were saying, Seth," I prodded him.

"Not much else to say, Jessica," he said, pulling out a photocopy of that assembled headline fragment reading AMED PRIN F THE Y. "After I struck out with a manual review of the issues, I tried the site's search engine. Got no hits when I put in the whole fragment and too many when I put in each part individually. It's like the story up and disappeared."

"I suppose it could've been deleted," I told him.

"By who? And why? I never thought I'd speak the words, but where's Evelyn Phillips when we need her?"

"You have Evelyn's cell number?"

Seth nodded. "Been trying it every hour on the hour. I'm thinking I should ask Mort to check her house. Could be we're up against some kind of conspiracy here."

"A newspaper headline hardly makes much of a motive for murder."

He frowned so deeply, it looked like his jowls had been pumped full of air. "Maybe you should read something other than mysteries, Jess. That kind of thing happens all the time in thrillers."

"This isn't a mystery or a thriller, Seth. It's real life."

He shook his head. "Since when can you tell the difference?"

I took a taxi over to the Cabot Cove Country Club and felt my heart thudding against my chest when I stepped out of the car and approached the entrance. I was used to book events and the myriad Cabot Cove functions connected to the library. I almost never had call to attend gatherings where I had no prescribed role or place. I knew in my heart I would have likely found an excuse not to attend Wilma's party if not for its connection to Ginny Genaway's murder.

That connection was Wilma Tisdale, and as soon as I spotted her across the lounge, where the cocktail reception was being held prior to dinner, I was struck by how little she had changed from my memory of her. I had seen her at that book signing she'd attended around ten years ago, but in my mind, Wilma was unchanged from when I'd last seen her at Appleton High. Of the remaining guests, I recognized very few, due to either how much they had changed or the fact that I'd never met many of them in the first place. By my count, Wilma had taught in Appleton for nearly fifty years. She was several years my senior and had been one of those who respected my efforts to make a difference as a sub, instead of just going through the motions, since she'd started out as one herself.

I could feel numerous eyes upon me, whispers being exchanged when the guests became aware of my presence. Unlike the vast majority of fiction writers, I'd enjoyed the good fortune to have appeared on numerous television talk shows discussing not just my books, but also the real-life investigations in which I'd often become embroiled. The end result was to make me far more recognizable than I would have preferred, and I was glad for a brief respite in the sitting area that held the gift table, where I deposited a colorful bag with a gift certificate to Cabot Cove's local independent bookstore tucked inside.

"Jessica!" I heard a familiar voice call out, and there was

Wilma Tisdale bounding across the room in her heels and wrapping me up in a big hug.

She was an inch taller than I, and I'd forgotten how strong she was; she'd once pushed her car from a snowdrift while I stayed behind the wheel working the gas pedal. She'd been an athlete of some repute in college, back in the days when female athletes garnered none of the respect they deserved and enjoyed today.

"Why, you haven't changed a bit!" She beamed, holding me at arm's distance after we finally separated.

"You either, Wilma."

She waved me off, looking down at the one part of her that had changed over the years. "You mean, except for those twenty pounds I keep losing only to gain back. I have no idea why I even bother." She gave me a closer look. "You, on the other hand, look like you haven't gained a pound."

"All that biking does wonders for the waistline, I guess."

She nodded. "Maybe I wouldn't have to keep losing that same stubborn twenty pounds if I'd never gotten my driver's license either."

I smiled. "I'm surprised you remember that."

"Almost everybody drives, Jessica. It stands out."

"Well, I can fly a plane, and not everybody does that."

"Point taken."

She shared my smile this time. "It's a wonderful party, Wilma."

She joined me in sweeping her gaze about the lounge, beyond which was the dining room, where we'd be having dinner a bit later in the evening. "How many of the guests do you recognize?"

"Not as many as I thought I would, actually. Maybe my memory's gone bad."

"Twenty-five years is a long time, Jessica. People come and go. A lot of these are the ones who stayed but most of them started after you deserted us for Cabot Cove. Wasn't long after you solved Walter Reavis's murder, was it?"

"No, not long at all. Just a couple months, until we closed on the house."

Her expression sombered. "I read about the fire, by the way. Terrible about all the damage. I can't imagine losing so much I'd cherished for so long."

I nodded. "I was lucky to get out with my life."

"To think," she said reflectively, "that it all started back in Appleton . . ."

"The writing didn't really start until after Frank died. Something to fill the time and all the space, too, I guess."

"Did you ever wonder how much writing mysteries may have sprung from solving one of your own?"

I recalled that girl from Bill Gower's sophomore English class who thought, after reading my "anonymous" story that had been rejected by every magazine to which I'd submitted it, that it might be a mystery.

"Not at the time, of course, but over the years I did, yes," I told her, failing to mention that I'd left that fact out of every interview I'd ever done. "I felt I owed it to Walter Reavis to do right by him, the way he had done for me."

Wilma smiled. "You know, after your first book became a bestseller, you were quite the talk in the teachers' room."

"Was I?"

"One of our own making good."

"I wish I could remember her name," I reflected, hearing the wistfulness in my own voice.

"Whose name?"

"The girl in Bill Gower's sophomore English class who told me I'd make a good mystery writer." And then, just like that, it hit me. "Missy—her name was Missy!"

Wilma smiled again, wider, coming up just short of a laugh, at least a chuckle. "Could you have stayed in Appleton the way things ended? If you and Frank hadn't bought your house here in Cabot Cove, I mean."

"I don't know, Wilma. I've thought about that a lot over the years, and I'm not sure I could have just picked up where I left off. People weren't looking at me the same anymore."

"It would've passed."

"Maybe. I think everything worked out best for all concerned."

"Not all," Wilma corrected me, turning her gaze to the lounge's French doors, which overlooked the patio and the golf course beyond. "Step outside with me a moment, Jessica."

"And take you away from all your guests?"

"This can be your gift to me, Jessica."

"I already left it on the table with all the others."

"I'm talking about another gift," Wilma Tisdale said, squeezing my forearm in her bony fist. "One only you can give me. How it all ended twenty-five years ago, how you caught Walter Reavis's killer. I need to hear the story."

Chapter Twenty-one

Twenty-five years ago . . .

Hi, you've reached the Dirkson residence. Please leave your name, number, and—"

Amos Tupper reached down and hit the SPEAKER *button to end the call. "Looks like we need to have a talk with Appleton High's acting principal, Mrs. Fletcher."*

Alma Potts offered to buzz Jim Dirkson on his walkie-talkie to call him back to the office, but Amos Tupper told her we preferred to wait. That wait took all of twenty minutes, through the next break in class, the hallways emptying as quickly as they had filled. Jim Dirkson stepped through the door to the main office with his ever-present bullhorn in hand, which made me think of his annoying blares down the long school halls to get kids to move along from their lockers and friends. I'd heard a few years back that the seniors had stolen the bullhorn and filled it with powder as a prank, so the next time Mr. Dirkson had used it, he was showered in white. The offenders were never caught.

He was a handful of inches taller than my five feet eight, with a slight paunch protruding over his belt, which made his shirt sag out of his pants. He'd coached football for a time and played it for years prior to that, leaving him with a big chest and neck. But his hair was dry and thinning, crusted with white flakes.

Dirkson's eyes froze on Amos Tupper, and he barely regarded me at all.

"What can I do for you, Detective?"

"Yes, Mr. Dirkson, well," Amos stammered, "we just had a bit of follow-up we needed. You know, some follow-up questions."

"'We'?" Dirkson questioned.

Amos looked my way. "Mrs. Fletcher has been kind enough to assist me in the investigation."

"'Assist you'?" Dirkson said, now glaring straight at me. "On what basis?"

I thought Amos might fold like a cheap suit then and there. Instead, I saw his spine stiffen, and suddenly he was almost as tall as I.

"I'm the lead detective on the case, Mr. Dirkson. So the basis of Mrs. Fletcher's assistance is my call and no one else's. We have two options here: cover a few routine matters here in your office or down at the station in mine. I'm going to leave the choice of which to you."

Amos shot me a wink at that point, which made me realize I'd been staring at him through his entire monologue. Jim Dirkson, meanwhile, stood before us like a statue, his grip tightening around the bullhorn in his hand. His breathing had picked up, and I could see his nostrils flaring every time he inhaled.

"My office, then," he relented, striding past us down the short hall toward his office without inviting us to join him.

I shot Alma Potts a look, and she flashed me a thumbs-up sign. Then I followed Amos Tupper into Dirkson's office, his west-facing window accounting for the lack of sunlight compared with Walter Reavis's office farther down the main office hallway.

Gazing at Walter's closed door brought to mind something about that sixth-period meeting I'd had with him, something I couldn't quite grasp but sensed was important. I knew this would continue to plague me until I latched onto it, but for now I had to focus on the task at hand.

"Close the door, please," Jim Dirkson said to me after I'd followed Amos Tupper into his office.

I obliged him, and without being invited Amos took one of the matching chairs set before Dirkson's desk. I took the other one, followed by Dirkson's glare the whole way.

"This shouldn't take long," Amos said, flipping through his memo pad and having trouble finding a blank page.

"It had better not, Detective. It's just me and my assistant running the building now, and we were already shorthanded from an administrative standpoint."

"We just have a few matters to clear up. We can have you back on the job in a few minutes, no more."

"So?" Dirkson said when Amos stopped there.

"'So,'" Amos repeated.

"These matters you needed to clear up."

"Of course, yes. Mrs. Fletcher and I have just come from an interview with our suspect, Tyler Benjamin. You identified him entering the building—is that correct?"

Dirkson frowned. "You took my statement, Detective."

"Apologies, sir. I don't have it in front of me."

"The answer's yes, then. I identified the young man entering the building when I was in my car preparing to drive off."

"Would you mind if I asked you a question, Jim?" I chimed in, much to Amos Tupper's visible relief.

"Since you're here in an official capacity assisting the investigation, perhaps you should call me Mr. Dirkson, Mrs. Fletcher."

"Very well then . . . Mr. Dirkson. My question is this: You knew the suspect, Tyler Benjamin, had been expelled for classroom outbursts. In other words, you had every reason to believe he was dangerous, yet you did nothing to approach him or follow him into the building when you saw him enter it. Would that be correct?"

"I suppose, but the fact that he had come here with violent intentions never occurred to me. I thought he'd returned to the building with permission to clean out his locker, given it had been barely a week since his expulsion. I never imagined he'd come to confront Walter and do him harm."

"Even though you championed his expulsion for those so-called threats of violence?"

"I wouldn't put it that way exactly."

"What way would you put it . . . Mr. Dirkson?"

"I believed that Tyler was a troubled kid and that he needed the kind of help we were not equipped to provide him."

"You were a football coach."

"Yes."

"But you never actually coached Tyler."

"No."

"Ever encounter any other violent football players?" I asked him.

Dirkson looked at Detective Tupper, as if hoping he'd intervene, but Amos left the floor to me.

"No others that committed murder, Mrs. Fletcher," he managed finally. "And Tyler had certainly shown a tendency toward violence off the field, not just on it."

"And yet, again, you say you drove off instead of following him into the building. So as violent as you believe he had the potential to be, you still left teachers and others still in the building vulnerable, not to mention Walter Reavis, whom the young man blamed for his expulsion when he should have been blaming you. Tell me, do I have that right?"

"No, you don't. Do I feel guilty over what happened, over Tyler killing Walter Reavis? Of course, I do. Would I have done things differently if given it to do all over again? Of course, I would. But that doesn't change the material facts here one bit."

"Oh, I believe it does, because I don't believe Tyler Benjamin killed anyone, Mr. Dirkson."

"No? Well, fortunately, you're in the minority."

"Only because of your claim."

Dirkson's forehead had become shiny with sweat. "Claim?"

"That you saw Tyler entering the building after hours, just minutes before the man you've now effectively replaced as principal was murdered. But Tyler says it was you who opened Walter's office door when he knocked. That you sent him away and he never even laid eyes on Walter Reavis that afternoon. Tell me, Mr. Dirkson, what do you think would happen if the boy agreed to take a lie detector test?"

The sweat on Dirkson's brow had begun to bead up, glowing in the light when he turned his gaze on Amos Tupper. "Is this how your department typically conducts an investigation?" he demanded, his tone more pleading than accusatory. "Are you in the habit of involving civilians in your murder investigations?"

"Mr. Dirkson," Amos said, giving no ground, "the last murder here in Appleton was a dozen years ago. A woman named Thea Dunwoody hammered her husband over the head with the same frying pan she'd used to cook the dinner he'd dumped in the trash. I was a patrolman back then, first on the scene, first to see the body. You asked me if I'm in the habit of involving civilians in my murder investigations. Well, sir, I'm in the habit of doing whatever it takes. And it just so happens Mrs. Fletcher's assistance has been invaluable so far. She's got a keen eye for killers, and right now she's looking straight at you."

Dirkson rose, slowly and stiffly, lifting his phone receiver from its hook. "This conversation is over. I'm calling the chief of police right now."

"Perhaps you should tell him about that argument you had with Walter Reavis I overheard from outside his office," I suggested curtly.

He stopped short of dialing, his grasp tightening on the receiver in a way that made me picture him holding the trophy that had been used to kill Walter Reavis.

"Would you like to deny it was you on the other end of the line, Mr. Dirkson?" Amos asked him.

"We had a professional disagreement," Dirkson said, plopping back down in his chair, the receiver returned to its cradle. "That's all."

"He phoned you at home," I jumped in. "That means you drove back to the school after the call ended. Tyler Benjamin putting you in the office around the time of the murder makes you as strong a suspect as the boy."

"Except my fingerprints weren't found on the murder weapon. Maybe you're forgetting that, Mrs. Fletcher."

"Not at all. But as a former football coach who continues to maintain close ties with the Appleton High program, you would have known Tyler's prints would be on the trophy. That would explain your choice of weapon. Whether you're actually guilty or not, how can you, as an educator, in good conscience condemn a boy to life in prison? If nothing else, Mr. Dirkson, you should at least come clean about denying Tyler entry to the office that day."

Dirkson's features flared, his chest puffed up, and his paunchy stomach seemed to flatten a bit. "I have come clean, Mrs. Fletcher, and I'm done explaining myself to a *substitute* teacher. Maybe you should choose who you work with more wisely, Mr. Tupper."

"That's *Detective* Tupper." He rose from his chair enough to lift the phone receiver from its cradle and extend it across the desk. "You want to call the chief, go right ahead. It'll save me the trouble of telling him about this interview myself. Maybe you'll even save me the bother of writing out my report."

Dirkson snickered, laying the receiver down. "Perhaps you should ask Mrs. Fletcher to write it for you. She seems to be the one in charge here."

His remark had been meant to get a rise out of Amos, but the detective simply smiled. "I know there're folks in this town who don't have a lot of respect for me. They're free to think anything they want, but after I solve this case, they're going to look at me differently."

"When you call the chief," I said, "make sure to tell him the truth about Tyler Benjamin. Giving false testimony is a crime, Mr. Dirkson. You could be hauled out of here in handcuffs."

"Over my dead body."

"That's the same thing Walter Reavis said to you, isn't it?" I said.

"He called you about something," Amos Tupper interjected. "Your home number was the last one he dialed, at a time that jibes perfectly with Mrs. Fletcher's statement."

The air went out of Jim Dirkson. His chest seemed to deflate, his whole body went limp in the chair, and his confident gaze turned fluttery and uncertain.

"Care to tell us the subject of your conversation?" Amos Tupper pressed Dirkson after shooting a glance my way.

"Walter Reavis was taking certain liberties with the school budget, Detective, particularly with the discretionary funds, and I have the documentation to prove it."

"Go on."

"Specifically, he was redirecting sums allocated to other areas to staffing, holding on to teachers who were supposed to be laid off and diverting funds to long-term-substitute-teacher costs that were strictly against administrative rules."

I felt my stomach sink. Not only had Walter Reavis been in my corner; he'd broken the rules to keep me in the building on a full-time basis.

"I'm the vice principal," Dirkson continued, "so curriculum falls under my purview. That's how I discovered the discrepancies."

"You threatened him," I couldn't help but say to him.

"I advised him to come clean, fess up to what he'd been doing so the school board could take proper action."

"By which you mean firing him."

"That would have been their call."

"But you were prepared to force the issue, weren't you, Mr.

Dirkson? And just whom do you think the board would have appointed to replace Mr. Reavis once he was fired or suspended?"

"What Mrs. Fletcher is saying—" Amos Tupper started.

"I know what she's saying," Dirkson said, his gaze boring into me. "I don't deny we had a heated argument, that Walter said something to the effect of 'Over my dead body' after I told him to come clean or I would. But that's where it ended."

"So the subject of these affairs he'd been rumored to have over the years never came up?" I asked him.

"Why would it?"

"Because it occurs to me, Mr. Dirkson, that you could have threatened to expose Walter for that if he didn't just resign on his own."

Dirkson smirked. "I could've done that anytime in the past ten years, if the rumors were true. But that's all they were—rumors. And I've heard plenty worse ones passed around about myself."

That was the first thing he'd said that I fully believed, but I wasn't finished yet.

"It didn't really end with that phone call, though, did it?" I challenged. "Because you got in your car and came back here. You say you spotted Tyler entering the building, and he claims you opened the door to the office after he knocked. Either way, you came back after a conversation you admit was heated. That's suspicious any way you slice it."

Dirkson rose from his chair, looking neither as tall nor as broad as he had just minutes before. Maybe the bullhorn made the man.

"I came back to finish my conversation with Walter in person and give him the evidence I'd found in the hope it would spur

him to do the right thing. But the door to his office was locked, so I assumed he'd left for the day."

"Even though his car was still in the parking lot?"

"To tell you the truth, I didn't notice. Now that I look back, it's clear that Tyler Benjamin had already killed Walter by the time I got back here. That's why he's pointing the finger at me instead, Mrs. Fletcher. Even an amateur detective should be able to see that."

In that moment, I so wanted Jim Dirkson to be guilty. Thanks to his antipathy toward me in particular, and the way he held substitute teachers and clerical personnel in thinly disguised disdain, nothing would have given me more pleasure in that moment than finding a clue that definitively implicated him in Walter's murder. Of course, it was as much about finding justice for a man who'd believed in me. But I also wondered how much I might be letting my animosity toward Dirkson cloud my thinking. He'd never bothered to disguise the extreme disappointment and anger he felt over not being appointed to a job he thought he deserved, and he had seemed to make it a point to take his feelings out on underlings like me, who couldn't push back. Being a bully, though, didn't make him a killer, no matter how much I wanted that to be the case.

"Are you going to release Tyler Benjamin?" I asked Detective Tupper outside the school office after we'd wrapped up our interview.

"From what I heard in there, Mr. Dirkson's sticking to his story," he reminded me.

"His statement is still the only thing linking the boy to the murder. It's his word against Tyler's."

"There're also Tyler's fingerprint on the murder weapon, Mrs. Fletcher."

"Sure, but he'd handled the trophy previously, remember? Of course, his fingerprint would still be there."

"That's a fair point. But we can't deny the fact that he threatened a teacher—"

"Something he denies."

"—and had those two previous classroom outbursts, establishing a pattern it's difficult to explain away."

"Tyler Benjamin didn't kill Principal Reavis, Amos," I said with more assurance in my voice than I had a right to include.

"How can you be so sure about that?"

"I don't know. I just am. Just assume for one moment that Tyler's telling the truth and Jim Dirkson really was in the office around the time Walter Reavis was murdered. This would be the same Jim Dirkson who admits he argued with Walter over the phone and then drove back to the school in what might well have been a fit of rage."

"So why lie about being in the office, Mrs. Fletcher?"

"Because Tyler showed up at the perfect time for Dirkson to set him up as the killer. He knew it would be his word against the boy's, and whom would the police be more likely to believe?"

"I see your point," Detective Tupper said, frowning. "But that doesn't give us nearly enough to make a case against the now acting head of the school, does it?"

"Not yet," I conceded.

After last period was over, I sat at Bill Gower's desk in a fog. The afternoon sun was streaming through the windows, just as it had during my last conversation with Walter Reavis in his office, because Alma Potts hadn't been there to close his blinds as was her custom. It didn't surprise me one bit that Walter had been diverting funds to avoid having to lay off teachers—cooking the books, as they say. He had more than gone out on a limb for me; he'd risked his job for me and others to do the right thing by the eight hundred students who filled the school a hundred and eighty days every year. He was an old-school educator and arguably not a great fit for an educational system that relied increasingly on test scores and that had made budget cuts the rule instead of the exception. He had been a teacher for fifteen years himself before moving over to the administrative side of things. I imagined he'd spent many days sitting just as I was now, doing the best job possible of reaching his students.

With the sun blazing into his eyes.

I got up and pulled the blinds down gently, so as not to disturb the tape that was already keeping them together. Maybe Walter Reavis had allocated the money for new blinds to holding on to more teachers, something I could hardy argue with, given that—

I felt something hit me like a pillow to my face. I thought I was about to lose my balance and actually clutched the radiator to stop from falling, my knees having gone wobbly. I felt something flutter in my stomach as an icy feather scratched at my spine.

Alma Potts's Chevrolet Cavalier thumped and bumped its way forward, belting out a final backfire before settling on its way. The buses, even the single late one, were long gone, so the parking lot was pretty much empty when I stepped out in front of the car before Alma could swing onto the exit drive leading to the street.

"Is something wrong, Mrs. Fletcher?" she asked, rolling her window down. "Do you need a ride?"

"No, Alma."

That was when she spotted Amos Tupper approaching from behind a nest of bushes set around a single maple tree, with Tyler Benjamin by his side. The two of them were trailed by a pair of Appleton's uniformed officers, Tom Jennings and another whose name slipped my mind.

"Son, is this the car you saw leaving the parking lot the afternoon Principal Reavis was murdered?" Amos asked when he was close enough for Alma to hear him.

The boy swallowed hard. "It's definitely the car I *heard* leaving. There's no mistaking that backfire."

I looked back at Alma.

"Come to think of it, Mrs. Fletcher," she said, "I did come back to the office to pick up some spreadsheets so I could work on them at home. But the young man was right: The office door was locked, and I'd forgotten to bring the right set of keys with me, I'd rushed out so fast."

I nodded, pretending as if I believed her. "Did you notice Jim Dirkson inside?"

"No, I didn't," she said with her eyes straying beyond Amos to those two uniformed officers.

"But for the record, you are confirming at least a portion of Tyler's story."

"I suppose I am."

"Then why didn't you do so earlier this afternoon when Detective Tupper and I interviewed Acting Principal Dirkson?"

Her eyes teared up. "I was afraid he'd fire me, and I can't afford to lose my job, the medical benefits and all. I'm a single mother trying to raise two teenagers."

"I understand, Alma."

"You do?" she asked, a ring of hope lacing her voice as if there might yet be a way out of this.

"Yes. I understand that you murdered Walter Reavis."

Alma just stared at me in response, a still shot as opposed to a moving picture, looking utterly frozen.

"I don't think you had any intention of killing him," I continued. "I think you did come back for those spreadsheets, just as you claim. Then, when you saw he was still in his office, alone, you decided to confront him. He was carrying on with another teacher, wasn't he? The rumors about him having tawdry affairs from time to time over the years, rumors I scoffed at, were true. Maybe you warned him to stop or you'd report him at long last. All because you were jealous. That's it, isn't it, Alma? That's why he brought you with him from the middle school when he was named principal of Appleton High. Because the two of you were having an affair at the time."

Alma Potts looked up at me from the driver's seat, her eyes welling with tears. She didn't bother denying a thing I had said; there was no point.

"Things spun out of control, didn't they? An argument ensued. Maybe it was Walter who threatened to fire you. That's when you grabbed the trophy from his shelf. The football must've popped off from the figurine's grasp, so Walter leaned over to pick it up. That's when you struck him, when he was starting to stand back up, which explains why it appeared someone taller than he killed him. You could only have done it in a fit of pent-up rage that had been building when he started carrying on with a woman who wasn't you."

Alma Potts sniffled. "She wasn't the only one over the years.

But I kept quiet the whole time, hoping someday he'd come back to me."

"You locked his office door on the way out, just the way Jim Dirkson found it when he returned to finish the argument he'd started with Walter over the phone. That's why Dirkson thought Walter had left for the day. The two of you must've missed crossing paths by mere minutes. And then Tyler Benjamin knocked on the main office door while our now acting principal was inside. The boy was telling the truth all along."

"It's a sad story you've spun, Mrs. Fletcher. You should try your hand at writing mysteries someday. Fiction, because you can't prove any of this."

"Except for one thing, Alma. When I met with Mr. Reavis a few hours before, during sixth period, his blinds were open and the sun was in my eyes because you weren't in school to close them. But when the body was found the next morning, his office blinds were closed." I hesitated, to make sure she could catch up with my thinking. "Who closed them? Who would have had reason to close them? You, Alma, as was your custom. Something you did every single day and couldn't resist doing just a few minutes before the confrontation that ended in murder."

Amos Tupper drew even with me. "Please step out of the car, ma'am, and keep your hands where I can see them."

Alma glanced at Tom Jennings and the other uniformed officer again before climbing out of her battered Chevy, slowly and with her hands in view. Amos signaled the patrolmen forward to take her into custody, one already with his handcuffs out.

"I didn't mean to do it, Mrs. Fletcher," Alma insisted, her voice cracking. "I didn't plan to do it. It just sort of . . . happened. One moment we were arguing, and the next he was lying on the floor and I was holding that bloody trophy. I wiped it clean as best I could with Kleenex and hid the bloody wad in my bag. I wish I could take it back. How I wish I could go back in time and change everything."

Tom Jennings fastened the cuffs in place and started to lead Alma toward his squad car, the second officer falling into step behind him. Alma ground her feet to a halt and looked back at me one last time.

"I loved Walter. If I hadn't loved him, this never would have happened."

"'It's only in love and murder that we still remain sincere,'" I said.

Alma regarded me quizzically. "Did you make that up?"

"No, it's a quote from the playwright Friedrich Dürrenmatt."

"I'm impressed, Mrs. Fletcher."

"Well, Alma, I am an English teacher."

Amos Tupper drew closer to me, and together we watched her being placed in the back of the squad car.

"You know," he started, "that bit about her closing the blinds never would've held up in court."

"Of course, Amos, but I also knew it wouldn't have to. Once Alma Potts knew we had her, it was over."

He nodded reflectively as the squad car drove off with lights flashing but no siren. "Maybe she was right, Mrs. Fletcher."

"About her not having planned the murder?"

He turned toward me, smiling. "No, about you writing mysteries."

Chapter Twenty-two

The present

When I'd finished, Wilma gazed out over the rolling, manicured golf course that had browned with the fall. A chill breeze whipped through the trees, making me realize how cold I felt after completing the story I hadn't told anyone in a very long time and had never committed to paper.

"I never knew all the details," Wilma said, shivering as she continued to gaze out over the golf course.

"She confessed after the prosecutor's office offered to reduce the charge."

"Did you believe her, Jessica?"

"I believe she never intended to kill Walter Reavis. I believe she came back to the school that day to plead with him to take her back. I believe she'd been in denial, and the anger had built up in her until it spilled over and she felt she had to act. I believe she told Walter she was going to report him if he didn't stop . . . or come back to her."

"That doesn't sound like Alma."

"Murder didn't sound like Alma either, Wilma."

"Anyway," she said, trying to change the tone, "Amos Tupper followed you to Cabot Cove, didn't he? After he left the Appleton police force just after Alma went to prison."

"He drove a bus for a time, figuring he was done with police work. But then the sheriff's job here opened up, and he was hired."

"Must not have been an impressive field."

"Amos was the only applicant. But his replacement, Mort Metzger, came complete with twenty-five years' experience with the NYPD. I'm working with Sheriff Metzger on Ginny Genaway's murder, if you have anything you'd like to share with us."

She finally turned all the way around, tucking her arms tight against herself to ward off the chill. "I should get back to my guests."

I blocked her way to the French doors. "What is it you're not telling me, Wilma?"

She tried to shrug my question off. "The only mystery here, you solved twenty-five years ago."

"Until Walter Reavis's daughter Ginny was murdered five days ago. And a detective I asked to look into the death of her older sister, Lisa Joy, the girl you used to tutor, found evidence that suggests she might have been murdered, too. No, Wilma, you invited me tonight after Ginny came to see you last week because you were scared. You invited me because you had something you wanted to tell me."

Turning, I could see our darkened reflections in the French doors, making us look more like shadows than like people. An almost surreal view in contrast to the full-bodied people milling about the lounge, plenty more guests having arrived since we'd come outside to the cold.

"I'm going back inside," Alma said.

This time I let her past me, in large part because I was freezing and wanted to get back inside myself, so I fell in step alongside her.

"Did Ginny share something with you about Alma Potts? Could she have been the one who murdered Ginny after being released from prison?"

Before Wilma could answer, she was swarmed by a group of guests who'd just arrived, bearing hugs and presents. I decided to back off and give her some space, let her enjoy her own retirement party until she was ready to share with me whatever had led her to mail me that invitation. I turned and found Jim Dirkson right in front of me, a bottle of beer in his hand.

"Jim," I managed.

And he managed a smile in return. He'd lost weight, a lot of it, and the new bent of his big-boned frame didn't seem to suit him. He still had a paunch, though it was smaller, like everything else about him seemed. He'd lost a great deal of hair and sported a comb-over that didn't quite reach, the patches of clumped-together hair looking glued to his scalp.

"Catch any killers lately, Mrs. Fletcher?" He looked as if he regretted the question as quickly as he asked it. "Bad joke. I'm sorry. I didn't expect to see you here."

"Wilma didn't mention she'd invited me?"

"I was surprised she invited me. You know, I retired seven years ago."

"Actually, I didn't."

Dirkson nodded. "After eighteen years as principal of Appleton High, even though they left the interim label in place for three of them. Didn't have to bump my salary up to what Walter was making that way."

"That doesn't seem fair, but then life seldom is, right, Mr.

Dirkson? Like it wasn't fair for Tyler Benjamin to be arrested for a murder he didn't commit based on your false statement."

The tension between us felt like a wool blanket, the years having done nothing to relieve the animus that had existed between us even before Amos Tupper and I had come close to accusing Dirkson of murder during our interview.

"For what it's worth, Mrs. Fletcher, I'm sorry."

"Sorry enough to apologize to Tyler Benjamin?"

"Would it matter if I told you I did?"

I shook my head, not able to simply smile and move on. In that moment, a tall woman with a spiky hairdo that would have made Loretta Speigel cringe sauntered up to the bar to order a drink. I was certain I'd never seen her before, but she looked vaguely familiar somehow.

"He transferred to a private school," Dirkson continued. "The district paid his tuition. I told them to take it out of my salary, but they refused." Dirkson shook his bottle. "I need another beer. Can I get you something, Mrs. Fletcher?"

"I'll get it myself," I told him, watching the tall woman with spiky hair leave the bar with a drink in her hand, "but I appreciate the offer."

We went our separate ways, and I don't think I've ever wanted to be out of someone's company more. Whoever said that time heals all wounds was wrong. I suppose I could take some solace in the fact that Jim Dirkson was clearly a sad, miserable man. And for some reason, I felt certain that had I checked the overflowing gift table, there'd be nothing left upon it from him.

I'd like to say I made the best of the rest of the evening, but that would be a lie. At dinner, I was seated at a table with a few former colleagues I barely remembered and a few younger teachers newer to the building. I joined them in small talk and dreaded the moment the conversation would get around to me and my books, which it ultimately did. I normally don't resist a conversation veering in that direction, but I was too distracted tonight to pay attention to their comments and answered their questions in a fashion so cursory, it clearly put them off. I tried to make up for it by engaging them in small talk of my own, but things had grown too strained. Coffee was served in the nick of time.

Speeches and some presentations followed, emceed by the younger principal who'd replaced Jim Dirkson after he retired. I forced a few laughs and made myself applaud at the proper times, then joined the crowd in a standing ovation when Wilma was introduced to make some remarks, as the lights were dimmed and a cake emblazoned with candles was rolled out on a cart.

The candles' glow radiated color on Wilma's pale visage, and she seemed genuinely overwhelmed as the new Appleton High principal led an improvised version of "For He's a Jolly Good Fellow," modified to suit her. She was truly beaming as someone handed her a knife to cut the cake, whatever fears had been plaguing her forgotten in that moment.

Then I saw her expression change as she completed the initial cut to another round of applause. I followed her gaze to the part of the room it had been focused on, wondering if she'd seen something that had disturbed her. Her remarks were terse; she sounded suddenly like she wanted to be somewhere else, her eyes scanning the still-dimmed room for whatever had left her unsettled.

Already on my feet, I started to move through the crowd clustering toward her and the cake to fetch their pieces; I wasn't even halfway there when Wilma burst out of the congestion of bodies and grabbed me by the arms. "She's here!"

"Who? Wilma, what's going on?"

Her eyes swam wildly about, ignoring the well-wishers who continued to offer their congratulations. "You're right, Jessica. You were right all along! I should have told you earlier, but I lost my nerve. Never thought you'd believe me, especially after—"

Wilma's eyes bulged at something she was gazing at across the room. "No . . . No!" She tightened her grasp on me, actually hurting my arms. "Call your sheriff! Call him now! She's here. Tell him she's here!"

Once more, I swept my gaze about, following her line of vision in search of whomever it was she'd spotted. But the dimness of the room kept me from gaining clear focus on anyone.

"Wilma . . ." I started.

And that was when the lights went out. Not just the lights, but all the power, because the music died, too. When the emergency lights failed to snap on, I knew something was terribly wrong even before a dark shape brushed past me, a flicker of motion set against the black backdrop. I heard a grunt, a gasp, and the start of a scream before something crashed into me and forced me to the floor.

I couldn't move, with something heavy pinning me down. Moments later, a flashlight beam shone down on me, illuminating a limp body pinning me to the floor.

Wilma Tisdale.

With the knife she'd used to cut the cake protruding from her back.

I reacted reflexively, shoving her off me. I think I might have been screaming myself. Hands helped me back to my feet as more screams and cries rang out, cell phone lights illuminating

Wilma's body for all to see. The crowd, not surprisingly, erupted into an all-out panic. The surge spun me one way and then the other, the mass of guests flooding from the dining room in an unbroken tide diverted only by a handful of guests kneeling by Wilma's side and trying to tend to her.

Except for a single, dark-clad figure moving in the opposite direction, toward the patio.

"Call nine-one-one. Somebody call nine-one-one!" a shrill voice called out.

I knew it was too late, knew Wilma's wound had been fatal, as I fought against the crowd's flow, shoving my way toward the patio and feeling the surge of chill air just before I reached the still-open French doors. The figure I'd glimpsed inside a few moments before was speeding across the golf course.

I jogged after the figure, putting all the hours of treadmill work in the Hill House gym to good use, and so relieved I'd worn flats to the party instead of heels. But the figure ahead of me widened the gap, and at that point I hadn't exactly considered what I intended to do if I did manage to catch up with Wilma's murderer.

It didn't matter. Instinct had taken over, that and my misplaced obsessive curiosity over a mystery I was convinced went back twenty-five years. Was this one of the guests I was chasing? Or was it someone uninvited whom Wilma Tisdale had glimpsed in the crowd?

Call your sheriff! Call him now! She's here. Tell him she's here!

"She"? Was I chasing a woman? If so, it was one at least as big as I and in good enough shape to keep my pursuit from closing. She'd know I was coming, the thumps of my footsteps as discernible for her as hers were for me, the only sounds given up by the night in between bursts of wind.

The adrenaline surging through me kept me from grasping the folly of this pursuit—literally. I was chasing a killer alone around a golf course under cover of night. And even more to the point, what if the killer simply turned and held his or her ground, intent on making me the second victim of the evening?

Still, my deliberate pace already slowing, I pressed on, clinging to the hope I might grab some glimpse of the killer that would give away her, or his, identity. I tried to recapture the panicked flight of guests. Had Jim Dirkson been among them, or might he be considered a suspect in yet another Appleton-related murder? And what about Alma Potts, assuming she'd been released from prison and was free to harm those she'd held a grudge against for all that time?

The trouble was, Alma would be at least sixty now, potentially even older, as I couldn't remember exactly how old she'd been when she'd confessed to and been arrested for the murder of Walter Reavis. The figure widening the gap between us with long, loping strides didn't appear even close to that old, which, I supposed, likely ruled out Jim Dirkson as well.

I continued the chase, grinding to a halt after the killer had drifted out of sight. Was he or she hiding, intending to pounce when I drew closer? The absurdity of my actions, together with the danger in which I now found myself as a result of them, hit me headlong, and I realized in that moment the extent of my vulnerability. A killer who'd already struck twice in less than a week would make no bones about taking a third life.

I thought of Ginny Genaway and her similarly departed sister, Lisa Joy. I thought of their father, Walter Reavis, and how much I'd respected him. Three murders in a span of twenty-five years, dual generations that had each found a time for murder.

The wind blew through the golf course's trees, howling in a way that sounded like a woman screaming. Back up the downward slope of my pursuit, sirens blared and lights flashed through the night, announcing the arrival of a bevy of squad cars. The extra light and looming law enforcement threat made me feel safer, though not safe enough to continue chasing the killer I'd somehow lost a few minutes back. I backpedaled in the direction of the Cabot Cove Country Club clubhouse, so as not to leave myself totally vulnerable to an attack. And by the time the patio on which I'd told Wilma the rest of the story about catching Walter Reavis's murderer came within clear view, my feet felt swollen to twice their normal size, and agonizing bolts of pain shot up through the bottoms of both.

Then I spotted a figure charging toward me from around the side of the building. I lost a breath and then a heartbeat before I recognized the flapping holster, the department-issue jacket, and the hat that the man held pinned to his head as he surged my way.

"Two murders in one week, Mrs. F.," Mort Metzger said, eyeing me derisively. "Looks like you and I have a lot to talk about."

Chapter Twenty-three

The fast arrival of the Cabot Cove Sheriff's Department on the scene had prevented all but a few of the guests from screeching out of the parking lot in their cars. The vast majority of them were still gathered in the parking lot, mingling about in search of updates on Wilma Tisdale's murder and the investigation already under way.

Meanwhile, Mort and I stood back a bit from Wilma's body while Seth Hazlitt crouched over to perform a preliminary examination of the corpse.

"Wilma told me to call you, Mort," I said, gazing down at her body. "It was the last thing she said."

"Well, you should have. Earlier."

"And what would you have told me?"

"That your overactive imagination was acting up again and to just enjoy the party."

"That's why I didn't bother calling. Earlier."

"Why'd she tell you to call me, Jessica?"

"She'd spotted someone in the crowd I think she believed killed Ginny Genaway."

"Another uninvited guest?"

"Hey, I was invited."

"Right," Mort groused. "Better late than never, I suppose. What exactly was it that Mrs. Tisdale said when she asked you to call me?"

"She was in an all-out panic," I told him, "utterly terrified. 'Call your sheriff,' she said. 'Call him now! She's here. Tell him she's here!'"

"But who could *she* have been?"

"I have no idea. The only obvious name that comes to mind is Alma Potts."

Mort's expression tightened. "That name rings a bell."

"The product of my first murder investigation over in Appleton twenty-five years ago."

He nodded. "That explains it."

Seth Hazlitt looked up from the body to us. "Well, looks to me like the knife slid through a pair of ribs and punctured her heart. Death doesn't get much more instant than that."

I shivered, recalling the feeling of Wilma's literal deadweight pinning me to the floor, the coppery scent of her spilled blood filling my nostrils.

"Why Wilma Tisdale?" Mort wondered.

"You asking me?" Seth said, pointing to himself.

"No, our sleuth in residence here."

"Wilma obviously knew more than she shared with me, likely connected to that visit she received from Ginny Genaway last week. I think she knew, perhaps without realizing it, the identity of Ginny's killer. Someone's covering their tracks here, Mort. I think that's what these murders were about."

"Tracks going back *twenty-five years*?"

"Walter Reavis's murder was the start of all this, the catalyst."

"But Alma Potts would be a hundred years old now."

"Mid- to late sixties," I corrected Mort.

"And guilty of a crime of passion a quarter century ago, not first-degree murder with a gun and then another with a knife. Who does that leave us with exactly?"

"No one comes to mind."

Mort took off his hat and ran his hand through his still-thick hair. "We're bringing the guests we've been able to round up all back inside the club to take their statements and figure out the names of those who left so we can track them down to get their statements, too."

"Somebody must've seen something, maybe several somebodies. Put their stories together, and we might have at least a general description of the killer."

"The woman, you mean, at least according to Wilma Tisdale. Did anything you saw out on that golf course tell you anything else about her?"

"Not a thing, including the fact that it was definitively a 'her.'"

"What about in the moments before Mrs. Tisdale was murdered?"

I shook my head. "Nothing. I was facing the wrong direction, and the lights went off just as I turned to follow Wilma's gaze."

"And this was the first time you believed her to be scared?"

"'Terrified' would be a better way of describing what I saw in her eyes. She was scared when we talked on the patio earlier. She was scared when she invited me here in the first place."

"You think she knew a killer was going to crash the party?"

"No, but I think she knew, or at least suspected, who the killer is and was struggling with whether or not to share her suspicions."

"And that's why she invited you?"

I shrugged. "Maybe she changed her mind. Could be she'd come to doubt whatever conclusions she came to in the wake of Ginny's visit. Now that I think about it . . ."

"What?"

"She mailed the invitation days before Ginny Genaway's murder, so it couldn't have been that that spooked her so much. It had to be something Ginny had told her, and whatever it was explains what lured Ginny back to Appleton and then brought her to Cabot Cove." I looked down at Seth finishing up his examination of Wilma's corpse. "Seth drew a blank on that headline."

"So he told me. Which leaves us back five or six months ago again, with whatever Ginny had uncovered that ultimately led to her being murdered."

"Alma Potts, Mort. We need to check her out."

"But you just said—"

"I know what I said, but she spent twenty-five years stewing over her past and her future. Who knows what came out through those gates?"

"She was released?"

I shrugged. "She must've been. She accepted that guilty plea and was sentenced to twenty-five years, all of it to serve. Her prison term would have ended—"

"Don't tell me," Mort said, fingering his chin dramatically. "Around six months ago maybe?"

"Maybe even sooner, if she got time off for good behavior, or whatever they call it these days. I also seem to remember Alma

Potts had two teenagers when she was arrested for Walter Reavis's murder. Twins, I think, a boy and a girl. I heard they went to live with an aunt and uncle when their mother went to prison. You may want to look into their whereabouts, too, Mort."

"Any other orders?"

"No, that should do. For now," I added, enjoying the rise that got out of him. "But if Alma Potts really did kill Ginny Genaway and Wilma Tisdale, how do we know she's finished? Maybe she's got a longer victims' list, many of whom are still here right now."

Mort nodded deliberately. "I'd better call in some more deputies."

"I suspect so."

"And, Mrs. Fletcher?"

"Yes, Sheriff Metzger?"

"Don't stray too far yourself."

"Worried for my safety, too?"

"No, ma'am. You're not just working the case now. You're the only witness I've got, and I need to take your statement."

Viewing murder from a distance, either writing about it in fiction or coming in on it after the fact in reality, leaves a far less indelible mark than the up-close-and-personal experience I'd had that night. I tried to remember another time—in reality, anyway—when a murder victim had literally fallen into my arms. It wasn't something I'd soon forget. In fact, I shivered now just thinking about it.

Because I was a material witness myself, Mort told me that under no circumstances could I participate in the interviews with all the potential witnesses.

"But I know these people," I said.

"No, you don't, Jessica."

"A few, anyway."

"Our killer went to great pains to avoid being seen," Mort reasoned properly. "I wonder if we can take that to mean he or she was afraid to be recognized."

"I had another thought on that subject," I told him. "What if the killer was one of the invited guests?"

"You think he or she may have come complete with that dark outfit to change into at the proper time?"

"Wilma was pretty adamant about it being a 'she,' Mort."

She's here. Tell him she's here! I recalled her pleading to me.

"Interesting, Mrs. F., because, if you're right, the killer would be one of the guests we won't be able to account for after the murder took place."

I recalled the surge of panicked guests streaming for the exits. "I'm guessing several would have just jumped in their cars and gone home."

"We need to account for them as well as those who are still on the premises now. Try to get a notion as to where everyone was at the time of the murder."

"You may also want to have your men lock down the parking lot. The killer ran off, but their car would still be here. That means any vehicle that's still here after all the guests are freed up to leave might belong to our killer."

"Gee, I hadn't thought of that," Mort said sarcastically. "Those twenty-five years with the NYPD didn't teach me a darn thing."

"What about the entire guest list that you obviously won't be able to get from Wilma Tisdale herself?"

"No, but the club has a version of it that includes the main-course selections. They're making me a copy, and I believe there were seventy-two names on it. Any way you can think of determining which of them actually showed?"

"The gift table would be my first thought."

"I do believe you've done this before," Mort said, flashing a wry grin.

"Unfortunately. Cataloging the gifts should go a long way toward determining who'd already arrived and who was a no-show by dinnertime."

"One of my deputies is already in the process of sorting through all that. I'll add the gift table to his to-do list."

"I'd think he should pay special attention to the women on the list," I said, recalling that Wilma Tisdale had clearly indicated it was a woman who had so terrified her.

"Can you say whether the figure you were chasing was definitively a woman, Mrs. Fletcher?"

"No."

"Then, if you don't mind, we'll pay the same attention to all the names for now," Mort said, gloating ever so slightly.

"I also wouldn't rule out any of the no-shows as suspects," I told him.

"That's where a careful check of the cars left over in the lot could come in very handy, indeed."

"The killer couldn't have escaped across the golf course and made it back to the parking lot before your arrival, Mort. It's impossible to build a timeline to that effect. That means if the killer's on the premises now, she or he would've almost surely joined those who'd gathered outside a bit later, hopefully late enough to stand out."

"I'll make sure questions to that end are included in the queries we pose to everyone."

As we spoke, his deputies continued checking for evidence, a painstaking process in which the upgrades in personnel Mort continued to incorporate at the Cabot Cove Sheriff's Department were clearly on display. All three deputies currently crisscrossing the room were wearing evidence gloves and, to a man or woman, had plastic evidence bags at the ready. But their efforts seemed fruitless at this point; none of those bags contained anything of note, save for a number of cloth napkins lifted from the table close to the area where the dark-clad phantom had seemed to originate. Those napkins would provide the fingerprints of anyone who'd used them, among which might be our killer's. I doubted that, given the clear precautions the killer had taken. But Mort's thinking was spot-on when it came to first determining, above all else, who among the guests gathered couldn't definitively account for their whereabouts around the time of the murder.

"There's one guest, by the way, who's already said he'll only talk to you and you alone," Mort told me.

"Who's that exactly?"

Mort checked his magical memo pad, which never seemed to run out of paper. "Jim Dirkson."

Mort's deputies, eventually to be supplemented by the Maine State Police, were using the club lounge, where cocktails had been served prior to dinner, to conduct their interviews with the guests, who were being kept as comfortable as possible in the lobby as they awaited their turns on what promised to be a very long night. I imagined plenty of them were grumbling about being held in such a fashion, and that would only get worse as the hour drew later.

"I don't trust those cops," Jim Dirkson said, seated across from me at a two-person bar table with matching stools on either side.

"But you trust me?"

"Your investigative abilities. Don't forget I've seen them at work firsthand."

"I don't recall you ever being much of a fan of them or of my efforts to help find Walter Reavis's killer, especially when I exposed the story you fabricated."

"You just made my case for me in that respect, Mrs. Fletcher. I don't want to end up a suspect in yet another murder, and I've got something to say I don't want lost in the cracks by these yokels."

I let Dirkson's remark slide. "Pertaining to what, exactly?"

"Were you aware that Wilma Tisdale and Alma Potts had a bit of a history between them?"

"No, I wasn't."

"Come to think of it, most of it transpired after you'd left our fair town for Cabot Cove. Alma had worked twenty years as a school secretary, first at the middle school and then at the high school. Back in those days that would've meant she had a sizable pension coming, and her lawyer fought to secure it for her children."

"Twins, weren't they?" I recalled.

"Yes, but they went to a different school system since Alma didn't actually reside in Appleton. I don't remember how old they were at the time or whether they were boys or girls."

"I'm guessing they never got the money."

"No, they didn't. And as head of the Teachers' Retirement Board for the state, Wilma Tisdale played a very big role in the union's refusal to pay out, under the circumstances. Nothing like this had ever happened before, so there was no precedent to follow. The decision wound its way through some lower courts and was affirmed every step of the way."

I looked at Dirkson atop his matching stool. "Our sheriff's department is checking on Alma's current whereabouts, in the likelihood that she was released from prison after serving her time."

Dirkson looked at me differently than he ever had before, the stubborn bravado replaced by what looked like admiration, or at least respect. "And to think that twenty-five years ago was your first experience with all of this . . ."

"All of what?"

"Murder. I know you hated me for not following through on Walter's plan to bring you on full-time to replace Bill Gower, but I probably did you the greatest favor anybody ever did. Who knows, Mrs. Fletcher? Maybe it's me you owe more than anyone else for becoming rich and famous."

Chapter Twenty-four

When I got back to my suite at Hill House, Joe and Nails were camped out in chairs on either side of my door.

"Boss called," Joe explained, rising. "Told us to protect you on account of what happened tonight."

"And how did Mr. Genaway find out so quickly what happened tonight?"

Joe shrugged. "Beats me," he said, opening the door for me in true gentlemanly fashion. "Anyway, we're supposed to stand watch."

"For how long?"

"Until the boss tells us to stop."

"I assure you that's not necessary."

"Said the woman who almost got turned into a campfire marshmallow a while back."

I didn't argue the point. "I noticed you opened the door without a key," I said instead.

"Who needs a key?" Joe smirked.

"Apparently, not you."

"Nails, actually," he said, tilting his eyes toward the ever-silent man still seated on the other side of my door. "Just one of his many talents."

I slid by him through the doorway into my suite.

"You need anything, Mrs. Fletcher, just holler," Joe said, sitting back down and easing a well-worn paperback reprint of one of my mysteries from his jacket pocket.

"Please thank Mr. Genaway for me," I said, and closed the door behind me.

I was exhausted, but much too keyed up to sleep. I couldn't get my mind to shut off, and none of my tried-and-true means to drift off got me any closer. First, I tried channel surfing on the television, then reading a magazine and finally a book. But I couldn't rein in my thoughts about the murder of Wilma Tisdale earlier in the evening and what it might mean. The killer had now struck twice in less than a week, and I was starting to seriously consider the possibility that the same person was behind the death of Lisa Joy Reavis as well. Why else would Ginny Genaway have sought Wilma out with questions about her older sister the week before she was murdered?

Now they were both dead, and whatever information Wilma had shared with Ginny might well have explained the motive. Harry McGraw's astute analysis of that butane found on the remnants of the blown tire indicated that the accident that had killed Lisa Joy was almost surely murder. Beyond that, I was convinced Wilma Tisdale had been on the verge of telling me far more than she had already when she was murdered.

Call your sheriff! Call him now! She's here. Tell him she's here!

I couldn't shake Wilma's final, desperate plea from my mind, and I fixated on the *she* part. Who could *she* possibly be? Had Wilma been on the verge of identifying her killer to me, fleshing out exactly what she and Ginny had discussed in Appleton last week that had led her to invite me to her retirement party?

I found myself suddenly glad for the presence of Joe and Nails outside my door. When it was clear that I was fighting a losing battle to fall asleep, I switched on the computer in search of information about Alma Potts. There wasn't much outside of her arrest, given that she had never formally stood trial in the wake of her plea agreement. That said, a few of the articles made mention of the fact that she had two children, teenage twins at the time. A boy . . . and a girl.

She's here. Tell him she's here!

Alma Potts's daughter targeting Wilma Tisdale over a lost pension didn't add up for me, but plenty of murders don't make any real sense. That made me think of the newspaper headline fragment AMED PRIN F THE Y that Seth Hazlitt and I had found in Ginny's apartment. The headline should have matched one from the *Cabot Cove Gazette*, but Seth's efforts had thus far failed to produce it, and we still hadn't heard back from Evelyn Phillips, the *Gazette*'s owner and chief editor.

So with night at its darkest, I jogged my computer screen to an online Scrabble game and began trying to assemble the remainder of the headline. The problem, of course, was that I had no idea how many words preceded AMED and how many came after the word that began with "Y." But it gave me something to do to while away the time, and—wouldn't you know it?—the process finally made me begin to drift off after I failed miserably to assemble any combination of words that made any discernible sense at all. That said, something had started to occur to me—something I could almost reach out and touch but kept slipping away before I could get my mental hand around it.

Slumped in my chair, I awoke to the sun streaming through the windows and my cell phone ringing. I grabbed for it, feeling the kink that had formed in my neck from dozing off awkwardly in my desk chair.

"How many times have you been my wake-up call?" I greeted Mort Metzger.

"Far too many, because they've all involved a murder. I've got some news I thought you'd want to hear immediately."

"What time is it?" I asked him, trying to stretch the stiffness out of my neck.

"Just after nine o'clock. What happened to Jessica Fletcher the early riser?"

"She didn't fall asleep until after six a.m. Nerves."

"I knew I should've put an officer at Hill House."

"No need. Vic Genaway's men have been camped outside my door all night."

"You really should consider keeping better company, Mrs. F."

I cleared my throat to clear the sleep from my voice. "So, what is it you have to tell me?"

"We can safely cross Alma Potts off our suspects list. She died a month after being released from prison."

"Cancer," Mort continued, "before you get any ideas."

"She had two children, Mort—twins, and one of them was a girl."

"Named Kristen, but everybody called her Kris. She became one of the greatest female athletes in the history of her high school and later went on to coach several sports at a number of schools where she taught gym over the years."

"Where is she now?" I asked him, figuring Kris Potts would likely be in her late thirties or early forties now.

"That's just it. We don't know. She's moved around a lot through a number of teaching and coaching jobs, and we haven't been able to locate her yet."

"And should we read anything into her moving around a lot?"

"She had a temper that got her in hot water a few times but nothing actionable, if you know what I mean."

"In other words, she was never arrested and charged with anything."

"Not that I've been able to find, no. I've got a picture of her from the last school she taught at, apparently the most recent photo available."

"Can you e-mail it to me?"

"It's on the way . . . now."

"Did you manage to take all the statements last night?" I asked Mort while I waited for the picture to arrive.

"Finished up the process just before dawn. The last batch of guests was none too pleased."

"Can't say I blame them."

"Well, it couldn't be helped."

"Did anything they have to say help?"

"Not as far as identifying characteristics go. We did get an idea of the direction the killer came from, specifically an area consistent with an emergency exit door we believe may have been propped open. Those who witnessed anything recalled only seeing a shape move purposefully past them."

"'Purposefully'?"

"That's how one of the guests described it."

"How many of those present were you unable to interview?" I asked Mort.

"Around a dozen. File them under 'unaccounted for,' Jessica."

"Which makes them our top suspects."

My computer pinged, signaling the arrival of a fresh e-mail in my in-box. "Hold on—that picture of Kristen Potts just got here," I said, jogging the screen back to my e-mail.

I clicked on the attachment and waited for the picture to download. It must've been a large file, because it took longer than usual, the picture taking shape on the screen directly before me.

"Oh my," I managed, literally shivering even before Kristen Potts's face was fully formed.

"What is it, Jessica? What's wrong?"

"I recognize her, Mort. Kristen Potts was at Wilma's party at the country club last night."

The woman at the bar while I'd been talking to Jim Dirkson! She didn't have the same spiky hairdo in the picture, but it was definitely Kristen, daughter of the late Alma Potts.

"Did I just hear you right, Mrs. Fletcher?"

"If you have to ask me that, you know you did."

"I'm going to put out an all-points bulletin on her," Mort informed me, sounding as determined as he did surprised by this revelation. "I'm going to call in the state police to help us track her down."

I heard a knock on my door and tried to ignore it until it fell again, louder and more incessant this time.

"There's someone at my door, Mort."

"Genaway's thugs, maybe? I'm staying on the line."

I took the phone, and thus Mort, with me as I walked across the room, threw back the lock, and drew open the door.

"We caught this one snooping around the floor, Mrs. Fletcher," Joe told me, Nails behind him holding a figure by the arm. "We figured we'd best let you know."

Joe stepped aside, clearing my line of vision to the figure Nails held by one hand in a grasp that looked like it could have cracked walnuts. I dropped the phone, Mort's voice resounding up from the floor.

"Jessica, is everything all right? . . . Jessica?"

I didn't know what to tell him, because standing before me was Kristen Potts.

Mort sped over to Hill House with two of his deputies in tow after making me promise not to say a word to Alma Potts's daughter until he arrived, which took all of nine minutes. His men took her into custody, handcuffs and all, while Mort engaged in a staring contest with Joe and Nails.

"What's the charge, Officer?" a smirking Kristen Potts asked him.

"Let's start with suspicion of murder and go from there."

The smirk vanished. "'Murder'?"

Mort nodded. "And it's 'sheriff,' not 'officer,' by the way."

Down at the sheriff's station, the deputies escorted Kristen into the sole interview room and remained with her, while I pleaded my case to Mort to let me participate in the interview slash interrogation.

"Can you hold your tongue, just this once?" he relented finally.

"You know I can."

"No, I don't, because you've never been able to before in all the years we've known each other. Maybe you should consider sitting this one out."

"Got any duct tape in your office, Sheriff?"

"What for?"

"So I can cover up my mouth."

In the end, I decided to rely on force of will instead. Mort and I sat on one side of the table, the still-handcuffed Kristen Potts on the other, her face utterly blank.

"I didn't kill Wilma Tisdale, Sheriff," she said without being prompted, before Mort had even said a word.

"I notice you weren't on the invite list, Ms. Potts. Care to explain what led you to crash the party?"

"I wanted to give that woman a piece of my mind, that's all."

"Long trip for something you could've done over the phone. At last check, you were living in Pennsylvania."

"I've been moving around a lot the last few years."

"So your file says."

"Walter Reavis was principal at Appleton High," I chimed in, "where your mother worked. Did you ever meet him?"

Kris nodded a single time. "When I was a little girl and they both worked at the middle school. I was in the mall with a friend and her mother. I spotted them together at a restaurant. I was too young to realize what I was looking at, but I didn't stay young forever," she said, confirming her mother's motive for killing Walter Reavis twenty-five years ago.

"That make you mad?" Mort asked Alma's daughter.

"I was in denial."

"But you don't deny crashing Wilma Tisdale's party last night."

"Why bother?" she asked, fixing her gaze on me. "I practically bumped into the great Jessica Fletcher there."

"Thank you," I couldn't help but say, drawing a caustic stare from Mort.

"A real hero, aren't you? Made your bones getting my mother arrested for murder."

"She confessed, Kris," I said, sensing Mort's ire. "You should keep that in mind."

"That doesn't mean Wilma Tisdale had to steal the pension she'd worked her whole life accumulating from my brother and me, does it?"

"From what I hear, the money instead ended up going in one lump sum to the family of the man your mother murdered," Mort informed her. "How'd that make you feel, Kris? Upset enough maybe to kill Walter Reavis's two daughters: Lisa Joy fourteen years ago and Ginny last week after she somehow caught on to your involvement?"

I have to say that Mort was really impressing me here. I guess you can take the cop out of the NYPD, but you can't take the NYPD out of the cop.

"I have no idea what you're talking about."

"I wonder if the FBI might take an interest in you, too, Kris. As a matter of fact, I wonder if you'll be able to account for your whereabouts on the night Lisa Joy was killed in Alabama."

"I've never been to Alabama in my life, Sheriff."

"Then you've got nothing to fear from the FBI. Of course, if you come clean to me you'll find us local authorities a lot more willing to work with you than the feds. Believe me, I know of what I speak. And if you didn't intend to do Wilma Tisdale any harm, what were you doing at her party last night?"

"I already told you I was going to confront her."

"Get yourself a little satisfaction, then," Mort said, nodding.

"I guess."

"Why not get yourself a lot by sticking a knife in her back instead? Why else would you have fled the scene after the lights came back on?"

"Because I was already gone before they went off. I changed my mind after I spotted Mrs. Fletcher at the bar. Figured she might tell Wilma I was there."

"Except I'd never met you and had no idea what you looked like," I said, not able to help myself. Mort did not seem to mind my interruption this time. "So how was I supposed to tell anyone you were there?"

"I panicked, got cold feet. And Wilma Tisdale deserved worse than a knife in the back."

"I don't know how much worse it gets than that," Mort interjected. "Maybe you'll find out, Kris. We don't have the death penalty in Maine, but they still do in Alabama."

"Look, Sheriff," she said, her voice and her facade of bravado both cracking, "I've made my share of mistakes and done more than my share of stupid things, but I've never killed anyone." She shook her head, her expression laced with self-loathing. "You want to know the worst of it? My mother going to the ceremony honoring Walter Reavis as Principal of the Year. I think that was the moment that broke her, just a few months before she finally did the town a service by cracking his head open."

I didn't hear Mort's next question. I was too fixated on what Kristen Potts had just said about Walter Reavis being named Principal of the Year and on resuming the Scrabble game I'd played on my computer the night before.

AMED PRIN F THE Y.

In that moment, I knew the rest of that newspaper headline from the *Cabot Cove Gazette.*

And I also knew who'd killed Ginny Genaway and Wilma Tisdale.

Chapter Twenty-five

Sheriff, could I see you outside for a moment?"

Mort caught the look in my eyes and followed me out of the interview room, signaling a patrolman to watch over Kristen Potts.

"I know who the killer is," I told him, still feeling numb.

"I'm getting the impression it's not the woman in that interview room."

"Not at all."

Evelyn Phillips finally called back at that moment, her call probably the only one I would have even considered taking. "About time, Evelyn," I said after putting my phone on speaker so Mort could listen, too.

"Just make sure I get an exclusive on all these murders once you bring the killer to justice. Anyway, I got your messages. What you don't know is that there's a very good reason why Dr. Hazlitt couldn't find that headline in the *Gazette*. I've also taken over the local Appleton paper."

"I wasn't aware of that."

"Nobody is, because it hasn't been announced yet. Don't want to go creating a stir about consolidation and shrinking paper size and all. But the truth is, consolidating operations is the only thing that allowed the *Appleton Post* to stay in business. We piggyback the printing on the same press and run numerous articles of local interest in both papers. That's why you and Dr. Hazlitt recognized the typeface as the *Gazette*'s, because it's the *Post*'s typeface now, too. And the headline you're looking for reads in total—"

"'Cabot Cove Resident Named Principal of the Year,'" I completed for her.

"It got bumped from the *Gazette* for space reasons, when we were having all those zoning board issues," Evelyn told me. "The headline also included the principal's name."

"Jen Sweeney," I said, filling in that blank, too.

Mort couldn't believe it when I told him. "Are you saying Jen Sweeney killed Ginny Genaway and Wilma Tisdale?"

"Yes and no, Sheriff."

"It can't be both, Mrs. F."

"In this case, it can. You see, Jen Sweeney is really Lisa Joy Reavis."

"Well," Mort said, after letting that sink in, "I guess we can't arrest her for that murder, too, then."

"But we can arrest her for killing whoever she coaxed into

taking her car that night, but not before she filled the tire with butane to cause the blowout that forced the driver to lose control and crash into a tree."

Mort couldn't stop shaking his head. "Unbelievable. Why should I be surprised, though? It's always unbelievable with you."

"It should've come to me a lot sooner, but I kept missing it."

"Missing what?"

"After all those years Lisa Joy Reavis spent in Alabama, she couldn't help but bring some of the dialect back."

"You call that a clue?"

"I do when a woman who's supposedly spent her entire life in the North uses the phrase 'you all' as much as Jen Sweeney does. And when I ran into her and Seth at Mara's not long after Ginny's murder, she said something didn't 'amount to a hill of beans these days,' another phrase that's predominantly spoken south of the Mason-Dixon Line."

"Pretty thin for evidence."

"Which is why it didn't register with me . . . until now, until everything else fell into place."

"Like what?"

"Like that article running in the *Appleton Post*, accompanied in all probability by Jen Sweeney's picture."

"Which, you're suggesting, Ginny recognized."

"Enough to arouse her suspicions, anyway. Lisa Joy must've gone to great lengths to change her appearance, become another person entirely, when she came back to Maine to take the principal's job in Cabot Cove. But Ginny must've seen something she recognized in the picture, enough to make her suspect Jen Sweeney was the older sister she thought was gone for good."

"Hold on," Mort said, not quite grasping it all. "You're telling me Lisa Joy Reavis came back to Maine after all these years and took a job maybe twenty miles away from where she grew up."

"No, Jen Sweeney took that job because in her mind Lisa Joy Reavis really was dead and buried. You've heard the same stories I have about her growing up. What I'm saying is consistent with all that. She was so convinced she'd successfully become another person, she must not have even seen coming back to Maine as a risk. Or maybe she enjoyed that risk, since we now have strong reason to believe she's killed at least three people?"

"'At least'?" Mort repeated, incredulous at the notion.

"There are a lot of years unaccounted for between the time Lisa Joy supposedly died and Jen Sweeney took over as principal of Cabot Cove High."

"Just don't go calling her a serial killer. I know you've always wanted to catch one of those, but let's not turn Lisa Joy Reavis, Jen Sweeney, or whatever you want to call her into that. I'm having enough trouble buying into the possibility that she'd dare move back so close to home, never mind so close to the one person who would almost surely recognize her for who she really was: her sister."

"I don't think that even registered with her, and she might have had no idea that Ginny was still living in the general area. Or if she did, it was part of the challenge, the fun. To stick it in all our faces, become the high school principal in a town a stone's throw from where her family had been destroyed."

"So, that article runs, making Ginny wonder if Jen Sweeney just might be her long-lost-and-thought-to-be-dead sister."

"And if we dig deeper, we'll probably find that Ginny was spending time in Cabot Cove, watching Jen Sweeney whenever she could. From a distance for sure, but maybe even up close.

Check the school security cameras, and I'll bet you'll find Ginny somewhere on the recordings."

"But what clinched it for her? What led her to visit Wilma Tisdale and then interview you in the guise of a high school student?"

"I don't know, Mort, not yet. Something we haven't figured out, a piece of the puzzle that's still missing."

He nodded to himself. "So, Ginny finally confronts her. They meet at that rest stop—"

"Scenic overlook . . ."

"—and Lisa Joy shoots her own sister in the car. But that doesn't explain why she killed Wilma Tisdale, Jessica."

"I think it does, Mort, because I think Wilma was the one person who knew the truth. Maybe she figured it out on her own, or maybe Jen Sweeney had paid her a visit upon her return. Wilma was her tutor during high school and middle school as well, likely the one adult in her life she felt close to."

"Something Ginny would have remembered."

"She showed up at Wilma's house to confront her about what she already believed she'd figured out. I think Wilma intended to come clean at her retirement party. That's why she invited me at the last minute. But Ginny's death must have scared her out of doing it. And by the time she spotted Lisa Joy, aka Jen Sweeney, at the party and changed her mind, it was too late."

"But what was it that confirmed it all for Ginny, Mrs. F.? What did she see or hear that convinced her beyond all doubt that Jen Sweeney was her long-lost-and-thought-to-be-dead sister?"

"There's only one person who can tell us that, Mort."

* * *

But Jen Sweeney was nowhere to be found. Mort looped in the MSP on our suspicions, and within minutes every law enforcement officer in New England was looking out for a person matching Jen Sweeney's description. Mort and pretty much all his deputies showed up at the high school, where they were met by a janitor who unlocked the main entrance for them and handed Mort the school master key, given that it was Sunday.

"Stay here," Mort ordered.

I wasn't sure if he was speaking to me or to the janitor, so I followed him through the door. The search warrant Mort had managed to obtain on a Sunday after three hours of trying to reach an appropriate judge allowed us to search the Cabot Cove High principal's office, but we found nothing indicating Jen Sweeney was anyone other than who she claimed to be. Not a shred of evidence providing any indication of her past life as Lisa Joy Reavis.

"You ever write about this kind of thing in your books?" he asked me, stripping off his evidence gloves.

"What?"

"Someone effectively becoming another person."

"If you read my books, you'd know, Mort."

"Can you just answer the question? In this day and age, I thought it would be impossible."

"But Lisa Joy Reavis must've become Jen Sweeney around fourteen years ago, when she set up someone else to die in that car accident." I shook my head. "Three murders, then. How many does it take to brand someone a serial killer?"

Mort grimaced, no doubt recalling that he'd expressly told me not to call her that. "The resident expert on murder doesn't know?"

I shrugged. "Because I've never written about one."

"Not even once?"

I shook my head. "They scare me."

"I didn't think anything scared Jessica Fletcher."

"Clowns scare me, too. Clowns and serial killers."

"Well," Mort said, enjoying the moment, "as I live and breathe. Maybe I'll share that information with Evelyn Phillips."

"Are you blackmailing me?"

"Not yet."

"Good," I told Mort, "because I trust your search warrant includes Jen Sweeney's home as well."

He checked it, as if to make sure. "Wait a minute. I recognize this address. There was a break-in not too long ago. One of my deputies handled it, but nothing turned out to be missing."

We headed to Jen Sweeney's house straight from the school, as the late-afternoon sky darkened ahead of dusk with an approaching nor'easter the weathermen had been warning about for days. The wind had started to howl, and the first big fat raindrops began to dapple Mort's windshield, a portent of what was to come.

The rain had picked up slightly by the time three Cabot Cove and two Maine State Police vehicles ground to a halt in front of Jen Sweeney's simple slab of a ranch house located near the old Cabot Cove quarry in one of the least desirable residential areas in town. That had the positive effect of making the homes out this way modestly priced. The area qualified as a slum in Cabot Cove even though Jen Sweeney's simple home featured well-manicured, modest grounds and what looked like a fresh coat of paint and a new roof.

"This time, you need to stay put, Jessica," Mort told me, sounding genuinely sorry. "That's the MSP talking, not me."

"If she's inside . . ."

"You'll hear gunfire soon enough. Only way I can see how this ends."

As he walked away, I tried to envision a similar scenario with Amos Tupper in charge back when he was sheriff. In spite of his simple nature and down-home modesty, Amos had been a better sheriff than people realized, though not one who could've handled the rigors of the new Cabot Cove. We'd been very lucky to get Mort to replace Amos when he retired, never more so than today.

I waited in his SUV, holding my breath for much of the time. I tried to spot what I could between the blinds, but caught only flashes of motion as the four officers from the MSP and our sheriff's department, plus Mort, moved about the interior with guns drawn, likely going from room to room. In the end, there was no gunfire, were no any hints of a struggle whatsoever coming from inside the house. I wasn't surprised. A psychopath like Jen Sweeney, formerly Lisa Joy Reavis, would maintain no true attachments, even to herself. She'd already be gone without a trace, ready to disappear into another identity, after murdering the only two people in the area linked to her past. I believed that past was what she was actually killing once and for all when she shot her sister and stabbed Wilma Tisdale to death. And now she'd wipe the slate clean of Jen Sweeney, too, burying her in the same figurative grave as Lisa Joy Reavis.

I knew they hadn't found her inside when Mort emerged alone and retraced his path to his SUV. His expression was more dazed than anything else, making me wonder what he'd found inside the house, if not our killer.

"Something you need to see, Jessica," he said in what sounded like someone else's voice.

I followed him inside Jen Sweeney's modest ranch house. It felt sterile and cold, with a strange sense of not having been lived in. Most unusual was the fact that it seemed to have no smells at all. No hint of the previous night's dinner or lingering air freshener—nothing bad and nothing good. Just nothing at all, something I could never recall encountering before.

My muscles tensed as I trailed Mort into the home's combination living-and-dining room, which featured an empty space where I would have expected the dining room table to be.

"Oh," I managed, the rest of my words choked off by what I found myself looking at.

Lighthouses—the room was utterly dominated by them. Paintings and photographs featuring lighthouses hung from the walls. Scale models of various sizes cluttered the coffee table, battling for space. And a big one, almost as tall as I was, rested in front of a curved bay window, dominating the room. As I tried to process what I was seeing, one of the officers accidentally tripped the switch on the big lighthouse, activating the light, which flashed intermittently just like a life-sized version.

I turned toward Mort, knowing he was thinking the same thing I was.

"You wanted to know what clinched it for Ginny Genaway," I

said to him, sweeping my gaze about the room again. "What convinced her that Jen Sweeney was her sister, Lisa Joy. Ginny must have been the one who broke into this house, Mort. Once she saw what we're seeing, she knew for certain."

Mort followed my gaze. "I think we know where we can find Jen Sweeney, Mrs. Fletcher."

Chapter Twenty-six

The storm grew in intensity as our convoy of five police vehicles, with Mort's SUV in the lead, raced, lights flashing but no sirens screaming yet, down the highway toward Cape Elizabeth, ninety minutes away. The wind blew sheets of rain onto our windshield, the wipers hard-pressed to keep up with the increasing onslaught. Thunder crackled, sometimes loudly enough to shake the SUV. Bolts of lightning flashed regularly, leaving brief bursts of luminescence to brighten the night.

A single car was parked in the Portland Head Lighthouse lot on Cape Elizabeth; the driver had utterly ignored the lot's lines and markers in favor of just leaving the car in the first convenient place. Although I didn't know what kind of car Jen Sweeney drove, this vehicle could only be hers, because she had come here to eliminate the last person with whom she bore any connection at all before disappearing again, this time for good.

I noticed the entire facility and lighthouse itself had gone dark, likely due to a power failure in the raging storm that was just reaching its peak. The Cabot Cove sheriff's deputies and Maine State policemen had all donned rain slickers, something neither Mort nor I had handy, so he and I got soaked as we followed a path illuminated by flashes of lightning to reach the front door.

The door was open, blown by the wind backward against the adjoining wall. Mort entered first, his flashlight beam illuminating the path up the stairs toward Maddie Demerest's apartment. A ship's foghorn began to blare desperately in the waters beyond, sounding dangerously close to the rocky shore, since the power failure had knocked out the massive flashing light that would have otherwise steered it from harm.

The foghorn blared again, more loudly, which meant the ship had strayed yet closer to the deadly rocks that composed the shoreline. This as Mort reached the door at the top of the narrow stairs, a tight cluster of uniforms grouped behind him, while I held my ground maybe halfway up. Mort squeezed himself as much as he could to the side of the closed door before rapping hard on the wood.

"Police, Mrs. Demerest! Please open the door!"

No response followed, so Mort rapped again, louder and harder. And this time, when no response came, Mort nodded to the officers behind him before throwing his shoulder into the closed door and knocking it inward. I held my breath against the possibility of gunfire, as the uniformed officers from both Cabot Cove and the MSP filed forward in Mort's wake.

I could barely lift my legs up to follow, because the world had gone heavy and sluggish around me, as if the air was soaked in molasses. I finally pushed myself on when the last cop disappeared through the door, with still no gunfire coming from inside.

I glimpsed a dark figure. Then the door at the top of the stairs slammed shut, and the figure seemed to soar downward, crashing into me and knocking me to the side. I staggered but managed to avoid falling and swung all the way around to find Jen Sweeney, born Lisa Joy Reavis, illuminated at the foot of the stairs by a flash of lightning from the storm beyond. She followed the path we'd taken and vanished into the blackness of the night.

Someone—it sounded like Mort—was banging on the door at the top of the stairs from the inside. Jen must have jammed it somehow, trapping Mort and the other officers within.

"Jessica!" I heard him cry out as I rattled the knob.

"What happened to 'Mrs. F.'?"

"Just open the door!"

I rattled it again. "I can't. It's locked. And since you're currently indisposed—"

"Don't say it, Jessica!"

"—I'm going after Jen Sweeney."

She'd left the heavy door to the lighthouse open, as if she wanted me to follow her up the narrow, spiraling steel staircase. I could see that the door at the top accessing the lantern room itself was open, too, and in the distance, I heard the oncoming ship's foghorn blaring in a more rapid and desperate fashion than moments earlier.

I spiraled up the steep stairs until I came to the lantern room, where Maddie Demerest, formerly Reavis, was strung to the massive Fresnel lens with some kind of wire, and was irradiated by the flashes of lightning that pierced the night. Her daughter Lisa Joy, the woman I knew as Jen Sweeney, stood just to her side, a squarish pistol of some kind pressed against the side of Maddie's head.

"I guess this means you're not coming for Career Day, Mrs. Fletcher," she managed, flashing a smile bred of pure evil and hatred.

"You don't have to do this, Lisa Joy," I said. "Your secret's out. There's no reason to take another life."

"Let her," her mother rasped. "Doesn't make any difference anyway. She'll be doing me a favor."

The ship's foghorn blared louder still, sounding as if it was virtually upon us.

"You must've been to my house," Lisa Joy Reavis said, her eyes wide but empty. "Did you like my lighthouse collection?"

"I don't think this one would fit on your coffee table," I told her. "Now let your mother go."

"I can't, Mrs. Fletcher. I have to complete the circle. People will be talking about the tragedy of the Reavis family for years, how they were all murdered. Guess my brother was the lucky one, since he got to die in the war."

"You need help, Lisa Joy. Let me help you."

"Would you ever use such a lame line in your books?"

"I suppose not, but this isn't one of them."

She pressed the barrel tighter against her mother's temple, giving me the opportunity to draw inside the doorway. "Ever create a villain like me?"

"Not quite, no. My villains tend not to be psychopaths. They don't enjoy killing nearly as much as you do."

Lisa Joy Reavis narrowed her gaze. "Trying to get a rise out of me, Mrs. Fletcher?"

"Let your mother go, Lisa Joy. You and I can finish this alone."

She aimed the gun my way. "You want me to shoot you instead? You can make that deal if you want."

"I don't have to. You need me to live to tell the story of all this—a story far more incredible than anything I've ever made up."

"Going all the way back twenty-five years to my father's murder. I might have killed him if Alma Potts hadn't beaten me to it. She saved me the trouble."

"Where'd you come up with the butane idea?"

Her eyes narrowed, looking almost playful. "What, you think that was my first? You underestimate me, Mrs. Fletcher."

A chill coursed up my spine. "Why do you do it, Lisa Joy?"

"Why do you write?"

"Because I enjoy it."

"There you go."

I looked toward Maddie Demerest and met her milky gaze, which looked sharper than it had just a moment earlier. I finally noticed her upper body was lashed to the huge light, but her legs were free. She wiggled her slippered feet as if to draw my attention to that fact, her presence seemingly forgotten by her daughter, who now focused solely on me.

"How many more murders were there?"

She winked. "I'll never tell. Ask my sister. Oh, that's right. You can't, because I killed her, along with that snoop Wilma Tisdale. Once you and my mother are both dead, too, I can go on my way and become somebody else again."

"Kill me and who's going to tell your story?"

"Think you can do me justice?"

"I doubt anyone can," I said.

That's when Maddie kicked out with both legs, dual thuds landing on her daughter's back, which pitched Lisa Joy forward. The pistol, gone from her grasp, skittered across the floor, glinting briefly in a fresh flash of lightning that illuminated the massive ship bearing down on the coastline, still desperately blaring its foghorn. Lisa went for the gun, forgetting about me in that moment, which allowed me to pounce.

She was about the same height as me, but younger and stronger. She shoved me backward as she tried to kick my legs out. I managed to avoid the sweep of her legs, backpedaling through the door onto the landing beyond as we continued to struggle. Lisa Joy spotted the pistol within easy range, but as she went for it, I twisted her around toward the stairs and shoved myself against her. I tensed for the impact I knew was coming as we pitched over onto the iron stairwell, and tumbled down with our positions alternately reversing. I felt each thump and bump on my back, legs, and head; some sharp edges tore at my clothes and skin.

At the bottom, our momentum carried us through the door and out into the storm. Lisa got the better of me, regaining her feet ahead of me and striking me hard on the shoulder and the stomach, the latter blow stealing my wind. I felt myself hit the rocky ground, smelled the wet undergrowth, and twisted around on my back to see Lisa Joy with a huge rock held overhead in both hands.

"Too bad, Mrs. Fletcher. My story would've been a bestseller for sure."

The foghorn blared again in a deafening fashion, and Lisa Joy Reavis twisted to see a massive freighter crashing over the rocks and mounting the shoreline, heading straight for us. I just managed to roll aside as its dented bow crested the shore and surged forward, as if the ship were on wheels. The woman I knew as Jen Sweeney tried to dive aside, her hateful eyes rooted on me when she stumbled and nearly lost her balance.

The ship rose over Lisa Joy Reavis, dwarfing her in its shadow before swallowing her altogether en route to crashing into the Portland Head Lighthouse and sending a shower of rubble into the air to mix with the pelting rain. The entire structure seemed to waver before breaking apart. I rolled and then scampered away, barely managing to avoid the biggest chunks of the crumbling structure.

The ship finally ground to a squealing, earth-ripping halt smack-dab in the middle of the lighthouse structure. I saw no sign of Lisa Joy Reavis, aka Jen Sweeney, and pictured her entombed by the rubble. But enough of the stairwell was intact for me to mount the stairs, which quaked under my weight, and climb them as quickly as I dared.

At the top, Maddie Demerest lay on the floor of the lantern room, her frame perched over the top edge of the wavering stairwell, which had been torn loose from its mounts. She was only semiconscious when I reached her.

"Maddie, Maddie!" I cried, shaking her lightly, but she barely stirred.

I had no choice but to take her in my grasp atop the precarious perch outside the lantern room, because the lighthouse structure seemed to be disintegrating around us. A quick glance downward through the spray of the freighter's deck lamps revealed the frontmost portion of its bow literally inside the lower levels of the structure, having embedded itself there after crashing through, its now barely recognizable name stretched across the near side of the bow. I heard panicked voices intermixed with the now scratchy, deafening blare of the foghorn, which had stubbornly clung to life.

I started down the spiraling stairs, leaving it to sway one way and back the other. It came to rest at an awkward angle beneath the lantern room and the watch room immediately beneath it, where fuel, supplies, and replacement bulbs had been stored in previous eras. Today the room was empty, save for what looked like a heavy, coiled rope that I assumed must have been the old-time version of an escape ladder.

With the iron stairs no longer secure enough to trust, I realized that rope might be my only chance to escape before the entire Portland Head Lighthouse collapsed around us. I couldn't go without Maddie Demerest, though; nor could I risk her deadweight causing both of us to fall to our deaths. So I slapped her across the face.

"Listen to me!" I blared, holding her by the shoulders when her eyes snapped alert. "If you want to die here, tell me now so you don't kill me, too. What's it gonna be, Maddie?"

"Help me," she managed, pleading. "Please."

"You need to hold on yourself so I can get that rope in there. Can you do that, Maddie?"

She nodded and eased out of my grasp. Then Maddie wrapped her arms around the nearest step of the teetering iron stairs, freeing me to push myself far enough into the watch room to grab hold of the rope. With the storm and the freighter's deck lamps cutting through the night and providing all the light I needed, I reached up and looped the rope through a hole in the mount where the stairs had broken free and tied it tight, using a nautical knot I'd learned from research for a book whose title escaped me at that moment. Then I dropped the rope downward and watched it scrape the freighter's sharply angled bow and then dangle all the way to the rubble now composing the lighthouse floor.

If I'd thought any further about what I needed to do next, I might not have done it at all.

"Hold on, Maddie," I told the woman, who now seemed desperately to want to live. "Hold on tight!"

She clung to me, closing her eyes. I doubt she weighed more than a hundred pounds—a godsend in this case, since I was able to hold fast to the rope and start our descent while she dug her fingers so tightly into me, I thought my skin might tear. Rubble from the lighthouse's circular roof was falling, grazing me and leaving the residue of stinging pain in its wake. I felt I could handle anything other than a direct blow to the head. I was also fearful that that kind of impact to Maddie would force her to let go of me and likely plunge to her death.

Around the halfway point, I thought I heard the entire structure creak, seeming to sway around me. The rope started to swing from side to side, driving us up against one side of the lighthouse and then the other; each impact was more stunning than the last. I looked up to see the mount through which I'd fastened the rope starting to break free. Not fancying the idea of a thirty-foot drop, I glanced down, chancing the queasy flutter that passed through my stomach.

The sway of the rope carried us over the peak of the freighter's deck, not much of a target but all Maddie and I had right now if we were going to survive this intact.

"Get ready to let go, Maddie!" I told her. "Get ready to let go when I tell you!"

She nodded her understanding. I could feel the rope beginning to break free above, and I knew we had just seconds left before we plunged downward. I struggled to manipulate the rope's sway, turning it so it carried us over the ship's deck before rocking us back in the other direction. The timing of what I needed to do next had to be perfect; there was no margin for error at all.

So the next instance that the rope's swing brought us over the deck, I cried out, "Now! Now!"

Maddie and I let go in the same motion, falling a total of less than ten feet and just catching the lip of the bow atop the very edge of the decking. We went down hard, landing in a jumble of limbs that twisted us into each other. The rubble continued to plummet, the side walls of the Portland Head Lighthouse giving way now as I pulled Maddie to her feet and dragged her across the freighter's deck back outside into the storm.

The deluge instantly soaked us to the bone, one flash of lightning after another revealing the collapse of what remained of the lighthouse, the massive lens and lamp bulb exploding on impact and sending a shower of sparks hurtling into the air in rhythm with the thunder that crackled overhead. I glimpsed Mort, his deputies, and the MSP officers rushing our way through the storm. I caught him shaking his head when his gaze locked on me waving to him from the freighter's deck.

He came all the way around to the aft side, shaking his head again as he looked up at me. "And I thought you hated boats, Jess."

"I do now," I told him, glancing again at the rubble that had entombed Lisa Joy Reavis.

Chapter Twenty-seven

"You're not going to like this, Jessica," Mort said, joining Seth and me at our usual table at Mara's Luncheonette the next day. "I just heard from the MSP. They haven't been able to find Jen Sweeney's body."

"You mean Lisa Joy Reavis's."

"Same body, last time I checked. Either way, she's gone."

"She couldn't have survived that, Mort. I watched her get buried alive."

"Well, she must've dug herself out, because they haven't found a single trace of her besides some torn swatches of clothing."

"You plan on ordering pie?" Seth prodded when our server came back to the table.

"Just coffee, please," Mort said.

"Good—more for me," Seth said, apparently prepared to give up on his diet. "I'll have my usual. Same for the lady here."

"What happened to your diet?" I asked him.

"If the past week has taught me anything, it's that life is too short to deny yourself the pleasure of pie, especially strawberry-rhubarb."

Mort leaned back, after our server took her leave. "Well, that was a strange one even for you, Mrs. F. Murders twenty-five years in the making."

"Hmmmmmm . . ."

"What?"

"'Murder in the Making'—can I steal that for a title?"

"Knock yourself out."

"I'll pass, if you don't mind, Mort. Came too close to that happening, literally, yesterday."

"You saved that woman's life," he told me. "I hope she's thankful enough to make the most of the years now."

"Only time will tell. If nothing else, she's going to have to relocate."

Seth shook his head. "Well, I can't imagine one of my kids killing another one, *ayuh*."

"That's because you have no kids, Doc," Mort noted.

"No," Seth said, patting my arm, "I have Jessica here instead."

I looked toward Mort. "He bandaged up all the scrapes and cuts last night left me with."

"Two required stitches. That's why I'm celebrating with pie. I still have the touch. I'll bet they don't even leave a scar."

Mort looked toward me. "Maybe somebody stitched up Jen Sweeney, too. On the other hand, there's still plenty more rubble to sort through. Jen Sweeney's body might turn up yet. Or maybe it got washed out to sea, something like that."

"Maybe," I echoed.

"But you don't think so."

"She's a survivor, Mort. And if she lived, more murders will follow wherever she goes."

"I'd better put a man on your room at Hill House," he said. "You know, just in case she decides to pay you a visit."

"Save the overtime," I told him. "I've got Joe and Nails."

"They're still around?"

"I'm starting to wonder if they're ever going to leave."

"In that case," Mort said, letting himself smile, "I hope Jen Sweeney shows up."

"You know, Mort, you just gave me an idea."

Two days later, Seth drove me to the New Hampshire State Prison for Men because I didn't want Mort to know I was making the trip.

"Does this mean I'm sworn to secrecy?" he asked me when we got there.

I nodded. "We can take a blood oath later," I said, holding up my hand.

Seth cringed. "As a licensed physician, I can tell you that's not a safe practice."

The door to his old Volvo opened with a lingering creak, and I climbed out. "You don't have to come inside with me, Seth."

"That's good, because I wasn't planning on it."

Vic Genaway sat across from me at the same table as on my other two visits to see him.

"Thank you for all those books you sent down to the library, Fletch. Not just yours, but all those others."

"Overflow from the Cabot Cove Library. I'll make sure to send more down here regularly. And thank you, too, by the way, for Joe and Nails."

"Least I can do for a friend. You got the woman who killed my Ginny." He shook his head, looking suddenly vulnerable. "Her own sister. You ever hear of such a thing?"

"All too often, unfortunately."

"Yeah? Well, not in my world. We may not be angels, but at least we don't eat our own. Anyway, if nothing else comes out of this, at least I got to meet you," Genaway said. "That almost makes it worth it—not losing Ginny for good, but everything else."

"It's not finished yet, Vic."

"Come again?"

"They still haven't found Jen Sweeney's body."

"You mean Lisa Joy Reavis's body," he corrected me.

"I do, yes. I think she got away. I think she's still out there, and it'll be time for her to murder again before you know it. And I don't think the police have any chance of finding her."

"Yeah?"

"I was thinking you might know a few people who are better at such things, the kind of people she'd go to to buy a new identity for herself."

"I just might, Fletch." He looked down at the steel table, then back at me. "You'll come to see me again, right?"

"I'll deliver the next batch of books in person."

"I'd like that. New books aren't in the prison budget, but thanks to you, the library shelves are overflowing. You made me a star in here among all these cons and killers."

"There's still another killer out there who needs to be brought to justice."

"Yeah," Vic Genaway said, his expression chiseled in cold stone now. "I was thinking the same thing."

My landline rang five weeks later while I was doing edits on my latest book.

"Hey, Fletch."

"Hello, Mr. Genaway. What can I do for you?"

"It's what I can do for you. Since you're a writer, I'm sure you have a pen handy, so get ready to write down the address where you can find Lisa Joy Reavis."

"Portland?" Mort quizzed, after I'd relayed the information to him.

"As in Oregon, not Maine."

"I'll make a few calls, Mrs. F., and bring the FBI in, too. You got this from Vic Genaway?"

"Yes, I did. And by the way, don't call me 'Mrs. F.' anymore. I've warmed up to a new nickname."

"What's that?"

"Fletch, Mort."

I placed another call as soon as I'd hung up with Mort.

"That you, Mrs. Fletcher?" Amos Tupper's voice greeted me.

"See, you really still are a great detective, Amos."

"Nah, it's just that nobody else calls me, especially from the good old two-oh-seven area code."

"I've got some news," I told him. "That case we solved together twenty-five years ago, the murder of Walter Reavis, has finally come full circle."

"Really? You got the latest killer you were looking for?" he asked in a way that made me wonder whether he recalled the details.

"I did," I said, and proceeded to lay them all out for him, the former Appleton detective and Cabot Cove sheriff hanging on my every word.

"Wow," Amos said when I'd finished, "that's really something, isn't it? I appreciate you letting me know, Mrs. Fletcher. Makes me feel like we're still a team, putting the bad guys away. I miss those days. I miss them real bad."

"You need to come for a visit, Amos. You can stay with me. I could use the company."

"Really? I'd love to." His voice sank just slightly. "Though it might be best for me to stay at Hill House so people don't get to talking about us. We don't want that, do we?"

"Let them talk," I told him. "'Rumor is a pipe blown by surmises, jealousies, conjectures, and of so easy and so plain a stop that the blunt monster with uncounted heads, the still-discordant wavering multitude, can play upon it.'"

"Hey, that's Shakespeare, isn't it?"

"I'm impressed," I told him.

"I told you I've been reading him, didn't I? I remember his quote that 'Cowards die many times before their deaths; the valiant never taste of death but once.'"

"Oh my . . ."

"What is it?"

"The *Valiant* was the name of the freighter that crashed through the Portland Head Lighthouse."

"Small world, isn't it, Mrs. Fletcher?"

"It is, indeed, Amos. It is, indeed."